Impeding Justice

M. A. COMLEY

OTHER BOOKS BY
NEW YORK TIMES BEST SELLING AUTHOR
M. A. COMLEY

Blind Justice (Novella)

Cruel Justice (Book #1)

Mortal Justice (Novella)

Impeding Justice (Book #2)

Final Justice (Book #3)

Foul Justice (Book #4)

Guaranteed Justice (Book #5)

Ultimate Justice (Book #6)

Virtual Justice (Book #7)

Hostile Justice (Book #8)

Tortured Justice (Book #9)

Rough Justice (Book #10)

Dubious Justice (Book #11)

Calculated Justice (Book #12)

Twisted Justice (Book #13)

Justice at Christmas (Short Story)

Prime Justice (Book #14)

Heroic Justice (Book #15)

Shameful Justice (Book #16 coming May 2018)

Unfair Justice (a 10,000 word short story)

Irrational Justice (a 10,000 word short story)

Clever Deception (co-written by Linda S Prather)

Tragic Deception (co-written by Linda S Prather)

Sinful Deception (co-written by Linda S Prather)

Forever Watching You (DI Miranda Carr thriller)

Wrong Place (DI Sally Parker thriller #1)

No Hiding Place (DI Sally Parker thriller #2)

Cold Case (DI Sally Parker #3)

Deadly Encounter (DI Sally Parker thriller series #4)

Web of Deceit (DI Sally Parker Novella with Tara Lyons)

The Missing Children (DI Kayli Bright #1)

Killer On The Run (DI Kayli Bright #2)

Hidden Agenda (DI Kayli Bright #3)

The Caller (co-written with Tara Lyons)

Evil In Disguise – a novel based on True events

Deadly Act (Hero series novella)

Torn Apart (Hero series #1)

End Result (Hero series #2)

In Plain Sight (Hero Series #3)

Double Jeopardy (Hero Series #4)

Sole Intention (Intention series #1)

Grave Intention (Intention series #2)

Devious Intention (Intention #3)

Merry Widow (A Lorne Simpkins short story)

It's A Dog's Life (A Lorne Simpkins short story)

A Time To Heal (A Sweet Romance)

A Time For Change (A Sweet Romance)

High Spirits

The Temptation series (Romantic Suspense/New Adult Novellas)

Past Temptation

Lost Temptation

KEEP IN TOUCH WITH THE AUTHOR

Twitter
https://twitter.com/Melcom1

Blog
http://melcomley.blogspot.com

Facebook
http://smarturl.it/sps7jh

Newsletter
http://smarturl.it/8jtcvv

BookBub
www.bookbub.com/authors/m-a-comley

ACKNOWLEDGMENTS

As always love and best wishes to my wonderful Mum for the role she plays in my career. Special thanks to my superb editor Stefanie, and my wonderful cover artist Karri. Thanks also to Joseph my amazing proof reader.

Licence Notes.

Chapter One

At the sound of helicopter blades whirling in the distance, Detective Inspector Lorne Simpkins leaned over the steering wheel and peered up at the sky. She couldn't see the chopper but judged it to be hovering beyond the towering buildings to her left, which bordered the Thames. She imagined the armed response team crouched inside it, guns locked and loaded, waiting for her call.

If this tip-off turned out to be good, precious minutes would be lost getting the team to her. For the millionth time, she rued the fact that she and Pete couldn't carry guns on these missions. *Damn politics!*

For the second time, she drove past the alley: still quiet, nothing suspicious. She eased the car to a standstill.

Pete shifted uncomfortably in the seat beside her.

She turned and asked, "Nervous?"

"No. As usual, the dry cleaners sent these trousers back to me a size smaller than when they went in…"

"Yeah, right, Pete. The fact you've gained about twenty pounds lately wouldn't have anything to do with them shrinking, I suppose?"

"Hey, it takes a lot of calories to keep my shape, you know. Besides, I eat more when I'm stressed, and these wild goose chases don't help."

"Let's hope this one's for real and we finally nail the bastard."

"Fifty quid says it's another Brixton?"

"No thanks. Take the far side of the alley, get into position, and stay put until I give the all clear—Christ, Pete, fasten up your bullet-proof, and start taking this seriously, will you? If it turns out to be another dud lead, so be it, but—"

"The bloody thing gives me indigestion, squashes me in like a fat thigh in a stocking. I've had a bigger one on order for yonks. One of the vest-type that fastens at the side, but—"

"Look, zip up, and shut up, 'cause if this is for real, we'll be sussed before we get out of the car."

Lorne took up her position, leaned forward, and surveyed the long, narrow alley. The stench of urine and the rotting, fly-infested waste spewing from overturned bins tinged her nostrils. She motioned the all clear to Pete, waited for him to dash across to the other side before she checked the alley again and gave him the thumbs up.

They picked their way along the graffiti-stained walls. A skinny dog, hunting for its next meal, growled at them, but hunger won over conflict, and he grabbed a chicken carcass and made off with it.

Lorne released the breath she'd been holding and mouthed to Pete, "Anything?"

"Not a fucking dickey bird. If you'd taken up the bet, I'd be fifty—"

A crack split the air.

Pete slumped to the ground. Horror held Lorne rigid as his bullet-proof flew in all directions. *Oh no, Pete, no! You didn't do the bloody thing up.*

His body jerked as he took another hit. Lorne bent over, making herself as small as she could, trying to cross over to him, but a sting vibrated off her face and spun her to the ground.

She swallowed back the rising panic and delved into her inner resources. *Everything by the book, Lorne—make the call!*

She grabbed her radio. "Backup needed... Officer down!"

The sound of the helicopter changed from a distant hum to an urgent drumming, and its blades chopped the air faster as it sped towards her and Pete.

Pete groaned.

Thank God, he's still alive... But he needed her help. Another spray of bullets echoed down the alley. Dust and rubble jumped into the air. Lorne looked around, desperate to find a way of getting to him.

A large steel rubbish bin stood just inside the backyard of one of the shops behind her. Its contents bulged out of the top, but the wheels looked in good condition. She positioned it between her and the gunman as more bullets ricocheted off the walls and the ground. Some hit the bin. Splinters of plastic bottles, tin cans, and debris showered her, but her shield held, and she made it across to Pete.

His throat rasped as she ripped open his shirt. A ragged hole in his stomach and a wound near his heart put the fear of God into her.

Shit... this is bad.

After whipping off her jacket, she removed her blouse, tore it in half, then used it to plug the holes. Her hands trembled as she pressed on the wound.

Bullets rained down around them. A tyre blew on a nearby delivery van. Sweat flowed from her pores. *Jesus, where's the bloody response team?*

"Lorne…" A cough stopped Pete's croaky voice. Blood trickled from his mouth.

No… Oh, please, God… Let us both get out of here alive…

"It's too late, Lorne… I'm…"

The tears she'd held back trailed down her nose and dripped onto his chest.

"Don't try to talk. Everything's okay. The team is on its way…"

"It's… It's not…"

"Look, you idiot. I'm the boss around here. If I say…"

"I… I've got… I… must tell… you…"

The helicopter swooped into the airspace overhead and hovered above the building from where the shots had come. Two officers slid down ropes from the helicopter and landed on the roof.

"Stay where you are. Don't move," a voice ordered through a megaphone.

"Like we're… planning on… going anywhere…"

Pete's dry, cracked lips stretched into a half smile. Lorne smiled back at him, appreciating his attempted humour.

"How's the pain? Is it bad?"

"It's nothing… Listen, I…" The ambulance siren's whine joined the helicopter's racket.

The gunfire had ceased. Had the Unicorn escaped again, or had they finally caught him? She hoped it was the latter.

She sat back on her legs and looked up. An officer on the roof gave her the thumbs up, and the helicopter moved away. For a moment, the chaos descended into an eerie silence, then a bin crashed behind her. She turned and saw two officers kicking at rubbish and throwing bins to one side. The ambulance crew followed just behind them, laden with equipment and a stretcher.

Thank God…

A smile of hope froze on her lips as she looked down at Pete. His head rolled to one side. A throaty breath gurgled from his lungs. Through half-closed lids, he looked up at her, staring, but not seeing her. Everything that had been Pete fell into an expressionless, waxy mask.

The cold lining of her jacket around her shoulders chilled her as strong hands helped her to stand. She didn't resist. Standing to one side, she stared at the paramedics, willing them to revive him. Then she heard the words she'd been dreading.

"Dead on arrival at the scene."

With an officer supporting her on each side, Lorne stepped into the ambulance. She sat up and watched them load Pete's covered body into a second ambulance. It pulled away, not bothering to use its siren. A paramedic tended the wound on her face, cleaned her bloody hands, and injected a vial of something into her arm.

She did little to stop the tears flowing. She thought of the information relayed to her as she left the scene. The Unicorn had escaped. The bastard had been a thorn in her side for too long, and now he'd taken her dearest colleague and friend from her. Every nerve and sinew of her body screamed its hate and her need to take her revenge.

As she drifted off into a drug-induced sleep, she repeated the same words over and over again... *I'll take care of things, Pete. I'll get him, I promise..."*

Chapter Two

"He's here, Pete. I've finally caught the bastard…"

"Oh God. What…?"

A loud bang catapulted Lorne from the terrifying dream. The unfamiliar, sterile white walls reflected her fear.

Where am I? A fog clouded her brain, obscuring any answers. She turned her head as a waft of cool air brushed her face. *Tom.*

The door swished closed behind him. Her fear eased as her husband walked towards her.

"Awake, at last. How are you feeling?" he asked.

"I'm okay. How long have I been asleep?" Memories she'd rather forget flooded her fuzzy mind.

He didn't answer.

"God, Tom. How long?"

She threw back the covers and swung her slim legs over the side. She winced when the iron bedstead dug into the back of them.

"What are you doing? Darling, you have to stay in bed…" Before she had time to think, he pounced and tucked her legs back under the covers.

Words failed her. She glared at him.

"Tom for God's sake, tell me how long?"

"Twenty-four hours…"

"What?"

"They thought you were suffering from shock. Sean and I agreed with the doctor to knock you out for a while to let your body recover from the ordeal. After all, you were injured…"

"Injured? It's a bloody scratch… You and Sean? Since when did you become bosom buddies with my boss?"

He thwarted her second attempt to leave the bed.

"I must get out of here. You and Sean have already cost me valuable time."

She pushed the heels of her hands against his chest, but he refused to budge.

"Look, I know Sean and I have never really seen eye to eye, but in this instance… after what happened to Pete—"

"Oh right, so you do *know* about Pete, then? Well, I must say, you hide your bloody grief well. Didn't it occur to either of you that

Pete's murder is exactly *why* I didn't need drugging up to the eyeballs? Pete's *killer* is out there somewhere. How the hell am I supposed to catch the bastard when I'm confined to a hospital bed? Jesus Christ, the shit has a head start on me. One hour is enough for him. What in the hell was Sean thinking of? Am I the only one around here with any brains?"

"No, you just think you are. It's always the same cry—Lorne against the rest of the world. I've heard the same bloody argument more than a thousand times over the years."

As his words sunk in, regret swept through her. Yes, she had put him through the mill at times. He had never grasped the dedication she showed her job, the priority she gave it over her family.

His look changed to one of angry resignation. Not exactly a truce, but at least he'd given in. He fetched her clothes from the locker. Sometime during her imposed sleep, he'd had the foresight to replace her bloodstained suit with a fresh outfit.

She pulled up her skirt over her rounded hips. Her legs wobbled. She reached out to the hospital bed to steady herself. As she zipped her skirt at the back of her slim waist, Tom's growing annoyance filled the room with sighs.

Bloody childish.

"I need to get to HQ. Will you drive me, or would you rather I get a taxi?"

"Cut the crap. You'll probably find this hard to believe right now, but *I'm* not one of your many enemies. Don't take your frustrations out on me. I'm as gutted about Pete as you are. He was a good mate of mine, too, remember?"

She turned to challenge him, but the pain stretching across his handsome features shocked her. *Oh, God, I'm a selfish cow, at times.*

He flung out an arm and marched heavy-footed towards the door. "What's the bloody point? The doctor will need to give you the all-clear. I'll see if I can find him."

Shocked, she retaliated. "Don't bother. No one is going to stop me checking myself out of here. No one, do you hear me? Just do as I ask, and bring the car round the front."

Needing to lash out, she attacked her shoulder-length brown hair with her brush. The pain went some way to lessen her anger.

Lorne burst out of her room and marched down the hallway. The blonde middle-aged ward sister sprinted around the desk. "Mrs. Simpkins, you can't just up and leave."

"You want to bet on that? Watch me."

"At least let me try and get hold of Dr. Carter. He's due to start his rounds." She tried to turn Lorne back to her room.

But Lorne shrugged her off. "I've wasted enough time as it is. Just get me the release form to sign to get me out of this dump. No offence."

The sister thrust the release form under Lorne's nose.

"Thanks. Now, which is the quickest way to the mortuary from here?"

"Take the first left, then the second door on the right. The lift will take you down to the basement. You'll find the mortuary at the far end of the corridor on the right."

No more bedside manner then?

She was filled with trepidation and hoped her good friend and occasional colleague, pathologist Jacques Arnaud, would be on duty.

She hadn't gone far when she needed to lean against a wall to catch her breath. *Did that sister say second or third on the right?*

The jerky ride on the lift left her shaken up. Once more, she took solace against the cold painted brick wall of the corridor. *What the hell is wrong with you, girl?* She knew the answer. This would be the last time she ever laid eyes on her partner, her *dead* partner.

"*Ma chérie*, how are you?" Jacques startled her. His voice came from behind a mountain of reports. He placed them on the desk, then approached her, his arms outstretched.

Her cares and worries eased as she nestled into his embrace, clinging to him. He caressed her back and whispered in his native tongue into her ear. In his adopted language, he said, "Ssshhh… *chérie*, everything will be okay."

She wanted this moment to last forever. She could tell he felt the same way.

Why does life have to be so damn complicated?

She pushed away from him, trying to deny the stirring feelings. She refused to let this happen. Not here, not now.

They had known each other for years, but over the last twelve months, their friendship had deepened.

"Is he here, Jacques?"

"He's here, yes. But I don't think it would be wise for you to see him."

Puzzled, she looked up at him. Her heart threatened to betray her, and his words annoyed her, but she shivered away the feeling.

Why does everyone think they know what's best for me? Why can't anyone, even Jacques, give me credit for keeping my emotions in check?

Anger fuelled her exit. She headed down the hallway towards the changing rooms. Jacques followed her, making no further protest.

"I'll be the judge of that. Has he been opened up yet?" she said, flinching at her callous words.

She tore off her jacket as she walked, preparing to don the regulation protective suit before entering Jacques' theatre. "No greens, no admittance," he'd told her the very first time they'd met.

"*Oui*, I performed the post-mortem this morning. If it is any consolation to you, Lorne, not only would he not have survived an operation due to his injuries, though his heart was strong, he, well—"

"What you're trying to tell me is his cholesterol-filled diet would have killed him soon, anyway."

"I try to be tactful. I wouldn't necessarily have put it quite like that myself. But yes, that about sums up his state of health. Did he have any family?"

"Yeah, me... No, *only* me. He had a sister, but she died three years ago from a heart attack. That's why I nagged him about his poor diet. Maybe I should've left him to his own devices, at least he would've died happier—"

"Pete had a happy life. He loved his job. You know he was besotted with you, yes? I know, I watched him. I saw the way he hung on your every word. Um... he warned me off you, too. Made it clear he did not think I was 'good enough to wipe the drips from your nose'. I thought it a funny expression at the time. I had to ask a colleague what it meant. Once I knew, I thought he was probably right."

Was this what Pete had tried to tell me? Why hadn't I seen it if others had? The thought of them discussing her behind her back didn't sit well with her. *When and why had they been discussing me? What gave them the right?* She didn't feel in the proper frame of mind to challenge Jacques about it. Instead, she tried to reassure him of Pete's motives.

"Don't take it personally, Jacques. He was like a brother to me. We looked out for one another. My family was as much his family. He was just protecting Tom and Charlie. Oh God, I feel as though I've lost a limb. I'm going to miss the old sod."

Jacques didn't speak. Not often lost for words, he was struggling to know what to say. Maybe if she spoke French, he could convey his feelings, but then, she knew he would respect her wishes not to offer shallow words of comfort. He knew how close she and Pete had been. They had a true understanding that rarely happened in the Met.

After donning their pathology greens, they walked in silence towards the pristine, newly equipped post-mortem suite. Covered by a green sheet that stopped just short of the floor, Pete's unmistakable shape lay on the nearest stainless-steel table.

This is it. Hi, Pete, I'm here.

Her hand shook as she folded back the sheet, but her dread gave way to relief. The fear and pain etched on his face in his final moments had gone. Pete's chubby features were now angelic, pure, and peaceful.

Jacques lingered behind her. "Are you okay?" He squeezed her quaking shoulder.

She welcomed the support, and when she raised her shoulder, her cheek rested on the back of his hand. "I'll survive, Jacques. "

The comforting moment lasted for a few minutes.

"What happens now? When will his body be released for the funeral?"

"We need to carry out a few more tests first. A couple more hours should do it. The funeral home will collect him around five o'clock. Do you know what his preference was? Burial or cremation, I mean?"

"Now there's a question. It's not something we ever discussed. The subject never cropped up. Why would it? We regarded ourselves as indestructible." The mood had changed. She turned to face him. "I guess he'd prefer cremation. He once helped in the garden at home and squirmed when a long worm crawled across his hand."

"I think you are right. Cremation appeals to me more and more nowadays. I take it the police force will give him a good send-off?"

"They'd better, or I'll have something to say about it. Look, I have to go. Tom's waiting outside for me." Her cheeks flushed as she mentioned her husband's name.

Facing Pete's body again, she kissed his icy forehead, then whispered in his ear. "So long, sweetheart. Thanks for all the times you took care of me. Sorry I wasn't able to repay the favour."

As they left the post-mortem suite, Jacques said, "Lorne, you must not blame yourself for what happened. He had several near misses in the past, and going in with a jacket not properly done up—"

"I know. I'm mad at everything at the moment. Pete for flouting the rules, myself for not challenging the screwed-up system we work in, but then, if we'd had guns, we still couldn't have done much. We walked into a trap."

"And your one-woman campaign stands very little chance after the hoo-hah of the De Menezes case. I think it'll be a while before this country thinks of arming its police. Now, go home, try and get some rest. Let me know when the funeral has been arranged. I would like to attend, and, *chérie...*"

She had stripped off her protective suit and was about to slip on her shoes, but something in his tone caused her to search out his ocean-blue eyes.

"I was going to say, you know where I am if you need a shoulder to cry on." He tapped his shoulder and gave her a cheeky wink.

After stepping into her shoes, she walked over to him, kissed his cheek, and embraced him in a bear hug. "Thanks, Jacques. I'm so lucky to have you as a friend."

Without waiting for a response, she walked towards the exit, afraid of what the consequences might be if she stayed around him any longer. She allowed herself one peep back before closing the door behind her. The dejection outlined in the slope of his shoulders tugged at her heart, but what could she do?

Chapter Three

"Shit." She'd driven straight through a red light. The sound of the indignant honking of the driver's horn behind her was still ringing in her ears as Lorne turned into the police station. She needed to pull herself together. And now, she would have to contend with the sympathetic looks and the meaningless condolences. Shutting the door on the reception and outer offices, Lorne closed her eyes and thanked God things hadn't got out of hand. She'd coped well with the nods and patronising smiles.

Her agenda to solve Pete's murder took priority over everything. Now, to make that clear to her colleagues in the Major Crime Squad, she entered the room with determination.

Silence greeted her. A rehearsed spokesman, Sam O'Connor, stood up and cleared his throat. "Ma'am, we're sorry—"

Lorne lifted her hand. Disappointed in their reaction, she spoke harsher than she'd intended. "Right, take it as read, we're all damn sorry, no one more than me. But what I want from you is action. Pete's gone, and while there's a breath left in my body, he'll not be forgotten. But now we need to nail the bastard who murdered him. I want one hundred and fifty percent from all of you. Our focus has to be on tracking the Unicorn. When we've caught him, then we grieve, right? In fact, if I catch anyone doing so before that, I'll suspend them on the spot. Have I made myself clear?"

No one answered. She turned her back on them. One more milestone needed to be tackled.

Lorne opened her office door and hesitated for a moment. The air held a tinge of Pete's Cool Water aftershave. They'd shared this cardboard box of a room for the past year due to refurbishments taking place in another section of the station.

"Free to speak honestly, ma'am?"

Detective Sergeant John Fox's voice came from behind, forcing her to step into her office.

"Yes, come in and take a seat. Is there something troubling you, John?"

"Um... A little harsh out there weren't you, ma'am?"

He sagged into the seat as if his reprimand had sapped his strength. She hoped he had more balls than that, considering he'd have to step up into Pete's shoes for a while.

"It needed to be said, John. I've seen better teams than mine crumble when a colleague has been lost in the line of duty. It's better to acknowledge how upset everyone is and quickly move on rather than let things fester. Pete would've wanted that too. You of all people should understand that."

"You're right as usual, boss. The gangs meeting down at the White Swan after work to have a commemorative drink for old Pete. You're welcome to join us."

"We'll see. Let's get down to business, shall we? What have you uncovered so far?"

He took his notebook from the top pocket of his black jacket, the same jacket he'd worn every day in the six years she'd known him.

"Right, this guy should be calling himself the Magician, the amount of tricks he's got tucked up his sleeve. It looks like he deliberately lured you and Pete into that alley."

"That fits the bastard's mentality, and I'd already come to that conclusion. Okay, give me what you have?"

"On the roof, SOCO found around thirty or so spent shells from a machine gun, rigged up to rotate at regular intervals, firing off three to four shots per second. If they hadn't stopped it when they did, it would've fired several hundred and kept you pinned down longer."

"So, he set off the machine gun to cover his escape. The crafty little shit. But judging by the amount of rounds fired, he couldn't have got away much before the response team got there. If only they'd been a little bit quicker... What else? Any idea how he escaped?"

"There were prints found on the weapon, but we know from past experience they'll turn out to be forged, so I don't hold out much hope on that front. It seems most likely he made his getaway down the fire escape."

"Where does it lead?"

"Market Street. I've got a couple of guys looking through the CCTV footage now."

"Good work. But there's one thing puzzling me. How did he know we'd sent for backup? Oh, I know, it's natural we would, but he wouldn't know we had it close by. The noise from the helicopter could have been anything. They're always hovering over London. Anyway, John, keep me informed as things develop."

"Will do, ma'am. By the way, the DCI popped in earlier, said he wanted a word with you as soon as you arrived." John rose as he spoke.

Lorne's conscience prodded her. He looked weary. She may not have wanted sympathy herself, but she had a duty of care towards her team. *Bugger. She'd mucked up...*

"John, how are you holding up?"

"Fair to middling, ma'am. Pete was a good man, one of the best. I'm gonna miss the old git. Been buddies for years, in the same class at Hendon, we were." Tears glistened in his eyes.

"I know, John. It's going to be hard for all of us over the next few weeks. Hey, I'm going to be relying on your support."

Taking him in her arms came natural to her. They all went back a long way. They jumped apart when the phone rang on her desk. Lorne turned back to answer it.

"DI Simpkins..."

"Ah, Lorne. How nice of you to answer my call personally..."

She immediately recognised the Unicorn's smug voice. "You *bastard.*" She covered the mouthpiece and indicated to John to trace the call.

"One step too far, Lorne. You only have yourself to blame for that. You had enough warnings to back off, and yet you chose to ignore them. Tut tut. Perhaps you'll be more vigilant next time, and I'm confident there will be a next time, dear Inspector."

His laughter sickened her.

"Just get on with it. Why are you ringing?"

"Am I keeping you from something, Lorne?"

"Yes," she snapped back.

"Very well. I've had my fun, now let's get down to business. I want twenty million pounds. No, let me correct that. I'm demanding twenty million in cash be deposited on the roof of Great Ormond Street Hospital, within the next twenty-four hours—"

"Twenty million... Is this a joke?"

"Remember, remember, the fifth of November... Only I, dear Lorne, am not your Guy Fawkes. I won't fail."

"That's ludicrous. You wouldn't dare."

"Doubt me at your peril, dear lady. In twenty-three hours and fifty-nine minutes, and oh, thirty seconds, London will see the biggest firework display ever. Speak later, dear."

The phone clicked.

Lorne stood as if she were encased in ice. *The Houses of Parliament.*

Chapter Four

"Is he in?"

Lorne anticipated the secretary's move to bar her way and marched towards the chief inspector's office.

"Yes. But he's in a meeting."

"With whom?"

"Superintendent Greenfall. And I have strict instructions they're not to be disturbed."

The secretary lived up to her nickname, Wily Fox, as by the time she'd said this, her sly, hop, skip, and jump had her positioned in front of DCI Roberts's office before Lorne could reach it.

"Get out of my way." Tugging Wily Fox's cardigan achieved nothing but a resounding bump louder than a knock on the DCI's door.

If Lorne had been a lesser woman, she would have given in under the look Wily Fox gave her. Instead, she tried a shove. The other woman's resistance had them locked tight against the door.

"I have urgent news for the—" Her words became lost in a mouthful of shirt as a gaping hole sucked them both in. Mortified, Lorne could do nothing. A few wobbly moments later, the chief regained his balance.

"What in God's name…"

It took Lorne a moment to disentangle herself from Wily Fox.

"Sorry, Chief. I've just received a call from the Unicorn and thought you should know about it straight away."

"Well, if it's that important you'd better come in. Thank you for trying, Margaret. Perhaps you can rustle up some refreshments for us?"

Wily Fox's protest stayed locked behind tight lips. Another deadly look and the door slammed behind her.

"Lorne." Superintendent Greenfall acknowledged her with a curt nod. His balding head shone like a beacon beneath the office lights, his face a picture of disgust at her abrupt intrusion.

"Sir."

"Take a seat, Lorne," the chief said.

She sat down next to Superintendent Greenfall, the man she despised most in the Met.

"Before we find out what made you barge in here, I would like to offer my condolences for the loss of your partner. Pete was a fine man... One of the best."

"He was, Chief. He'll be hard to replace." Anxious to keep her composure, she said, "About the Unicorn—"

"Of course, Inspector. Surprise us," the superintendent stated in a bored tone.

"He's holding the Houses of Parliament to ransom."

"That's absurd!" Greenfall shifted uncomfortably in his chair.

Detective Chief Inspector Roberts ignored him. "Go on."

"He's demanding twenty million pounds in the next twenty-four hours... Actually, make that twenty-three hours and fifty minutes. He warned that unless we meet his ultimatum, he'll blow up the Houses of Parliament. I think we should take him seriously, sir. It's not in his genes to make idle threats."

"I see..." The DCI sounded calm, but his pen raced over his pad.

"Well, I don't," Greenfall snapped.

"With respect, sir—"

"Lorne," Roberts warned.

"With respect, sir, havoc is this man's middle name. I should know. I've been on his tail for the past eight years. Only a *fool* would take what this man says lightly." Lorne narrowed her eyes.

"The inspector has a point, sir. She knows this man better than anyone else on the Met."

"Is that right, Chief Inspector? Then answer me this. Why is it that DI Simpkins has been unable to capture him? After eight bloody years. The fact is this terrorist has avoided capture for that long. The inspector here has let him slip through her fingers."

Lorne's pulse thumped. *How dare he question my detecting skills!*

"Have you any idea what type of person Unicorn is, sir?"

"I've read the reports, Inspector—"

"You may have read the reports, but—"

"That's enough, Lorne—" Roberts jumped in.

"I will not stand for insubordination, Chief Inspector."

"I'm sorry, sir." Roberts said.

"I didn't mean from you, man, but from your inspector here."

A smile threatened, but Lorne managed to suppress it. She found it priceless watching the superintendent huffing and puffing like a raging bull.

"Perhaps you can make an exception, in light of what happened to her partner. This isn't Lorne's normal behaviour."

"Sir, I—"

"Leave it, Lorne."

"No, let her speak. Let's hear what the wise inspector has to say."

The superintendent's smugness tortured her. She clenched her fists tightly again; the temptation to wipe the self-righteous grin off his face was so great, her fingernails dug into her palms.

"The fact is, sir, the Unicorn has resources at his disposal which, frankly, leave us standing. He alters his appearance more times than I change my underwear. He clicks his fingers, and helicopters, boats, or even private jets seem to appear in minutes. He has guns the Russian army would be proud of owning. Whereas, I'm forbidden to even look at a bloody gun, let alone put my hands on one. Even protective vests are in short supply due to the cutbacks. If they hadn't been, my partner wouldn't be lying in the morgue at this very moment, because the one he had didn't bloody fit."

"It's your duty to society to arrest this man at the earliest opportunity."

The pompous bastard didn't even acknowledge the difficulties.

"How? We thought we had him cornered yesterday, but he'd set us up. What I need, *sir*, is special dispensation to carry a gun. I have the necessary training. I gained these skills in my own time with a force instructor."

"Out of the question, and besides, you had no right to the training. The ranges are for selected staff. I demand to know the name of your instructor," Greenfall said angrily.

Shit. "I'm… er… I can't remember his name, sir."

Roberts coughed awkwardly. "Actually, sir, I think Lorne has a valid point, and I'm personally asking you to consider her request. I'll take full responsibility, as her senior."

Lorne held her breath. She could see Greenfall mulling it over in his mind.

"Okay, I agree if it's the only way to capture this criminal. But the commissioner will need to give the all clear. What's your next step, Inspector?"

"My team's looking through the CCTV footage from yesterday's incident. Our priority is to get an ID on this guy. We have clips of him from other scenes, and the forensic guys are trying to use facial recognition software to make a match. Unfortunately, to our knowledge, he's only been spotted on camera at three other locations."

The superintendent stood up and headed towards the door. He threw a needless order over his shoulder as he left the room. "Keep me informed of *any* developments."

"Yes, sir." Lorne spoke in unison with the chief.

The instant the door shut behind him, Roberts demanded, "What the fuck was all that about, Lorne?"

"He's a prick, Chief. We both know that."

"I agree, but you've got to curb that temper of yours, or he'll have you off the force quicker than you can say, 'I've got tickets for the policeman's ball, want to be my partner?'"

"Similar to the way he forced my father off the force, you mean?"

"Let it go, woman. God knows, your father has."

"Has he? How the hell would you know? When was the last time you visited him? It's pitiful the way he spends every day sitting in his conservatory, staring out at his garden. A garden he used to tend with pride, which now resembles a miniature jungle in the middle of suburbia."

"Lorne, your father left the force two years ago, and you know as well as I do, his decline has only happened since your mother died." He came around his desk, sat in the seat the superintendent had vacated, and placed both his hands on top of hers. The show of concern affected her, and tears trailed down her face.

"Come on, sweetheart, let it out."

Roberts' hypnotic voice transported her back to a family party five years earlier. She could see her beautiful mother, fussing over a table laden with food. It was a hot July afternoon, and they'd all gathered for a barbeque. Dad, dressed in the latest obscene apron, turned the sausages and burgers while Pete, guzzling cans of lager, talked to Tom about Arsenal, their favourite football team. Charlie, her angelic little daughter, helped her grandma, carrying cardboard plates and plastic knives.

And what had become of those fine people? Pete was dead, Mum had been stolen from them by breast cancer ten months

24

previously, and Dad was acting as though he couldn't wait for the day he'd join her. Her own marriage was at breaking point, and Charlie was having a ball living up to the terrible-teenager tag.

"Don't be nice to me. I'll be all right in a minute. It's just dealing with arseholes like Greenfall. It makes me question if it's all bloody worth it."

"Look, Lorne. You could do with a break—"

"No!"

"Okay, relax. I just thought—"

"I know, and I appreciate the thought, Chief, but I can't afford the time. Not now. Not with the Unicorn active. I have to be on hand to deal with his latest threat. I would be letting Pete down if I bowed out. Besides there is something I haven't told you."

"What?"

"I think we have a mole in our midst…"

Chapter Five

The moment Lorne walked through the swinging doors, she made for DS Fox.

"John, that CCTV footage, anything come of it?"

"Yes, boss, a bit of a breakthrough. We have a full-on mugshot from Marks' camera. Forensics are comparing it with earlier shots, *and* a four-by-four on the edge of an alley just off Market Street. They're running the plates through the system. Storey, got anything yet?"

"Give us a chance, boss. Hey, wait a minute. Yes."

Lorne and John crossed the room and looked over DC Storey's shoulder.

"UNI 123 is licensed to a Russian businessman, Sergei Abromovski. He lives in the heart of the city. Runs a business called Trelgo Oil. I'll start a background check on both."

"Good job, Storey. I'll put a pint behind the bar for you later. That's if our send-off to Pete is still on. Any decision on that yet, boss, in light of us being in the thick of it all?" John said.

"Yep, I think we should go ahead as planned. I've told the chief about it. He didn't object and said he'd join us for a while."

"Great, so what do you think of this little lot?"

"It sounds too bloody good to be true to me. What the hell is he playing at? He never makes mistakes like this," Lorne replied thoughtfully.

John nodded. "Well, let's hope he has. Surely not even he can be on top of his game all the time."

"I'll drink to that one. Right, let's go see what Mr. Abromovski has to say for himself. Give me a ring when you get more info, Storey."

* * *

The lift reached the penthouse office at breakneck speed.

"Shit, good job I didn't have that full English."

"Wimp." Lorne mocked him, despite the unsettled feeling in her own stomach.

The plush foyer had several doors leading off it. They chose the one marked Mr. Abromovski's Personal Assistant. Flashing their IDs at the buxom blonde behind the desk, Lorne asked, "Is he in?"

"Yes, but—"

Lorne nodded to John. Together they barged through the ornate double doors behind the PA's desk.

"Hey, you can't... I'm sorry, Mr. Abromovski, they just—"

The office's brightness startled Lorne. Everything in it glittered, giving the impression of a room made of mirrors.

"Mr. Abromovski, I'm Detective Inspector Simpkins, and this is my... my partner, Detective Sergeant Fox. We need to ask you a few questions."

The man sitting behind the thick glass desk looked to be in his late fifties. She focused on him for a moment. Apart from her distrust, the view through the wall-sized window behind him, though magnificent and far-reaching over the capital, did nothing to stave off her queasy feeling. This vast expanse of light reflecting in the desk had formed her first opinion of the office, but when she glanced away, she saw the other three walls held floor-to-ceiling books, stacked library fashion. All leather bound and of the legal and encyclopaedia type, they relieved the dazzling effect and settled her stomach.

Abromovski stood up and shrugged into his expensive jacket.

He spoke with a thick accent. "Police? What can I do for you? And why have you barged in here in this way? Am I under arrest? If so, it can only be because you British hold me responsible for the high price of petrol."

Lorne ignored his poor attempt at humour. "Where were you on Tuesday afternoon, sir?"

He gulped and turned towards the window. "I believe I was here all day. Of course, I would have to verify this with my diary." He spoke to his reflection.

Lorne went to stand beside him. Forcing herself to look out, she couldn't help being taken aback. He had a bird's-eye view of the Houses of Parliament. Any thoughts of him being an innocent bystander soon disappeared.

"Thank you. I'd like to see your diary. Did you have any meetings that day?"

When she looked back at him, she found his eyes scrutinising her body. She scowled at him, and a cold trickle of unease ran up her spine. He shifted his gaze, and she felt triumphant. He shuffled some papers as he answered her question. "Yes, I am a busy man. My life is a series of meetings."

"We'll need a list."

The Russian looked at her and quizzically raised an eyebrow.

"What type of car do you drive, sir?"

"Take your pick, Inspector. I am a very wealthy man."

"On *Tuesday*, what car did you bring to work?"

"Let me think. Ah, that's right, my chauffeur brought me in my black limo. The white one was in the workshop for a service. I prefer the white model, though. So much more stylish than plain black. So much more sexier, wouldn't you agree?"

"I'm not really interested in cars, Mr. Abromovski. I tend to see them as a reflection of a man's ego."

He laughed. "Inspector, I am a very busy man. Tell me what this is all about."

"Do you own a black four-by-four, licence plate UNI 123?"

"Yes, I do…"

"Did you lend that vehicle to anybody or notice it missing at all on Tuesday of this week?"

Lorne stepped towards the retreating Russian, trying to unnerve him, an old trick her father had taught her at the start of her career, one of many he'd written in a notebook. Her father had mastered the art of dealing with unsavoury characters with something to hide. It worked. Abromovski stepped backwards and bumped into his chair.

"No… No… As far as I know, the car remained at my home."

Her mobile's high-pitched buzz interrupted the conversation. With her eyes fixed on Abromovski, she flipped the lid.

"Storey, ma'am. I've dug up some stuff on Abromovski. I think you should give him a wide berth at the moment and get back to base ASAP."

"Elaborate for me?"

"He is already under surveillance, and we could be stepping on some very important toes."

"Right. We're on our way."

Abromovski's relief was evident in his smirk.

"We'll have to leave it there, sir. Something has come up." She couldn't let him think he had the upper hand. "We'll be back. I'm not convinced by your obvious attempts to put me off course—"

She caught John's eye. His gaze held a warning. He must've guessed the phone call had warned her to back off.

When they left the room, Lorne could feel Abromovski's steel-cut eyes boring into her back.

"Guys like that make my skin crawl."

John didn't comment.

Chapter Six

The Unicorn traced a finger along the scantily clad girl's thigh. A whore, a high-class one, but still a whore, she'd serve his purpose for now. He had better things lined up for the very near future...

His phone juddered the tune he'd assigned to the Russian. The interruption to the pleasure he'd anticipated rendered his patience tauter than a hangman's noose. As he flipped the lid, he told the girl to take a hike.

"Sergei?"

The Russian's part as a useful link in his plans would soon end.

"The police have just left here. They know my car was used by you on Tuesday—"

"Calm down, Sergei. What exactly did they say?"

Sergei Abromovski relayed in full his conversation with the two detectives and how the phone call the woman detective had received caused her to abruptly end their meeting.

"So... Just what, exactly, are you worried about?"

"What's going on? Are you listening to me? You were careless. You've implicated me in your little game. I demand to know what you intend doing about it."

"Trust me. My plan is about to get interesting."

"What the hell do you mean by that? Did you incriminate me intentionally?"

The Unicorn bit off the end of a Havana cigar and lit it with the solid gold lighter lying beside him on the antique mirror-topped bedside table. Another few hours, and it'll all be worth it. Tomorrow will be the start for him. He thought about the yacht he would acquire and sail to Monaco, where he would surround himself with beautiful rich people. For the Russian, it would be his last day...

"Sergei, would I do something like that to you, my great friend? It was a genuine accident, I assure you."

The lie sounded convincing enough, and after a moment, the Russian accepted it and rang off. The Unicorn reclined on his bed, a smile curling his lip. *My father would be proud of me.*

Thinking of his father triggered the pleasing memory of his sixteenth birthday. On that day, he'd savoured the sweet taste of revenge for all the lessons of 'use and abuse,' which had been ground into his very soul after years of watching his father's fists, large as melons, brutalise his mother into submission. Then, when she cowered at his feet, a bloodied heap of nothing, he'd beat him, his only son, as a warning of what he'd get if he stepped out of line.

But his day of retribution had come. A mercy killing some might say. His father *had* begged for mercy. He'd begged in hollers, loud, hoarse, and deeper than screams, drowning out the crack each of his chubby fingers as they broke in two.

Inhaling smoke deep into his lungs, the Unicorn blew rings into the air and watched them disintegrate. His mind replayed pictures of his father's entrails as they spewed out, like overgrown worms. Tears of blood had seeped from his father's eyes, red drops trickling down his ugly face. He'd drawn and quartered the bastard.

Describing the incident in graphic detail with the intention of keeping greedy business associates in line had had the desired effect. Associates always thought twice about double-crossing him.

He thought about the Russian, replaced his father's image with Sergei Abromovski's, and allowed his imagination to act out the torture once more. He experienced a pleasure far deeper than any the whore would have given him.

Chapter Seven

"Whose toes will we be stepping on?" Lorne asked as they returned to the squad room.

"MI6, ma'am," Storey said.

John let out a high-pitched whistle. "Them are pretty big toes, boss."

"How did you find out, Storey?"

"I was doing the background checks on our friend Sergei and his company, ma'am, when my computer crashed. Next thing I knew, my phone was ringing, and this guy announced he was from MI6 and told me to back off. When I asked why, he told me to ask my superior to ring him ASAP. His name's Tony Warner, ma'am. That's his extension number right there."

Lorne took the post-it and noted the number Storey pointed to amongst several scrawled on it.

"Sounds ominous. I'll give him a ring. I wonder what our Russian friend has been up to."

* * *

"Is that Tony Warner?"

"It is. Who wants to know?"

"Detective Inspector Lorne Simpkins."

"Who?"

"Cut the crap, Mr. Warner, you know damn well who I am and why I am ringing. Do you have a problem?" She suspected he had more than just the one.

"We should meet."

"I haven't got time. I'm on a tight deadline."

"I'm well aware of your deadline, Inspector. You're barking up the wrong tree with Sergei Abromovski. He has nothing to do with this."

"Oh? What makes you so sure about that?"

"I've said enough over the phone. Meet me in fifteen minutes in the White Swan car park."

"Right. I'm driving a Vauxhall Vectra—"

"I know what you drive, and I'll have no trouble recognising you. So no need for the white rose in your collar. Oh, and come alone."

Just who the hell does this guy think he is? All this cloak-and-dagger bollocks.

"John, I'm going out. It looks like our hands are tied on this investigation until I've heard what this guy has to say."

"I'll just get my jacket—"

"No. You're not needed."

"You're meeting this guy alone? Where?"

"The White Swan car park, and I'm sure I don't need an escort or a bullet-proof. He's MI6, a supposedly good guy."

Lorne arrived first. Not long after, another Vauxhall Vectra, not dissimilar to her own, pulled into the space alongside. Out the corner of her eye, she observed the thirty-something fit man staring straight ahead of him. Warner, no doubt, and sitting there with an arrogance that demanded she should join him.

Sod that. You want to speak to me, buddy, my car is just as warm.

Eventually, the penny dropped. He got out of his car and banged the door shut. He threw himself into the seat beside her like a rebellious teenager.

Jumped up little prick.

"Enough foreplay, let's have it, Warner. What have you got to tell me that couldn't be discussed over the phone?"

"We've had Trelgo Oil and Sergei Abromovski under observation for a while."

"Why?"

"MI6 don't need to give a reason."

"Bollocks. Stop wasting my time. Either you tell me now, or I'll take things higher."

"Ah, spoken like a woman who always gets her own way. Well, not this time, Inspector."

"We'll see about that. What's the point of our meeting? You may as well leave. I've more important fish to fry than to sit here bandying stupid words with you."

"Okay, you win. Let's just say he's been a naughty boy."

"Not good enough—"

"Christ, I'd hate to come up against you down a fucking dark alley."

"Don't play games. I'm not in the mood. You probably know why. Just give me the details."

"He surfaced at the end of 2004, started sniffing around a premiership football team. A couple of our overseas agents asked us to keep an eye on him. He has his fingers in many pies. Drugs, guns, people, you name it. His name appears to crop up all the time."

"What do you mean, 'people'?"

"Trafficking, but he's pretty shrewd, never leaves any kind of trail. Maybe he has friends in high places we haven't found out about yet. Anyway, roughly six to eight months ago, he started meeting up with this guy. Can't give you a name, I'm afraid. He's a bit of a mystery. We've tried several times to trail him, but he loses his tail every time. He's more slippery than a bar of Lifebuoy. I've got a photo of him if it will help."

He handed her a glossy ten by eight. "Any ideas?"

"Can't be sure, but it could be the Unicorn. Can I keep this copy? The guy has been on my radar for the past eight years. I'm not a hundred percent certain, though."

"Keep it. Now, it's your turn to spill the beans. Why are you after 'Mr. Nice Guy', Sergei Abromovski?"

"You told me you're aware of our deadline. How?"

"Don't you trust me, Inspector?"

"It's not that. It's just—"

"I know. You have a mole in your team."

"I think so, but how—"

"Lucky guess."

"And I'm supposed to believe that?"

"Well, let's analyse it. DS Pete Childs, your partner, is dead. This Unicorn guy has escaped your clutches, yet again. And escaped in the nick of time, despite him being cornered, correct?"

Lorne nodded.

"The whole scenario stinks of insider information," Warner said. "Take it from someone who knows. I'm a professional spy, after all. Any ideas on the mole's identity?"

"Negative. Everything is pure conjecture at this point, and with this damn deadline hanging over us, finding the mole is low down on our list of priorities."

"It should be your first. Sod the deadline. The mole must be flushed out."

"But—"

"Look, think logically about this, Inspector. Do you want the Unicorn to remain one step ahead of you?"

"Of course not—"

"Right, how many officers do you have on your team?"

"Um… twenty." His theory had blown her concentration. *Find the mole first.*

"And how many can you honestly say you can trust?"

That was the second time that question had cropped up today, and she still didn't have the foggiest idea.

"I take it your silence doesn't give a vote of confidence to any of them? A good starting point, otherwise, the very one you are sure it isn't will turn out to be the one it is, and you will have missed the clues pointing to them."

Her stomach churned. Christ, if she couldn't trust her colleagues, then who in this twisted world could she trust?

He carried on in the same vein, asking her questions: any new recruits, anyone seem more flush than usual, anyone not acting how they normally do or found in places they shouldn't be, and so on, and so on. He jotted down names into lists as she spoke.

She felt uncomfortable. "What's this all about? Why so much interest?"

"I'm going to do some digging for you."

"Why?"

"Because I'm a nice guy, and I'm at a loose end at the moment. Whilst you have a deadline to meet."

An MI6 agent at a loose end, that'll be the day. *Is it wise to trust him? But then, what other option do I have?*

"That's nice of you…"

"I sense a 'but'."

They stared long and hard into each other's eyes. Was it feasible to trust one another, given that they'd only just met? Lorne decided trusting him would be her best option at the moment, so she outlined the plan she and the DCI had regarding the get-together that evening.

He nodded his agreement. "Then what?"

"We start laying traps, I guess. Our plan is still in its infancy. We haven't had time to draw up anything concrete yet."

"This is what I suggest you do…"

He went into what he had planned. Besides digging into all their backgrounds and current finances, he wanted to know about anyone who hadn't shown that night, though he doubted there would be any.

Warner's take was that they were dealing with an intelligent copper, and if Pete was as popular as she said, then despite any other motive their mole may have, disrespecting Pete's send-off would risk too much animosity from the other Met officers.

"When I have something, I'll get back to you. Then you and the DCI can start laying traps, and let's see if the one it's nailed down to takes the cheese. Sound good?"

"It's good, but it goes without saying I'll need to run it past Chief Inspector Roberts. Now tell me, what's in it for you? Why are you so eager to lend a hand on this?"

His response of wanting a bit of action and being at a loose end didn't convince her. She had a gut feeling there were other motives.

They swapped mobile numbers before going their separate ways. Lorne went straight to DCI Roberts and filled him in with the details of her meeting.

"You think you can trust this guy, Lorne?" Roberts asked.

"About as much as I trust my own team."

"That much, huh?"

Chapter Eight

The décor of the bar at the White Swan looked as tired as ever. Lorne checked her watch. Just on six o'clock.

John spotted her and the DCI walk in and rushed over, offering to buy them a drink.

Her cynical side prodded her. She wondered if he could be the one. His offer could indicate his guilt. If he sucked up to his seniors, they'd never think of him as a mole.

For Christ's sake, girl, are you that screwed up that paranoia has set in?

The chief thanked John but declined his generosity, then walked over to the bar and gave the barmaid fifty quid. Everyone cheered. Someone shouted.

"To Pete, God rest his soul."

They all raised their glasses. The silence that followed was louder than the cheer.

Lorne surveyed the room. Officers either dabbed at their eyes or sat staring, allowing the tears to drip. Some of her pain eased when she saw how much the group had thought of Pete.

The DCI reminded them all they were due back on duty in thirty minutes. He grabbed Lorne by the elbow and guided her to a quiet corner, ignoring the disgruntled groans. They sat alongside the large inglenook fireplace, a new addition to the bar that didn't fit in with its surroundings. The heat from it made Lorne's cheeks warm.

The DCI faced her, putting his back to the group. She watched them over his shoulder.

"Right, Lorne, anyone missing?"

"Simon Teller isn't here, nor is Flash Harry…"

"Who?"

"Alan Jackson, so called because of his MR6 sports car. He's rumoured to like his women just as fast, if not faster than his cars. Everyone else seems to be here. Hang on—Laura Crane—she's not here. I overheard a conversation the other day concerning her. Now, what the hell was it about?"

She rubbed her temple, trawling through her fuzzy mind. The chief jumped when she snapped her thumb and middle finger together.

"That's right, she was talking to one of the men. It appears her life is one long stream of work and caring for her bedridden mother. I meant to have her in, point her towards the counselling service and benevolent lot to see if there's anything they can help her with, but all this blew up. I guess we can rule her out."

"Go and ring Warner, and give him all *three* names."

"Not Laura Crane's."

"All *three*, Lorne."

Lorne pushed open the door to the ladies' toilet. She hoped Laura might be in there, but she wasn't. Mobile in hand, she stepped into the last cubical, dropped the loo seat, perched her bum on it, and placed the call. Warner answered after the first ring. She gave him the names and a brief outline on each. His interest piqued when she told him about Alan and his playboy ways.

"On a copper's salary? Sounds a bit suspicious, don't you think? You never mentioned this earlier."

"You asked about anyone who has recently become flush. Alan's been like it for ages."

He showed the same interest in Laura. "The quiet ones are the worst."

"You'll be working all night, I take it?" he asked.

"Yes. Get back to me the minute you think you have something."

She spoke this last into a dead phone. "Charming. Goodbye to you, too."

Why do men always have to be so damn rude?

Chapter Nine

Lorne and the DCI arrived back at the station before the rest of the team.

"Shall we have a quick search around the desks?" She'd spoken to the DCI's back as he headed towards his office.

"No. We're not getting into the human rights, bloody palaver."

"Well, that leaves waiting to see if Warner gets back to us. In the meantime, I'd better ring home. I'm expected back tonight."

"Ditto," the DCI said.

She knew the call would piss Tom off and place yet more stress on their fragile marriage. Her recent workload had stretched Tom's patience to its limits. She thought of Jacques Arnaud and wondered if she would still be with Tom if it weren't for their daughter, Charlie. She didn't know, but didn't like the thought of her call making things a zillion times worse.

"Hi, sweetheart, it's me."

"What's up now? You only use endearments when you're about to tell me something bad."

"I'm sorry, Tom. I won't—"

"You're not ringing to say you're not coming home?"

The sound of saucepan lids banging came down the receiver. She imagined him with the phone wedged between his ear and shoulder while he continued to cook their meal. Guilt stopped her from answering. The silence stretched the gulf between them until the crash of pots landing in the sink broke it. Lorne stiffened, shocked by his reaction.

"Please don't be like that, Tom. Something big has come up. I can't go into details over the phone, but the whole team has to work through the night."

"Ever heard of delegation, Lorne?"

"Even the DCI is working through the night on this one."

"Ah, how bloody cosy for you."

Why in God's name did I mention Sean Roberts? Jesus. That's all I need, the past dredged up again. She wondered why every argument or disagreement always came back to this. She and Sean had enrolled in the force together, and after completing their training, they'd become partners in every sense of the word. Two years into the relationship, Tom had come on the scene.

A mechanic in his father's garage, he'd come to her rescue when her old banger had given up the will to live. Within an hour, Tom had fixed the fault and arranged a dinner date with her for that evening. Their courtship had been brief, intense, lustful, and passionate. They walked down the aisle six months to the day of their first meeting.

Sean had coped with being dumped by grabbing the promotion offered to him and moving to a force two hundred miles north. He'd reappeared twelve months ago. Lorne's professional world had turned upside down when she'd learned who would be taking over on the retirement of her old DCI. Her fears proved to be unfounded. He'd taken her to one side, told her bygones were bygones, and reassured her that her job was safe.

If the news of Sean's returning had worried her, it had *devastated* Tom.

"Look, Tom, how many times do I have to tell you? It's you I love. You have nothing to worry about where Roberts is concerned."

"Who are you trying to convince?"

"He's married, Tom. *We're* married. That's the end of it, okay?

"Yeah, but—"

"No. No buts, Tom. Listen, is Charlie home yet?

"Nope."

"Where is she?"

Charlie, their thirteen-year-old daughter, seemed intent on pushing teenage rebellion to the extreme.

"She rang earlier, told me a group of them were going into town straight from school. Before I could tell her to come straight home, she'd hung up on me, and her phone miraculously died when I tried to ring back."

Great. Yet another thing to worry about.

"I'll ask Sergeant Harris to get uniform to look out for her."

"And if they find her, are you going to bang her up in a cell all night?"

His attitude got to her. "If that's what it takes, Tom, that's exactly what I'll do."

"You can't do that."

"Like you give a toss. You've made it clear you don't want anything more to do with her discipline. Well, I've got news for you,

Tom. Kids stopped going to church and singing in choirs long ago. You piss me off with your holier-than-thou attitude. I can't help wondering who the child is in our family, Charlie or you."

The sound of the phone banging down made her realise what she'd said. *Shit. He'll be sulking for weeks now.*

Charlie had built a reputation for herself amongst Lorne's colleagues, one that caused Lorne embarrassment. But the way Tom used their daughter's antics as a weapon hurt her. She was fed up with him throwing the same insults her way. "If you were any kind of mother or if you were around more, she wouldn't be like this."

Maybe the ring of truth didn't help, but neither did the company Charlie kept. One or the other of them seemed to always be up before the magistrates' youth court. Charlie had been near to it herself, but Lorne's colleagues had come to the rescue just in time. One particular incident stood out. The CCTV footage of Charlie's so-called friend's behaviour had shocked Lorne, not in its contents, but to think her own daughter was involved in such hooliganism.

Her well-thumbed copy of *The Guide to Successful Parenting* hadn't helped either, as none of the suggestions had worked with Charlie. Even a professional counselling session had ended in disaster, when Charlie lashed out, both physically and verbally, and bolted from the room. On that occasion, they'd punished Charlie by locking her in her bedroom, but she had escaped through her window, almost breaking her neck in the process. Tom had given up after that and resorted to firing the blame Lorne's way every time Charlie mucked up.

Well, sod him. If it's down to me to sort out the little minx, then that's exactly what I'm going to do.

Before Tom could ring back for round two, Lorne placed a call to the front desk.

"Sergeant Harris? It's DI Simpkins."

"Yes, ma'am, gone missing again, has she? I'll get the guys to keep an eye out for the young whippersnapper."

"Are you sure you're not my guardian angel in disguise?"

"Damn! The secret's out. Don't worry, ma'am, my lot'll track her down."

"Thanks, Burt. I'll be sure to remember you at Christmas."

The banter calmed her. She liked the sergeant. She went back to what she'd been doing, confident one of the uniforms on the beat would find Charlie and get her home safely within the hour.

Chapter Ten

Lorne's next call was to Tony Warner.

"Have you managed to find out anything?"

Warner laughed. "I forgot to tell you I have a nickname."

"Oh, what?"

"Mole Catcher."

"Meaning you do have something. Well, get on with it. The suspense is killing me."

"First up, Alan Jackson, haven't you ever wondered where he gets his money from?"

"It has been bandied about, yes. Why? Are you about to tell me something bad?"

"No, Alan Jackson is the son and heir to the MP of Gloucester, Saint John-Jackson. A multi-multi-millionaire so far up the prime minister's arse he'd need an operation to detach the bugger."

"You're kidding me. What the hell is he doing in the force?"

"Daddy told him to make his own way in life. He's new to your team, isn't he?"

"Yeah, about six months, I suppose. Why?"

"Rumour has it Daddy used to give young AJ an allowance, but didn't like the way he spent it. So he pulled the plug. I'm discounting him, but watch your back, Lorne. He has influential links."

"Message received. Go on."

"Simon Teller is as clean as boiled undies."

"I think I know where this is leading. I can't believe it—"

"Believe it, Lorne. Everything points to Laura Crane being your mole. You said something about her living at home caring for her sick mother?"

"That's right."

"Wrong! Her mother died five months ago of cancer."

"Jesus, but—"

"It's true. Her mother left Crane the house in her will. I've gone through her bank accounts and found large payments credited to her account."

"How large, how many, and how often?" Lorne listened in disbelief as he told her.

"Ten grand has found its way into Crane's account twelve times so far, but no set pattern as to when. The intervals between payments varied. They started around May 2006."

"Shit! I'll have to check her personnel file, but I think that's about the time she joined the force. The question is, was she vulnerable and easy to turn, or was she planted?"

"I'd go for the first option. Money talks, I know, but when it's a woman being used as a mole, it's usually emotional not financial."

"You mean, he used the fact that she's no oil painting and had a lonely life to pull her in?"

"Exactly. She's stereotypical. He wines and dines her, screws her like she'd never dreamt would ever happen, and she's hooked. Add the 'never could earn as much money in her life' factor, and a mole is born. She'll do anything for him and has no inclination that one day, she'll outlive her usefulness."

"You mean he'll kill her?"

"Mess with evil, and you usually die by the hands of evil. That's been my experience."

"If we wanted to help her, how could we do it?"

"Don't set her up. Confront her and bang her up for a while for her own safety."

"I'll speak to the DCI. By the way, has there been anything on the bomb threat?"

"They did a thorough search of the area around the Houses of Parliament, but nothing has come to light."

"Maybe he isn't planning a bomb. We've had reports loosely linking him to terrorism, in particular Islamic extremists," Lorne told him.

"What? Why the fuck didn't you tell me this in the beginning?"

"We were talking moles, remember? And—"

"Fuck that, Lorne, you should have said. So we could be looking at a suicide bomber?"

"It's a possibility. Don't you think?"

"I think I'm spending far too much time on this damn phone with you."

She knew by now not to expect a goodbye. *Oh, God, I wish I had trusted him in the first place.*

Chapter Eleven

"Get Crane in here," Roberts ordered.

"I'm not sure that is—"

"Now, Lorne. Time is of the essence."

"Yes, sir. But I think you're going about it the wrong way…"

DCI Roberts glared at her. The news of Crane's identification as the mole had shocked him.

There was no sign of Crane in the squad room when Lorne entered. John informed her that Crane had called in and said she had to take her mother to the hospital.

"When I reminded her about the urgency of the case, ma'am, she seemed pretty upset about letting everyone down. She's volunteered to drop into forensics on her way back, see if they've had any joy with the facial recognition, yet."

"The minute she comes back, tell me. I'd like a word with her. Nothing important, just let me know."

The downright liar, how dare she hide behind her dead mother's skirt!

"Right. By the way, Sergeant Harris has been looking for you," John said.

Lorne went through to her office, closed the door, and rang the front desk.

"Sergeant Harris, it's me. What's up?"

"Do you want the good news or the bad news first, ma'am?" the desk sergeant asked, trepidation edging his voice.

"The good news first, I suppose."

She braced herself and tumbled into her chair. *What the bloody hell has Charlie done now?*

"We've found Charlie. Umm… I'm afraid she was with a gang of hoodies causing chaos in the town centre."

"Christ, Burt, if that's the good news, it doesn't bode well for the bad."

"No, ma'am. I suppose I'd better ask if you're sitting down first."

"Yes, Burt, I'm sitting. You're starting to worry me, man. Get on with it. What has that wretched girl of mine been up to now?"

"Well, it's like this, ma'am. A couple of my men saw the gang. They were about to read them the riot act when out of nowhere came a black four-by-four. It pulled up alongside young Charlie, the back door opened, and a man leaned out and grabbed her."

Shit. A four-by four, a black four-by-four? Fear smacked her in the stomach.

"Ma'am, are you still there?"

"Yes, Burt. This four-by four, give me the plate number." She gulped in a large breath and exhaled slowly.

"Er... Uniform, November, India—"

"One two three."

"You know this car, ma'am? We were just about to run a check."

"Yes, Burt. God, did no one try to stop him?"

"My men were on the other side of the gang and didn't stand a chance, but a couple of the youngsters tried to hold on to Charlie. One of them got a boot in the face and a broken nose. The officers in attendance called for immediate backup. We activated the nearest patrol car, but they lost the trail. Every patrol is on the lookout for the car, but one big setback is that Charlie's school bag containing her mobile dropped to the ground. If she'd had that on her—"

"Oh, Burt, the guy who has Charlie is an evil bastard. Oh, God. Sorry, Burt. I'll get back to you."

She knew her weakened legs wouldn't be able to carry her to the DCI's office. Through a sea of tears, she fumbled with the phone and called his direct line.

"Lorne?"

"He's got my daughter! The bastard has got Charlie!"

Chapter Twelve

"Everyone, as you were."

Lorne wiped her eyes. She felt relieved to hear the DCI take charge and clear her team from her doorway. John gave her shoulders a last squeeze.

"Right, Fox, settle the team down. Tell them I'll brief them as soon as I can."

"Now, Lorne, give me a full report."

She told him all she knew. "Sean, what the hell is he going to do with her? She's a thirteen-year-old girl, for fuck's sake."

"Let's not speculate. First, ring Tom and tell him. Get him in here if that's what you both want."

With shaking fingers, she managed to speed dial Tom. "Tom... Oh, Tom, Charlie... She's been snatched..."

"Christ, Lorne. What... Who?"

"It's to do with a case I've been working on, and—"

"Not that wacko bastard Unicorn?"

"Yes, Tom. He's got our Charlie. Oh, God."

"I told you, Lorne. You're to blame. I fucking told you to give the case up."

His reaction, though predictable, appalled her. "You can't blame me any more than I blame myself, Tom."

"Has he contacted you? Made any demands?"

"No, he hasn't contacted since, God. Is it still today? I mean..." She looked at her watch: 11:00 PM. "He contacted me earlier, before... that's why I've had to stay on."

"What did he say then?"

"I can't tell you, Tom. I'm sorry, security—"

"Fuck that. Did he threaten to take Charlie?"

"No."

"But you know what he's planning, right?"

"Tom. I can't say—"

"Then I'll find someone who can!"

Lorne sat staring at the telephone.

"Is he coming over?" Roberts asked.

"No, sir, at least, I don't think so. He thinks I know something and I'm keeping him out of the loop. I think he'll get in touch with my dad and use him to go over our heads."

"Well, if it keeps him occupied. His reaction is normal, Lorne, well normal-ish. I'm surprised he doesn't want to be with you—"

The phone rang, cutting him off.

"DI Simpkins."

"Inspector, how are you?"

"Where is she? Where's my daughter? She's nothing to do with this. Let her go."

Roberts tapped her shoulder and signalled for her to keep talking. He left the office, she suspected to try to trace the call.

"Why, Inspector, how rude of you to forget your manners. What you should've said was, 'let her go, *please*' or even *pretty please.*"

He laughed, and Lorne found it hard to continue the conversation.

Roberts returned. Seeing how Lorne was struggling, he placed the phone on speaker.

"This is Chief Inspector Sean Roberts. To whom am I speaking?"

"Nice try, lover boy. I am right, aren't I? You and the inspector there used to be lovers many years ago, didn't you? You see, I do my homework well. Nice for you two to be working alongside one another again. Plenty of chances for a quick shag over your desk, eh?" His cruel, bitter, and twisted laugh filtered down the line.

"Let the girl go. What do you hope to accomplish holding her?"

"You coppers have got to be the dumbest people on this planet. She's not going anywhere. Let's just say she's my insurance policy, shall we? If I hang on to her, then I know my request will be so much easier to achieve."

"Mum, help me!"

"Charlie, I'm here. Don't be scared, baby."

"Charlie. Such a cute name. Bit of a tomboy is she, Inspector? Never mind, we'll soon knock that out of her." His voice changed as he barked out an order to someone in the room. "Take her away, and get her ready."

"You lay one hand on her, you crazy fucker, and I'll—"

DCI Roberts waved his hands and shook his head. Lorne realised her mistake when she heard the Unicorn order, "Bring her to me."

Lorne froze as Charlie's voice, full of spirit, came down the line. "Leave me alone." Then, Lorne heard a spitting noise and Charlie scream. "Bastard!"

Lorne, held her breath. *No, Charlie, don't!*

"Why, you little—"

Lorne couldn't bear it as a thwacking sound that was almost drowned out by Charlie's harrowing cries filled her heart with dread. Before she had time to react, the line went dead. With her whole body numb with terror, Lorne's mind seared with the knowledge she could do nothing to help her daughter.

"Why did she fight? It only made things worse."

"She's her mother's daughter, Lorne. Let's hope her spirit helps her get through this and doesn't hamper her survival."

"What do you suppose he meant about getting her ready? What was that all about?"

Her own deductions concerning the Unicorn's method of carrying out his earlier threat hit Lorne like a bullet between the eyes. "No… Oh God, no… A human bomb. Christ, Sean, we've got to find her. Oh God, help us."

"Lorne, calm down. Okay, I know I'm asking the impossible here, but you must try. You're racing ahead of yourself. I'll get one of the officers to take you home. I'm taking over the case."

She didn't argue with him. She knew she wouldn't be allowed to handle things, not now. She also knew the chief had gone back into professional mode. She had to do the same. She had to block out the horrific theory pounding around her brain. If she didn't, she wouldn't be able to convince him not to send her home. She had to stay and have her finger on the button. Yes, he'd be in charge, but she could guide him, make sure he made all the right moves.

Chapter Thirteen

Opening the door to the squad room hushed the buzz of conversation, which Lorne guessed centered around the whys and wherefores of Charlie's kidnapping and the fact Tom hadn't arrived to be with her when she most needed him.

As they walked towards the room, she told herself to remain quiet and allow the DCI to take charge. That changed within seconds as the far door opened and DC Crane walked through.

A vile hatred welled up inside Lorne. "Arrest that woman."

The file Crane carried fluttered to the ground. The images in black-and-white print floated out. Crane stood stupefied in the doorway. Nobody moved until the chief reinforced Lorne's order. Crane turned to run, but two nearby officers grabbed her. Lorne reached her in seconds and hit out with a vicious swipe.

"You disgust me. I just hope it was worth it, Crane."

"Oh, it was, Inspector, it was." She licked the blood running from her lip.

"Laura Crane, you're under arrest for aiding and abetting a known criminal and knowingly hampering police whilst carrying out their duties." Lorne didn't take her eyes from Crane's as she continued. "Take her down. I want her held in custody overnight. We'll interview her later. Get the desk sergeant to read her rights to her and book her in. I want you two back here ASAP. The DCI has an important briefing for you all. Oh, by the way, tell the sergeant to put in his report that she slipped and banged her lip whilst trying to get away, but that she's not to be charged with resisting arrest."

No one objected to the lie.

A few minutes later, the two detectives were back, and the whole squad sat rigid with attention. "Right, can everybody hear me?" DCI Roberts asked.

The chief explained what they knew so far about the kidnap and how Crane had been uncovered as a mole.

"Therefore, you'll all understand when I tell you I am taking over the case."

"What's our next step, sir?" John asked.

"May I?" Lorne asked.

The DCI nodded and sat on the corner of the nearest desk.

"First, we check the file Crane dropped. DC Teller, I see you've gathered it up."

Lorne took the file from him and opened it. "It's not easy to be sure, but I suspect Crane has doctored them. Teller, after the briefing, take them back to forensics and get another set. When we've got the true results, we'll be in a better position of finding this scumbag. Right, I want you to hear it from me. The chief taking over is only temporary. I'll keep abreast of everything and stay close to the DCI, ready to step back into the lead once— Well…"

"Okay." DCI Roberts stood up. "We have to keep our eye on the ball at all times. Anything, anything at all you find, no matter how inconsequential you think it is, I want you to run it by me. Got it?"

"Yes, sir," the group shouted back.

"Time is of the essence here, people. So what do we know about this guy so far?" Pointing at the charts lining the far wall, he went through the main areas of knowledge.

"One. He became high profile about eight years ago, as a result of the murder of a drug baron in which he was implicated. Two. His methods are gruesome, as evidenced by the way this baron and subsequent suspected victims met their end. We have one burnt alive, others who had their throats cut, and two were found with their penises cut off and stuck in their mouths. The removal of the genitals had taken place *before* they died, and both loss of blood and asphyxiation contributed to the deaths. Three. He has killed two police officers. One of them just out of Hendon and a godson of Inspector Simpkins, the other, our colleague and Inspector Simpkins' partner, Pete." Roberts paced the floor a little, then continued, "To sum up, we're dealing with a thug who doesn't give a shit about human life and enjoys playing mind games. He likes to live on the edge and enjoys the thrill of just evading capture by the skin of his teeth. From his record of deals and takeovers, we can assume he desires wealth and power at any cost." For a moment, he stopped to take a sip of bottled water. "Now, for the worst trait of all—He is playing a terrifying game with Inspector Simpkins. His possible reason for this is to profile his personality traits, which he hopes will make us afraid of what he'll do next."

Lorne sat down heavily. The chief looked over at her. She nodded for him to continue.

"He's been one step ahead of us because of Crane's activities, but now she's out of the equation. Okay, is there anything I'm missing? Obviously, Inspector Simpkins has kept me up to date with regular briefings, but what isn't on the board?"

"We've a file of possible links, sir. I've mentioned some, and we've only charted the strong evidence of the Unicorn's involvement. The rest we've filed."

"Right, Lorne. Thank you. John, get those files to me after the briefing. Anything in particular that's getting near to going on the chart?"

"Yes, sir. A couple of years ago, the body of a plastic surgeon from Harley Street was found. His eyes and mouth had been glued shut, and his throat had been slit from ear to ear."

"Okay, John, so what makes you suspect the Unicorn has anything to do with that?"

"We had a sighting of him in the vicinity we were chasing him at the time. The theory is, he'd had a face-lift done by the surgeon and was afraid of him being able to identify him. We've gone along those lines a couple of times, as there's no other reason the facial recognition keeps coming back blank, but we haven't got total proof."

"Let's get that on the chart. And when we get the images from forensics, I want every known plastic surgeon in the country questioned."

"Yes, sir."

"Now, has anything new come to light from his most recent activity, not the kidnap, but the alley incident?"

"The bullets that killed Pete weren't from the gun set in motion on the roof. The Unicorn must've taken it with him. However, forensics traced the serial number of the one he left behind. It's from a consignment hijacked during transportation from the army base at Bovington." John closed his black book with a snap. "That and the CCTV footage concerning the getaway vehicle and its Russian owner, plus the images which you already know of is it, I'm afraid. Very little to go on."

"I wouldn't say that. We've a possible military connection with the gun and could have a mole in that quarter. Follow that up with the MPs ASAP. Find out everything you can about the theft—"

"And what about Charlie's abduction? Have you had a chance to look over the CCTV footage yet?" Lorne interrupted, trying to override her feeling of uselessness.

"We have uniform collecting all they can from the surrounding shops and the street camera, ma'am, and the social worker is booked for tomorrow when the other members of the gang are due to be questioned." John looked from her to the chief.

The chief nodded. "Good. Get someone onto that as soon as the films arrive. Plus, I want every car park within a four- or five-mile radius checked for Abromovski's car. We have to assume it's outlived its usefulness and he exchanged vehicles. Once it's found, check all CCTV of the area, and bring the vehicle in for forensics to give it a thorough going over. In the meantime, assign two of your best to question Crane. I want everything she knows about Unicorn on this chart by morning. His habits, how often he bathes, even how he screws—everything."

Lorne hadn't realised she'd been nodding during this last instruction until one of the younger members of the crew sniggered. The chief looked at her. Embarrassed, she dropped her head.

"That's it, for now. DS Fox, I expect you to delegate all that to the men and collate it before bringing results to me. That's yesterday, not tomorrow."

Chapter Fourteen

Back in Lorne's office, the phone was indicating an outside call coming in. She snatched at it, hoping it would be the Unicorn.

"Lorne, it's your father. What's all this I hear from Tom? Charlie's been kidnapped and you won't tell him why? He has a right to know, girl, we all do."

Her father's stern tone unnerved her. Where work was concerned, she had never put a foot wrong with her father. Family matters were a different ball game, though. Although he was proud of her achievements, he disapproved of the way, in his eyes, she neglected her motherly and wifely duties. To her father, it was a case of do as I say, not as I do. His hypocrisy at times drove her to distraction. *But then that's some men for you, isn't it?*

"Hi, Dad. Yeah, I'm doing fine, considering. Thanks for asking." She was hurt that he'd stomped over her in his size elevens without thinking what she must be going through. *If anyone should know what an invidious position I'm in, he should.*

"Yes, yes. Well, are you going to tell me what's going on?"

"What, so you can go running back to Tom and tell him? Grant me with some sense, Dad. I'm telling you like I told Tom. I cannot disclose what we know about the case because it is a matter of state secrecy."

"State secrecy? Huh. That's bullshit, Lorne, and you know it. Don't try and pull the wool over my eyes, young lady."

His tone at the end didn't bode well.

"You have to trust me on this one, Dad. If I tell you, then I risk losing my job. The chief has already pulled me off the investigation. He's in charge now. If it's any consolation, I really would like to tell you. I could do with your advice on a few things, but my hands are tied."

"Then I'll just have to speak to someone who will tell me. I still have some friends in the force, you know, influential friends at that."

He slammed down the phone, ending their confrontation. *Jesus, I'm surrounded by bloody angry men intent on hanging up on me. When are you guys going to give me a bloody break?*

Lorne buried her aching head in her hands.

"Penny for them?" The chief startled her out of her bout of self-pity.

"Come on, I'll treat you to a coffee and a Nurofen down the canteen. No arguments. There's little we can do around here for the time being. Five minutes, I promise. It'll help clear the cobwebs away."

"How can a girl refuse such a generous offer?"

Charlie's abduction had obviously swept through the station quicker than a bush fire in Oz. In the canteen, colleagues who usually stopped by her table for a quick chat looked uncomfortable and avoided eye contact with her. She followed the chief to a spare table at the rear of the canteen overlooking the car park. They sipped at the passable cup of warm liquid the canteen staff laughingly called Rich Roast Coffee.

"My day just seems to be going from bad to worse."

"How so?" the chief asked, tilting his head.

"Apart from the fact that my daughter has been kidnapped and is now in the hands of a murdering scumbag, you mean? Well, somewhere along the line, I've managed to piss off my husband, who is probably sat at home right now, fretting over his daughter's well-being, despising me as much as the man who's abducted her. And if that isn't bad enough, I've also managed to upset my father. He rang just before you came into my office."

The chief uttered meaningfully, "Oh?"

"Don't worry, I didn't tell him anything. That's why he's furious with me. I don't blame him. He should be in the loop as he's still bound by the Official Secrets Act. Anyway, he's taking it higher. God, as if having my daughter in that monster's hands and losing Pete isn't enough."

He reached across the table and rested a concerned hand over hers.

"You mustn't blame yourself, Lorne. Blame the system, by all means. But never blame yourself. If I had my way, I would get your father on board, bring him out of retirement. His experience would be a big help right now, but, as you know, that wouldn't be the superintendent's view. I'd never get him to agree to it."

Chapter Fifteen

"You're shaking, little one. Are you cold?" The Unicorn, as he'd told her to call him, mocked her. His dark, murky-brown eyes roamed her body. "Nice, and just coming into womanhood…"

Charlie stood before him; the seductive, sluttish clothes she wore were alien to her. The four-inch high heels were causing painful spasms in her ankles and to the backs of her legs. She strained to balance on them.

A huge hand shoved her in the back. The force sent her tumbling to the ground. She pulled her legs into her chest and lay as still as she could, but she couldn't stop her body quivering. New tears filled her eyes and tumbled down her flushed cheeks. All her fight and wild aggression had gone, beaten out of her by the man's brutish henchmen.

"Please, I'm only thirteen. Please don't hurt me."

The Unicorn and the four burly thugs in the room laughed at her, but as quickly as the sound had grated her ears, it stopped. The room fell silent. Confused, Charlie tilted her head to the side, daring to sneak a look at the Unicorn's face. He stared back at her. A fearful shudder shot through her aching spine. He nodded at the men standing behind her. Rough hands grabbed her and lifted her. Trying to understand, she looked from one to the other.

They smirked. They tore at her clothes. A scream from deep within released through her gaping mouth. With it came a realisation of what they intended to do. The strength that had abandoned her earlier came rushing back. She hissed, spat, and kicked out like a wild animal.

They showed only amusement. Her struggle exhausted her. The Unicorn's odious laughter filled the room.

"I like you. You have spunk, just like your mother. Now wouldn't that be something to have her here, too? What a dynamic threesome we would be. So, you are only thirteen— umm, just the right age for me, isn't she, boys?"

He bent closer to her. His breath smelt sweet. His tongue slithered along her lips. It felt funny. She shivered again. They all laughed. Her heart jolted, pounding her fear around her body.

Oh, God, please don't let him rape me.

He eased away from her but kept his eyes looking deep into hers. He gestured to the others, and they grabbed her arms. Her shoulders and ribs stretched as they dragged her across the room towards the large marble fireplace before lifting her and throwing her like a rag doll on the sumptuous, maroon and gold sofa. The soft cushions comforted her, but only for a moment.

Unbuckling his belt, the Unicorn swaggered towards her. His evil smirk twisted his face into an expression Charlie found impossible to read. Terror gripped her chest. She couldn't breathe or release the agony knotted in her lungs.

She watched his trousers fall to the ground. He stepped out of them then took off his tie and shirt and threw them aside. Still, she hadn't taken a breath.

He stood over her now. His striped boxer shorts stretched with a bulge she couldn't take her eyes off. He put both hands into the top of his boxers and pushed them down.

Only in pictures had Charlie ever seen a naked man, and only in diagrams in class had she seen an erect penis. It had been something to snigger over. But now, knowing what he intended to do with it, she couldn't laugh. Her scream turned to a holler. It ripped her throat and blocked out the light as she sank into a blackness that promised safety.

* * *

Sasha cringed further into the drapes as the door opened.

Two of the Unicorn's men dragged the limp body of the girl along the corridor. They were taking her to one of the houses.

Sasha had gone through every painful swipe and had experienced the deep stretching and tearing of her insides afresh as memories of her own capture had revisited her whilst she'd listened to it happening to this girl. But she questioned why this girl hadn't had the usual initiation? The one she and all of the other girls had suffered. Sasha wondered if this girl was someone special.

Usually, after the Unicorn was done, ten or more would take their perverted pleasure before the girl was taken to one of the houses to recover. But then, most of the girls didn't get the so-called privilege of being screwed by the Unicorn. She thought he perhaps intended to keep this one for himself, as she herself was kept.

Recovery meant a steady stream of drugs starting with cannabis and working up to heroin. Beatings around the body area ensured submission until the girls were hooked on the substances, when they resisted no more and worked hard to earn their fix.

Escape was impossible. Death was the only release from the grip of the Unicorn.

Sasha's survival instinct had her hoping the Unicorn did intend to have the girl take her place. Keeping the man satisfied took all her time. Time, even knowing the risks, she could spend planning her escape.

A choking sound pulled her back from her thoughts. She peeped out. The girl had come around and vomited. One of the thugs kicked her in the stomach. Her pitiful cry, no louder than that of a baby, ripped through Sasha's heart. The poor girl did not know what real suffering was. Not yet, but she would...

Chapter Sixteen

"Lorne, it's Tony Warner. How are things going at your end?"

"Not good. I'm not in charge of the case anymore. I—"

"How come? Has something happened that I should be aware of?"

"I thought the chief would've rung you. It's my daughter…"

She started to tell him what had happened, but didn't get past saying that the Unicorn had Charlie.

"*What?* When? How? Do you know where he's holding her? Why in God's name didn't you ring me straight away?"

"Whoa, hang on a minute. Tell me, did you learn your interrogation technique from the Gestapo?"

"Sorry, Lorne. I seem to be saying that a lot to you today, don't I?"

"Right, let's go through the answers one by one, shall we?" She ran through the incidents in the order they'd happened and finishing by telling him about the arrest of Crane and that the DCI had taken over the case.

"This DCI, he's all right, is he?"

"Cards on the table, I'm not going to lie to you. We've had our ups and downs in the past." She allowed herself a wry smile at this pun, but wasn't about to share with him any historical details of her relationship with the DCI. "However, all's been well lately. Yeah, he's a good man, Tony, but before you rush off to phone him, what did you ring about? I'm still keeping a finger in the pie, as you can imagine."

"Yes, well, look, I didn't say, but I'm sorry about what is going on. Try not to worry. We'll get the bastard. Look, a mate of mine in MI5 sent me what they have on this Abromovski. He's been a very naughty boy in the last few months. I told you before how he kept meeting up with this guy we presume to be the Unicorn? Well, that's not all they know about him. It looks like he's been supplying terrorists based in this country with explosives and arms."

"That ties in with our Unicorn theory, then, and gives us a reason for the link between the two."

"Yes, the information is these are British-born Muslims intent on tearing this country apart. We believe them to be responsible for the riots in Bradford a couple of years ago. And the general suspicion is that Abromovski supplied the explosives used by the terrorists in the Seven-Seven bombings. There's no hard factual evidence, but you were right to suspect the terrorist link."

"But it still begs the question, what the hell is a Russian hoping to achieve by supplying Islamic extremists with ammunition?" Lorne asked, the fear she'd dared not visit earlier clutched her stomach.

"Good question. We suspect he's 'a player.' A man with money to spend and a sadistic streak to feed, he wouldn't be fussed about who suffers or what beliefs or culture the people he's funding are from. He'd just crave the excitement and the pleasure when the deed is done."

"Sick bastard! If it's not a stupid question, why haven't your lot picked these guys up yet?"

"It's not from want of trying. We've picked up Abromovski a couple of times for questioning, but every time we bring him in, he comes heavily protected by a high-class brief, one who just happens to know all the appropriate loopholes needed to make a mockery of the justice system."

"So where do we go from here?"

"I can give you a few addresses that we know about, if that'll help. They're locations that Abromovski has either bought or rented out over the last few years, but you won't find it easy getting warrants to take a look inside. They're what you might call houses of ill-repute. And they're frequented by some very influential people. Though a stakeout might give you ammunition to get round the barriers."

"Bloody typical. Well, if I get an inkling Charlie is in one of them, no fucking influence will stop me getting in. Fire away with the addresses."

After giving her the last one, he said, "By the way, there's just one more thing. The sweep of the area is being extended to an intense one of the Houses of Parliament. It's in progress as we speak. Every device, including dogs, is being used—"

"And?"

"Nothing as yet."

"Great. What if he's leading us up the garden path?" Lorne cringed at the thought of what the commissioner would say if that turned out to be the case. But somehow, she didn't think the Unicorn was bluffing. She checked her watch. Less than eighteen hours to go…

"Can't answer that one, Inspector—"

The phone clicked and went dead.

Chapter Seventeen

"Bad news, I'm afraid, Lorne," the chief informed her when she stepped into his office moments later.

Not more bad news. I don't think I can handle any more today. She threw herself into the vacant chair opposite him.

"I've just heard that they've swept the area in and around the Houses of Parliament and found absolutely nothing."

She let out a breath she'd unconsciously been holding in. "Yeah, I know."

"You *know*. How do you know?" Roberts asked, raising an eyebrow in puzzlement.

"Before you ask, no, nobody from my team told me. You're the one in charge of the case."

"So how do you know about it?"

"Warner. He just rang me. He told me, and that's why I'm here. To tell you. He said they're just about to undergo a more thorough search. He seems to think we're barking up the wrong tree."

"If he's right, where does that leave us?" he asked. "Lorne, I'm concerned about you. You look drawn and pale."

"I'm managing."

"These last few days have been extremely difficult for you. Maybe you should—"

"No, I'm not taking time off." Lorne planted her elbows on her knees and supported her weary head in her hands.

"Do me a favour? Forget I'm the boss for a second and answer me honestly."

"Go on," she said, eyeing him warily.

"By the look of things, I'd say you're not holding up too well, are you?" he asked.

Feeling like a bolt of lightning had struck her, she sat upright, pushed out her chest, and extended her slim neck. "Stop worrying about me. I'm fine," she said, offering him a false, tired smile.

"Don't bullshit a bullshitter, Lorne. No one's going to think badly of you if you go home for a few hours—"

"No way. *Absolutely* not. Whilst there's a breath left in my body, I intend to do all I can to find my daughter. Please don't insist I go home, sir, because I'd hate to *defy* your orders."

"Of course, you'd never do that, would you, Lorne?" Roberts replied with a smile and a knowing glint in his smoky-grey eyes.

DS Fox knocked on the chief's door.

"Come in, John. Find anything interesting?" the chief asked as the other man stepped into the room.

"Well, we searched every car park in the area, like you said. Our guys were just about to call it a day when uniform located the car. The tape is being brought in as we speak."

"At last, could this be the breakthrough we've been waiting for? Get SOCO over there ASAP. Impound the vehicle. See if any matches come up on the DNA database."

"Yes, boss, I'll get onto it straight away." John was about to turn and leave when Lorne stopped him.

"John, on my desk there's a list of addresses. MI6 gave them to me. There's a possible link with Abromovski. I want a twenty-four hour surveillance put on each one."

Fox hesitated for a moment, unsure whether to accept the order. When Fox glanced at the chief, Roberts nodded his approval.

"Get on with it, Fox. What are you waiting for?"

"Me, sir? I'm not waiting for anything, sir. Ma'am… I'm on my way now, sir."

When John left the office, Lorne and Roberts exchanged awkward glances.

"Thanks for backing me up, Chief. I didn't have time to tell you that snippet of information."

He shrugged. "Don't mention it. Now all we have to do is find something to keep you out of mischief. Any ideas?"

"I'll tell you what I'll do. I'm going to grab a quick bite to eat, do a few miles on the treadmill in the gym, then have a long hot shower."

"Why, Inspector, I think that's a mighty fine idea. I'll see a renewed you in about an hour then."

"You could always join me." She blushed when she realised her mistake. She hastily corrected herself. "Um, I meant the bit about grabbing a bite to eat and visiting the gym, sir, not the rest of it."

"Oh, and there was me thinking you were inviting me to take a shower with you, for old time's sake," he teased, enjoying her obvious discomfort.

His laughter followed her down the hallway as she headed for the canteen. *You stupid, stupid woman, you're seriously losing it, Lorne.* She was still cursing herself twenty minutes later as she attacked her rubbery lasagne.

After only managing to eat half her meal, she pushed her plate away and, in a daze, sipped her warm coffee. She found herself focusing on the graffiti-plastered wall of the building opposite. For a while, tears misted her eyes as the black pattern somehow morphed into Charlie's terrified face.

Hold on, Charlie baby. Mummy's going to find you, just hang in there and stay strong, sweetheart.

Chapter Eighteen

Refreshed and rejuvenated after her gym visit, Lorne found the chief and the team engrossed in the details of the case once more.

The chief smiled at her. "I was just saying, Inspector, that AJ has been checking through the addresses Tony gave us, and something very promising has turned up. Actually, AJ, why don't you fill everyone in?"

The young man whose character had been in question only hours before stepped up to the board at the front of the room.

"Of the four addresses we were given, two of them flagged up as being of interest to the vice squad. In fact, they've had them under surveillance for the last couple of months. I contacted a mate of mine who works with that team, and off the record, he informed me that the 'clientele' enter the place as bold as brass, unconcerned, as if the building housed a public gallery or something and was not used for illegal activities. My mate thinks that the customers have been assured by someone who can be believed that the place will never be raided."

The chief shook his head in disgust. "Anything else, AJ?"

"Yes, there is, Chief. There was a disturbing incident outside one of these houses only last week. Apparently, one of the girls at the Knightsbridge house managed to escape. She didn't get very far, though. A couple of thugs jumped on her and dragged her back to the house. The surveillance team radioed for backup, but was instructed to leave well alone. After the girl and the two guys re-entered the house, they heard a girl screaming for a couple of minutes Then there was silence. They're assuming she was beaten up, maybe even killed, but on that score, nothing has left the building that could be said to be disguising a body. They have all entrances covered..." He trailed off as he looked in Lorne's direction.

Lorne had been hanging on his every word, and it must have shown. She hadn't meant it to. During her workout in the gym, she'd given herself a severe talking to about the importance of not overreacting, no matter how gruesome she found the details. She'd made a promise to Charlie to have a positive attitude at all times. It was the only way she could see of making it through this torrid time. She'd failed her first test.

The chief nodded reassuringly at her.

"There's something mighty strange and frustrating about this case, and the more we delve into it, the more I detest what we're uncovering."

"Corruption comes to mind, Chief."

"We have no evidence of that, DC Teller, and until we do, I'd rather any thoughts like that remained that way—as thoughts. Am I making myself clear?"

They all affirmed, but looking around them, Lorne realised from their glances at each other the entire team was of the same mind. Teller was the only one to have enough balls to voice his opinion, that was all.

Chapter Nineteen

Charlie's head felt as if someone had taken a swing at it with an axe. Confused, she looked below her and found she was lying on a wafer-thin mattress. The room spun when she sat up. She flopped back down and let out a groan. *What's happening to me?*

The edge of the bed squashed down. Someone had sat on it. Her heart thumped. A hand brushed her leg. Fear catapulted her to the top of the bed, where she scrunched up into a terrified ball against the cold, damp wall.

"Ssh, it's okay. I not hurt you," a young foreign girl whispered.

Charlie opened her eyes. The girl sitting next to her looked no older than Charlie. She had messy, blonde hair and wore vivid makeup.

"Where am I?"

"I don't know. We don't know."

"We?"

"Yes, look around you. There are many here." The girl appeared afraid and agitated, checking over her shoulder after every other word.

Charlie raised her muzzy head. Her stinging eyes took a while to grow accustomed to the darkness.

The room resembled a long, narrow passageway. The bed she occupied stood at the end, and on either side, right up to the door at the other end, forty or fifty prison-like bunk beds lined the walls. She could just make out the forms of girls, all of whom looked tiny, on each bunk. At the far end, a single bulb giving off a dim glow swayed on a wire suspended from the ceiling. Further light trickled in from two windows, which had metal bars across them.

The rank smell of stale body odour tinged her nostrils, causing her to gag.

"What's your name?"

"My name is Carma. I am from Romania. And yours?"

"It's Charlie. How long have you been here, Carma?" Taking guidance from Carma, she kept her voice as a whisper. She had so many questions she wanted to ask, but the sentences jumbled up in confused mind.

"I don't know how long, maybe two months, maybe three."

"My head feels funny…"

Carma's eyes brimmed with tears as she told her, "They have drugged you. See here." She pointed to a needle mark in the bend of Charlie's arm.

"It is heroin. They give it to us daily. It controls us as if we were a bunch of dogs. You'll get used to it."

Heroin? I don't want to get used to it.

Before Charlie could ask any more questions, Carma took flight back to her own bunk. A grating noise filled the room. The bolt on the door moved up and down. Each girl scampered down off her bed and stood to attention.

The door opened. Three huge men walked in. Charlie froze.

A whisper beside her urged, "Get up quick, or your life won't be worth living."

She tried to swing her legs over the side of the thin mattress, but fell back, defeated. As her limbs flailed out of control, her groan echoed in the silence.

The men worked their way up the line towards her. Her fear intensified.

"We have a party tonight, girls. Very, very important persons coming." The man spoke with a strong accent, not like the girl, but rougher.

Charlie's school had a Russian exchange student at school last year. This voice sounded similar, just older and deeper.

Charlie tried to see if she recognised any of the men; she didn't. Despair filled her as she watched them. *Where am I? What is this place? Oh, Mum, please come, please…*

The man continued to speak in seductive, melodic tones. "We have good time, all of us. You do me proud, especially you, Carma, my precious one."

He held Carma's chin in his hand. She tried to pull away from him, but his grip tightened, making her lips protrude as if she were a fish. He kissed her long and hard. She squirmed out of his hold and squealed. The man laughed, then punched her in the stomach.

"The next time I want kiss, you give me one, or I will…" He lifted his right hand, pointed his thumb towards his throat, and dragged it from left to right.

Charlie heard Carma sob, bend over in pain, and clutch her stomach. The man lifted her face and wiped away a tear from her flushed cheek.

"You do as I say, and you won't get hurt, you hear, sweetie?"

"Yes, Sergei," Carma replied, her voice trembling.

The man laughed and continued his journey, touching every girl he passed. Sometimes he ran his finger down a cheek, but mostly, his hands sought out the most private parts of their slim bodies. None of them objected, but Charlie knew they were afraid.

Now he was standing in front of her. His fingers clicked towards the two men who had followed his every step. They grabbed Charlie and pulled her to her feet. Her legs trembled, and her knees buckled, but before her body slithered to the ground, one of the men grabbed her right wrist and wrung it between his hands, giving her a Chinese burn. She cried out as the pain shot through her. But the cry strangled in her throat as the other man punched her hard in the stomach. She doubled over. Her breath left her body, draining all her strength. Her soul sank into despair.

"Ha, I thought he said this one is to be careful of? That she fight like a tiger."

His words mocked her courage, but didn't extinguish it. Her body may not have been able to help her, as wracked with pain and weakness and unable to breathe, she needed help to even stand. But that wasn't going to stop her from challenging him.

"What… what do you want from me? Who are you?"

"I ask the questions. Do you understand?"

His angry face almost touched hers. She gasped in his garlic- and cigar-laden breath. Her stomach rejected the vile smell. Vomit projected from her mouth. His ugly face took a direct hit.

Her body hit the cold, damp floor with a thud as the vicious swipe stung her ear and threw her off balance. She lay unable to move, unable to stave off the blows and kicks that rained down on her. She went beyond the agony. Her mind floated above her. Her blood mingled with tears, and snot filled her mouth. Then, a moment of clarity came to her. *This is where I die. Oh, Mum… Mum….*

Chapter Twenty

Lifting the receiver broke the agony of frustration the last couple of hours had given Lorne. At last, intelligence giving them new information came in, but they needed extra help.

"Tony? It's me. We've just heard there's going to be some sort of party at one of the addresses you gave me…"

"Yes, I know. We have it covered. I was just about to ring you. A mate of mine in vice contacted me. They have officers going in under the guise of being workers from a staff agency."

"Great, that's why I rang. My DCI wanted to get the same thing set up, but what you could've done given the timescale, I'd no idea, still not relevant now. What's the plan?"

"They haven't revealed everything, but as you'd expect, there's a surveillance van in place. I hope you don't mind, but I took the liberty of asking if you could go over there and join the team for a while in the van. But only say yes if you think you can cope. I told them you weren't the type to go all hysterical on them."

"Thanks, Tony. Yes, I'll cope, a lot more than I am here, doing nothing. Really appreciate that. Are you going to be in on it?"

"Yep, let's see, it's eleven forty-five. I'll meet you in the White Swan car park in fifteen. We should be there by midnight and catch most of the guests arriving. Our information has the party starting around twelve thirty AM."

"Right, see you there."

The phone clicked. This time, she felt relief rather than anger at his abrupt end to the call. She'd half dreaded him misreading her asking him if he'd be there and making some crass remark about holding her hand or something.

"Well, I can tell by your face you have news."

"Yes, Chief, they're already on it." She told him what had transpired.

"I'd like a word. In my office, if you don't mind, Inspector. The rest of you carry on digging up what you can. And, John, get someone to chase up the facial recognition team."

His face was like thunder. She wondered if she had gone too far making arrangements without running it past him first. He stormed ahead of her towards his office.

"I'm sorry, Chief, I should have—"

"Yes, you should have. You can't do it. I won't allow it."

The bang of his fist on the desk made her jump.

"But why? And why are you so damn angry with me?"

"Don't be so naïve, Lorne. By rights, you shouldn't even be on this case, but I gave you the benefit of the doubt. You promised me you'd take a back seat, and now *this*. You've got to be out of your tiny mind if you think I'm going to let you within twenty miles of that place."

She glared at him. He stood his ground, and his eyes lashed her with his anger. Memories she'd rather forget came to her. Their time as an item had been ninety percent fighting and ten percent making up.

"I beg your pardon, sir, but I think you're being unreasonable."

"Huh, *I'm* the one being unreasonable?" He flopped rather than sat down in his chair.

Lorne sat down, too. She could see he was beginning to weaken, so she pushed her advantage.

"I promise I'll not do anything untoward. Besides, Tony will be there to keep me in line. There'll be other officers there, too. They're hardly going to let me storm the place, are they?"

"God, you're impossible to deal with at times, Lorne Simpkins. I'm not in the least bit happy about this."

"I know, but I'll be okay. Please say I can go. I need to be there…"

His eyes softened. "Don't think you can wrap me around your little finger, Lorne."

"No, sir, of course not." She gave him her most dazzling smile.

Chapter Twenty-One

Sweaty bodies and rank remains of takeaways didn't exactly make the next few hours cramped in the Ford Transit, customised to look like one of the catering group's vans, appealing.

The four officers from vice greeted her with respectful nods. She recognised two of the officers from the Gripper Jones case she'd helped them out with the year before. Tony had obviously filled them in on her involvement in the case.

She picked up a pizza box and an empty curry carton from the only available seat. Tony had already grabbed one at the desk in front of the equipment.

"Thanks for asking me to dinner, guys," Lorne joked.

This lightened the tension and earned her an appreciative look from Tony. Three of the others grinned, and the third said, "Not exactly dressed for it. If you're hungry, there's some chicken chow mein keeping warm in the front there."

Before she had time to answer, one of the others said, "Heads up, we've got action." He reached forwards and manipulated some dials in front of him. "Falcon One, we are clear for take-off," he said into a tiny microphone.

They heard what appeared to be static in response. Tony leaned forwards and whispered in her ear. "That's one of the guys on the inside giving us the okay signal. We have six acting as waiters and one as a valet."

Scanning the half dozen monitors in front of her, she watched in disgust and awe as several dignitaries arrived at the Georgian-styled mansion. She recognised most of them, but one in particular shocked her.

"That's the aid to the Home Secretary, Paul Solomon. You'd think it was a film premiere. The only thing missing is a bloody red carpet," she whispered to Tony.

Appreciating her wit, he and the others all grinned. She now felt part of the team instead of an observer. Apart from the reason they were there, she enjoyed the experience. As stake-outs went, this was the luxury end. She remembered many a night cramped in her car with Pete, shivering from the cold and tired to the bone. The takeaway food was the only thing their operations had in common with this one.

The monitors covering the inside showed the guests being ushered into a large room located at the rear of the property. Male waiters handed out glasses of champagne and canapés to the guests who were standing around one half of the room and chatting in groups. The other half of the room housed several rows of red velour-covered seats arranged theatre style.

At twelve thirty, the guests fell silent, prompted by the slow hand clapping of none other than Sergei Abromovski bringing their attention to him.

"Gentlemen, it is a pure pleasure you should join us here this evening. I know you will not regret *coming*." He paused, smirking in sick appreciation of his own joke. A ripple of naughty-schoolboy laughter bounced through the microphones. Lorne gripped the rail of the chair she stood behind, but remained silent.

Sergei's voice droned on. "The proceedings for tonight's enjoyment will be as follows. I will ask all of you first to take a seat, then once you are all settled, the evening's entertainment will begin. The girls will be brought out one by one. You will bid for an evening of joy, and the highest bidder will win the girl. Rooms are available at a small extra charge, and all the money raised this evening will go to a charity close to my heart, the Children of Beslan Fund."

"Like hell, it will," Tony muttered. "There's only one charity he's interested in, the Sergei Abromovski Cayman Islands fund."

"Bastard."

"My sentiments exactly, Lorne. Hark at them clapping. They're so civilised, you'd think they were attending a state dinner with the Queen."

However, the men were not so refined when it came to choosing a seat. In fact, a few scuffles erupted as they vied for position nearest the front.

"Bloody, dirty old men." Lorne mumbled.

No one commented on her remark. Their attention was drawn to the gold silk curtains at the far end of the room, which swept back to reveal none other than West End actress, Dorothy Emerald.

"This is fucking unbelievable," one of the officers said. "What the hell is she doing here?"

"Acting as Mine Host, by the sound of her, and she is carrying it off like it's a regular job, which means she's involved in the whole scam. My God—"

Tony was interrupted by the appearance on stage of a very young, frightened girl who wobbled rather than walked down the red-carpeted catwalk. Her fear visible in her face, her body barely covered, she looked straight ahead. Whistles and cheering resounded through the mic, filling the van with a sickening feeling of wolves about to tear apart their prey.

Lorne gasped. "Jesus, she's no more than twelve or thirteen years old."

A picture of Charlie, which was never far from her mind, came to her, and her legs almost buckled. *Hold on, you're doing just great. Don't weaken now.*

Tony looked over his shoulder. "Okay?"

"Doing my best, but…"

He nodded. The others didn't acknowledge they'd spoken or that there might be something amiss. Lorne thanked God for their professionalism.

She looked back at the screen. A young, famous footballer walked the first girl out of the room. Another girl, this one huge-breasted, teetered onto the catwalk, struggling to walk in horrendously high heels. She stumbled and fell.

"Like a Christian to the lions. Poor bugger…" one of the officers said. They watched as men pawed her under the pretense of getting her back on the podium.

The bidding began at an unbelievable two thousand pounds and finished, with a rather rotund gentleman in his fifties, at four thousand. The girl visibly shuddered.

Lorne took a deep breath. In her career, she'd dealt with every vile, tragic, horrific, and sheer revolting situation one could possibly imagine. Her armour had been built of steel by her third or fourth case in her rookie year and had never let her down. A cop couldn't afford to let it. *But, this… and with my personal involvement… Maybe the DCI was right. This could crack me wide open.*

The sordid auction lasted for an hour and a half. Relief overwhelmed Lorne as Ms. Emerald drew the evening to a close, but it didn't stop her feeling distraught for the girls who had been bought that night. She hadn't wanted Charlie to be one of them. With all her heart, she hadn't wanted that, but part of her knew the experience hadn't taken her out of limbo. Questions pounded her head. If Charlie wasn't there, then where the hell was she? And the investigation now involved child trafficking for sex and paedophilia as well as the terrorist links and the numerous other activities they had tagged to the Unicorn and Abromovski. The implications were huge. And somewhere in the middle of it all was her baby.

Chapter Twenty-Two

The Unicorn kept his face fixed in a self-satisfied grin to match the one Abromovski wore as they watched the weaselly man, one of Abromovski's accountants, count the cash spread out on the kitchen table.

"Yet another success in the Abromovski world of corruption," Sergei gloated.

"Indeed."

The reply was distracted, but the Unicorn had numbers ticking through his brain—the ones to Sergei's Cayman Islands account. Another couple of hours and all of Abromovski's dirty money would become his. He clenched his fists in his pockets to quell the urge to rub his hands together.

For all his clever scams, the Russian's one mistake is to underestimate me, he thought.

"Where's the girl?"

"Which girl?"

"It's unwise to mess with me, Sergei." Another thing about the Russian: he never expected the unexpected.

The Russian's eyes widened with shock and bulged as the Unicorn tightened the pressure on his throat.

"You know which one. Now where is she?"

Two of Sergei's men guarding the door rushed forward. The Unicorn tightened his grip. The Russian motioned them to stay back.

"A rare wise move, Sergei." He released his grip and brushed the creases out of the collar of the man's black evening jacket.

"She's in my room. I thought I'd have a little fun with her tonight."

"Why wasn't she in the auction?"

"She's— she's still too feisty to introduce to our clients this evening. She hasn't had time to learn the rules."

The Unicorn could smell the Russian's fear.

"You mean you've bashed her to a pulp. Go on, admit it."

"I admit things did get a little rough, but I see it as a personal challenge to break her in. That is, providing you have no objections?"

"Just be careful. Keep the face clean like I taught you. What I really need is a photo of her. If she's a little roughed up at the moment, it happens to suit my purpose."

"My men will sort it." He signalled to the two men, but they looked at each other and back at the Russian. The Unicorn sensed they didn't want to leave their boss alone with him. Sergei waved impatiently at them. "Well, what are you waiting for? Make sure she's awake."

The goons left the room just as the accountant, who hadn't flinched or interrupted his work regardless of what had transpired around him, finished counting the mountain of cash. "Two hundred and fifty nine thousand," he announced.

Sergei whistled. "Not bad for one evening's entertainment, eh?"

"It'll do for starters. Get the photo to me ASAP. I'll be in touch soon."

* * *

Charlie fought to stay upright in the dark rolling tunnel, which jerked heavily and shook her body. She heard her own groans bouncing off the walls and coming back at her. Then something strong forced her upright. She could do nothing to resist. Sharp little pains attacked her cheeks and arms.

Someone is pinching me. As some consciousness came to her, so did the agony of her bruised and battered body.

She tried to form some words, tried to tell them to get the hell off of her and let her sleep. In sleep, the pain misted away, niggled from a distance. She could cope with that.

Flashes penetrated her closed eyes. *A camera?*

Chapter Twenty-Three

"Ah, DI Simpkins, you do take your job seriously. Glad to find you work through the night, too."

"You know what they say, no rest for the wicked. Is that why you're awake at this ungodly hour, too?" Lorne bit her lip. Her tiredness and worry had interfered with her professionalism. The last thing she wanted to do was antagonise the Unicorn.

His sick laugh grated in her ear. "Tell me, Inspector, does Charlie get her fiery nature from you or from her father?"

"What have you done to her, you evil—"

"Always the policewoman, aren't we, Inspector? Asking questions and more questions, then answering questions with further questions. Your daughter's a bit high-spirited, like I say. So it's taking a while to, shall we say, bed her in. But rest assured, we'll break her in the end. I can guarantee that much."

"You bastard! What the hell do you mean by that? Where is she? She's thirteen, for Christ's sake. Let me take her place. I'll be of more use to you than she is."

"Now don't treat me like an idiot, Inspector. You know as well as I do that your government doesn't deal with terrorists, although I don't really like putting myself in that bracket. This way, if Charlie remains with me, I have a better chance of my demands being met, because you'll kind of be on my side, won't you, Inspector?"

"I wouldn't bargain on that. You said it yourself, my government won't deal with terrorists. They know you have Charlie, but it's making no difference. I'm trying. You have to believe me, I'm trying, but there are no guarantees."

"I'm disappointed in you, Inspector. That's not exactly what I wanted to hear. You'd better start pulling in some favours if you want to see your little girl again."

The anger in his voice shot fear through her.

"Do you want to see Charlie again, Inspector? Maybe I'm reading the situation wrong here. Maybe you and hubby have had enough of the little tearaway. Is that why you're not pulling out all the stops to get her back?"

"I am pulling out all the stops." She decided she must give him some hope, some reason to keep Charlie alive. "I—I'm doing everything I can to meet your demands. Talks are taking place, negotiations—"

"Very well, then. As long as we have an understanding, now, give me your mobile number. I have something interesting to send you. I think it'll help you make some decisions."

She gave him the number. He hung up the minute she finished reciting the last digit. She sat staring at the receiver lying limp in her hand.

"Everything all right, Inspector?" DCI Roberts said from the doorway.

"That was him."

The chief walked around the desk, took the phone from her clenched fist, and replaced it.

"Okay, Lorne, what did he say this time?"

She took him through the conversation. As she finished, her mobile tinkled, indicating an incoming message. Their eyes met, and fear bounded between them like a high voltage electrical current. Roberts rushed to stand beside her. She tentatively opened her phone, afraid of what she would see.

"Oh God."

Charlie, a battered and bruised, spaced out Charlie. Her darling baby...

"Jesus, what the hell have they done to her, Sean?" She crumpled into his chest.

"She's strong, Lorne. We'll get to her soon. I promise you. Just hang on in there."

She could feel his hand stroking the back of her head as if she were a child. Her phone tinkled again. Roberts grabbed it and read aloud.

"If you want to see your daughter alive, get me thirty million by noon. Yes, that's right. The price just went up, Inspector."

Her fear and heartache melted away to be replaced with anger.

"Right, that's it. If that arsehole wants a fight, then he's going to damn well get one. When we track the bastard down, I'm going to rip his balls off one by one and shove them down his slimy throat."

"Thatta girl, Lorne. That's the kind of spirit I expect from you. Umm... promise me one thing, though?"

"What's that, Chief?"

He was standing by her office door with one leg crossed over the other.

"When we catch the bastard, just make sure I'm not around when you turn him from a unicorn into a eunuch. The mere thought of it brings tears to my eyes."

She laughed with him, but checked it as soon as it started. She dared not unleash any emotions, even lighthearted ones. If she did, she feared she'd not be able to stop. Laughter would turn to tears and tears to screams, and she would be crushed.

Chapter Twenty-Four

"Right, listen up."

A sea of tired faces stared back at Lorne and the DCI.

"The stakes have just been upped. The inspector has received a phone call and two messages from the Unicorn." The DCI went through the details of the call and the messages before handing the discussion over to Lorne.

Lorne first reported on what had happened during the stake-out. "Now, all of the so-called guests were very well known or high profile people. Vice are taking up the investigations into them, and all information is now to be shared between us. So we'll soon know everything about their lives and backgrounds. This is big, and it has to be handled with care. So no treading on the toes of the officers involved. One mistake, one hint we're on to them could prove to be disastrous. These are people who could shut the operation down in an instant. Our investigation stays with the Unicorn, and—and our main priority remains to find Charlie. Simon, see if you can pick up a trace on the messages."

She threw him the phone, and he almost dropped it.

"The inspector is right. We share everything, but we each have our own priorities, and like she said, Charlie is ours. Anything to report on the CCTV footage of the four-by four, yet?" Roberts asked.

"Yes, we've completed our search of the tapes. The vehicle was dumped on level two. Forensics scanned the area, and the vehicle is in and being stripped as we speak. So a report should be in from them very soon. There's a clear view of the occupants bundling who we assume to be Charlie up one level." John paused and looked at Lorne. She nodded at him to continue.

"From there, they broke into a Mercedes and continued their journey to wherever. It's been reported as missing, and the woman claiming to be the owner checks out. We have uniform keeping an eye out for it as well as alerting all manned CCTV operators, so any sightings will be reported back."

Roberts nodded. "Keep on top of that, John. There's every possibility the vehicle could lead us to the Unicorn."

"Hey, quiet everybody, listen to this." Julie Saunders, the youngest member of Lorne's team, pointed the remote at the portable TV in the corner of the room. The volume shot up, and everyone stared at the screen.

Sky News was running a yellow 'breaking news' banner along the bottom of the screen that read: A bomb has exploded in a building next to the Houses of Parliament.

A male reporter shouted a live update over the noise of the sirens and against a backdrop of flashing blue lights.

"As you can see behind me, half the front of the building was blown away in the blast. Sources tell me that no warning, I repeat, no warning call was received. Luckily, this happened at four AM this morning. Can you imagine what sort of casualties we would be looking at if this had happened four, maybe five, hours from now?"

"As you say, one can only imagine, Scott. Have the authorities given any indication who's responsible and why this bomb was planted?" the newscaster at the studio asked. His gaze was glued to the computer screen in front of him, keeping an eye on the news coming through the AP wires.

"I'm afraid it's chaos at the moment, as you can see. No one has arrived from any official source, and there is no spokesman from the emergency services as yet."

The correspondent signed off, giving the time as four twenty-five AM. The newscaster stated they would stay with the situation and update every few minutes or sooner, if something specific happened.

Chapter Twenty-Five

Every available phone in the incident room rang. Lorne looked at the chief and raised her eyes to the ceiling. *Here we go.*

"It's the superintendent for you, sir," AJ shouted.

"It's Tony Warner for you, ma'am," DS Fox said, offering Lorne his phone.

Lorne and Roberts both set off for their respective offices to take the calls.

"I take it you heard the news, Tony?"

"Yeah, any idea why he's pulled this stunt, Inspector?"

"Christ knows. He sent a photo of Charlie to my mobile and followed it with one increasing his demand to thirty million."

"Shit. Dare I ask how Charlie looked?"

"Pretty roughed up and full of drugs. Who would do that to a thirteen-year-old girl?" She swallowed hard.

"What can I say? You know as well as I do how dangerous this criminal is, Lorne. You say he's upped the price. Did he say why or give any other ultimatum?"

"I don't know, unless… It's a bit of a long shot. What if he found out the party was being observed tonight? That would piss him off."

"Um, unlikely. The vice guys we worked with are supposed to be the best. As far as I know, everything went without a hitch."

"What other reason should we be considering, Tony? I'm open to suggestions."

"Well, hypothetically speaking, what if one of the MPs we clocked at the party tonight told the Unicorn or Abromovski that the Houses of Parliament was being swept today?"

"Another inside job, you mean?"

"Could be."

"Look, I know we aren't supposed to step on toes, but vice might not keep us in the loop. So I'm going to get our guys to run checks on the partygoers. Just to make sure nothing's missed or, dare I say it… hidden. If for some reason our way is blocked, can I call on you for some help?" Lorne asked.

"Don't hesitate. I'll make sure our computers are at your disposal, on this case anyway. We've got till noon right?"

"Right." She glanced at her watch. It was four thirty AM.

"Let me consult a couple of my colleagues, see what we can come up with. I'll get back to you soon, okay?"

"Okay, speak soon." Not wanting to be cut off, she withdrew the phone from her ear, but not before she heard him finish.

"Hey, Lorne, keep your chin up."

She couldn't answer him. His unexpected compassion had hit a nerve. She slammed the phone down.

Chapter Twenty-Six

Lorne strode down the hallway to the chief's office. The brisk walk, though not far, did the trick. She snapped back into control again. With no secretary on guard at this ungodly hour, she wrapped her knuckles on the door and walked in.

DCI Roberts' usual healthy colour had drained from his face. His head shook in disagreement. "No, sir, no he didn't. Look, you'll be the first person I contact, sir."

Lorne hesitated by the door, unsure whether to intrude, but Roberts beckoned her in to take a seat.

"Yes, actually she's coping pretty damn well—far better than I would if I was in her situation. Yes, sir." He threw the phone back in its cradle.

"That bad, huh?"

"Forgive me for what I'm about to say, but that man can be such an arsehole at times."

"Go on, surprise me. What has our dear leader said now?"

"Apparently, we've, to put it nicely, messed up. He asked if we could've made a mistake along the way. Even suggested the Unicorn informed us his intended target was the building next door instead of the Houses of Parliament itself."

"He's a dipshit. What did he say about the party guest list?"

The chief took on the pose of Rodin's Thinker.

"You did tell him, didn't you?"

"Do you know what? What with the bomb and everything, it completely slipped my mind."

"That's shameful. You hypocrite. God, there'd be hell to pay if I ever kept you out of the loop like that, Sean Roberts."

"That's right, there would, so don't ever consider it. But on this occasion, I believe I'm doing the right thing. I'd rather go to him with the full picture in place. This is a case of do as I say and not as I do, Inspector, right?"

"As far as I know, you've told the superintendent everything."

"Good. So what did Warner have to say?"

"Nothing really. He was as surprised as we were about the bombing. I've told him our intentions, and he's volunteered to help if we come unstuck with anything flagging up 'classified information'. I can't help feeling a little blessed to have him on our side."

"Yes, he's a definite asset. Still wondering why he's helping us out."

"I guess we'll find out soon enough. Well, what happens now? Should we head over to the bomb site?"

"To be honest, we're caught between a rock and a hard place at the moment. We could go over there, but... look, there's something else. You probably won't be surprised, but the Unicorn's new terms are being given no consideration at all. We're expected to track him down before the deadline."

"And just how do they expect us to do that? We don't even know who this bloody character is, for Christ's sake," she said.

"I know, I know. There's got to be something obvious we're missing."

"Like what?"

"I don't know, Lorne, but there has to be something. Let's do some more brainstorming."

More brainstorming? Like we haven't done enough already. She arranged for a couple of coffees to be sent in whilst they set about re-evaluating every tiny piece of information they'd collected on the case so far.

"What about the plastic surgeon, Lorne? Do you think we missed something in his files?"

"I don't think so, but we could get one of the officers to go through everything again. It's all still archived. Nothing has been released back to the family or his partners as yet. Wait a minute. Laura Crane, has she been interviewed? Has anyone reported back?"

Roberts frowned. "Not that I know of, everything has moved so fast. I did schedule for DS Fox to interview her, but he may have low-prioritised it."

The DCI picked up his phone and buzzed the squad room.

"Right. Leave it with me. No, unless there is anything significant, leave it until the next briefing. Good." Roberts hung up.

"It seems they did try, but she's refusing to cooperate. Said something about not wanting the duty solicitor, but her own solicitor can't make it until the morning. Fox had held the news back for the next briefing. Told him that was fine. There's no need for him to bother us with every little detail. It'll only undermine any decisions he needs to take if we're tied up."

"Right, but what if we offered her some kind of deal? She's our best shot, sir. She knows him. Probably intimately. If we could get her to talk…"

"You mean a witness program deal?"

Lorne nodded. "Yes, scare her into realising how dangerous her position is."

"You're right, Lorne. You can almost feel sorry for the stupid cow. She's lost her job, the respect of her colleagues, and any friendships she made here, but that's nothing compared with what the Unicorn will have in store for her the minute she's released. She's a dead woman, and that gives us a strong bargaining position. Let's do it."

Chapter Twenty-Seven

"Wakey, wakey. Rise and shine, little one."

Lulled from her sleep, Charlie blinked. The bright lights above her pierced her fragile eyes as she adjusted to the light and became fully awake. Awareness gripped and locked her in terror. The man bending over her, his eyes brimming with hatred, featured in snapshots flooding her memory, and what he'd subjected her to filled her with horror. She remembered his name—the Unicorn—and wondered again why he had such a nickname.

"It's time for your medicine, little one."

His sour laughter vibrated through her and echoed off the walls, but then she realised it wasn't just him laughing. Two other men were standing near the door. Their stance made them look like guards, and each followed the Unicorn's lead in laughing at her.

She tried to concentrate. What did he mean *her medicine*?

Her surroundings came into focus as he straightened up. The rich and sumptuous room reminded her of the bedrooms of pop stars she'd seen in her magazines. Deep-gold satin sheets covered her naked body. Without warning, the Unicorn snatched the cover from her. It billowed out before landing in a heap behind him. She cowered in fear and embarrassment.

"No, no. Please don't."

The men mimicked her, and the Unicorn laughed. His eyes travelled the length of her slight body. She scrunched backwards into the pillows.

"Enough. Let's get on with it."

The room fell silent, and the men moved forward, one to each side of the bed. They grabbed her arms and stretched her out. She wriggled, kicked, and begged, but her strength didn't match theirs.

The Unicorn opened a drawer next to the bed. Something glinted in the light.

Charlie turned her head. Her voice wouldn't release the scream mounting inside her. It threatened to choke her as it strangled in her throat.

A spray of clear liquid squirted from the syringe. It dropped like raindrops onto her arm. Then the needle plunged into her skin.

Her mind calling out to her mum gave her the courage to speak. "Please don't. Please ring my mum again. She'll give you everything you want. She's a very important person."

"You should be a comedienne, little one. She's not so important, otherwise she would have bargained for your life by now." He emptied the vial into her.

"She is. She's in the police. She's an inspector, and my grandfather used to be a chief inspector. Between them, they have many contacts... Important people... Just ring her, *please*?" Her voice sounded strange, far away, like she was in a long tunnel and the words hadn't formed until they'd reached the end. Her head felt hazy.

"You stupid, bitch. Don't you think I know who your mother is and what she does? Why do you think I had you picked up? Take her to the bathroom."

She couldn't find the strength to struggle against the men dragging her. Steam dampened her face when they pushed her through the doors, and a gentler pair of hands steadied her. Gradually, the face of a pretty young woman came into focus. Her voice had a cruel edge to it, but her expression denied this. She winked and placed a finger to her lips, urging Charlie to be quiet and compliant.

"Come on, get into the bath. Hurry up, bitch."

Charlie felt a feeling of safety descend on her as the woman helped her climb over the side of the bath and sink into the hot, comforting water.

The woman leaned over to give Charlie the soap and a sponge and whispered, "My name is Sasha. I want to help you. Do as I say, and you won't get hurt."

Charlie nodded, but her fear made her question the woman's motives. *Is it possible someone could help me get out? Or is this girl with the face of an angel here to give me false hopes, to trap me into a false sense of security?*

Sasha smiled as she pushed one of the buttons on the edge of the tub. The water in the tub erupted like flowing lava escaping from a dormant volcano. Charlie relaxed, but after a moment, she felt repulsed and disgusted. She tensed as the bubbles tickled her in places she knew had changed forever and would never again be considered her *private and personal* parts.

Sasha gave her a look of pity that showed her understanding.

"We can talk better with the noise. Just enjoy it. It won't hurt you, sweetie," she said.

Charlie relaxed and allowed the water to soothe away the clawing pain between her legs. Her eyes closed, but her head started to spin, so she opened them again. She had the weird sensation she'd just come off a Waltzer ride at the fair.

"What have they given me?"

"Heroin. You will get used to it, although it will feel strange to begin with."

"I don't *want* to get used to it."

A loud thud on the door made her shudder with fear. She had spoken too loudly.

"What's going on in there?"

Sasha put her finger to Charlie's mouth and then took it away again.

"Sorry, the water was too hot, that's all. Everything is fine," Sasha shouted.

"I have a pain between my legs. Why is that? Have they raped me?" she whispered. Part of her didn't want to know the answer.

Sasha nodded, and her eyes welled up. "I am sorry. I could not stop them. I am just like you. They abducted me from my home town in Romania. They smuggled me here in the back of a lorry with fifteen other girls. Only they are all together, and I have to be here for him. He rapes me several times a day."

Charlie gasped.

"Oh, I… I shouldn't have told you. You are so young." Her hand brushed Charlie's cheek.

"It won't happen to you, Charlie. You have my word. I will help you to escape."

"How? And well, if that's possible, why haven't you escaped before now?"

"There will be a time. We will find an opportunity. You'll have to be patient. And me, I *can't* escape because they have my family. And if I even attempt to, they have warned me my family will be murdered. Burned at the stake…"

"Oh, no!"

The door burst open.

"Come on, that's enough. Now get out of there and get dressed," the goon ordered.

Charlie ducked under the water.

"Please, one more minute? I haven't washed her hair yet."

"You've got thirty seconds."

Unable to hold her breath any longer, Charlie emerged to find the man staring at her body. His eyes lingered menacingly. Her insides cringed, and she knew at that moment there were different types of rape a man could inflict on a woman.

"Be careful, Charlie. It is better you do as they say, then you won't get hurt. Just remember, I am trying to help you."

Charlie tried to take comfort from the words, but she couldn't.

Chapter Twenty-Eight

"For the tape. This is Inspector Lorne Simpkins. Also in the room are Chief Inspector Sean Roberts and our suspect, DC Laura Crane. The date is 23-10-2008. The time, four forty-five AM. Please sit down, Ms. Crane."

The woman pulled the plastic chair to another position. The scraping of its metal legs on the tiled floor sent a quiver through Lorne's tattered nerves.

"Ms. Crane, how long have you been divulging confidential information about the Met to the man known as the Unicorn?"

"No comment."

"Because of your selfish actions, a good officer and work colleague of yours died a couple of days ago. How do you feel about that?"

A slight smirk tugged at the young woman's thin mouth. Lorne tucked her hands into her lap under the table, quashing the temptation to knock the smirk off Crane's face.

"No comment."

"I wonder if you'll be saying that when we charge you as an accessory to murder?"

Crane's eyes opened wide. "You can't…"

"We're approaching the CPS with our evidence as soon as their office opens. We're confident it will stick. So let's see. Accessory to murder carries a five to seven stretch, but in your case, being a bent copper leaking confidential information, well…" Lorne turned to look at the chief, hoping he'd play along with her.

"Looking at the fact we've been after the Unicorn for eight years and his uncanny knack of knowing our every move, I'd say the judge would be very interested in where he's been getting his information from all that time. Um… let's see now, fifteen to twenty years in Holloway?"

The chief leaned forward. "And I wouldn't like to be in your shoes when the other inmates find out you were a copper, Crane. Doesn't bear thinking about really, does it, Inspector?"

"Rubbish. I've only worked for the police for two years. You can't pin what's happened over the last eight years on me. And I'm saying nothing more until my solicitor arrives. I know my rights. You bloody taught me them."

"Excuse me a moment." The chief stood up and motioned to the tape. "For the tape. Chief Inspector Roberts has left the room. Interview terminated at four fifty-two AM."

The tape machine clicked. The chief sat back down and looked Crane in the eye. "Off the record, Crane. You know you're in a hole, right? You have information we want. Okay, you know your rights, but you also know about the witness program—"

"You mean a deal? You're offering me a deal?"

"Yes, but time is limited." Lorne tried hard to take the edge off her impatience, but failed. "We cannot wait for your bloody solicitor to get here. Give us what we want, and we'll get you to safety."

"The Unicorn will—"

"He bloody won't, you stupid bitch—"

"Lorne!"

"I'm sorry, sir, but for God's sake, Charlie's life depends on her cooperating. Look, Crane. I'm sorry. I shouldn't talk to you like that, but wake up. The Unicorn won't help you. He'll kill you. Why do you think we kept you in the cells overnight, eh? For your own safety, that's why. He won't believe you haven't told us anything. If you're released from here, and you will be once your solicitor gets his teeth into us, you're dead."

"You're insane, the pair of you. If you think you can hide me somewhere he won't find me, the very fact you have will tell him I've talked. Oh, no. I'd rather face the consequences the force is going to throw at me than the wrath of the Unicorn. You truly have no idea what this guy is capable of, do you? Well, I do." Crane gave a short laugh.

"Yes, you do, don't you? Two years..." Lorne said, looking at the chief. "Sir, it seems unlikely to me that anyone working for the force for only two years was any use to the Unicorn. I mean, taking in her training period and her move to our department, that took some time, and then, how much would she know at first? Just enough to tell him how many sugars we had in our tea, I should think, but if she was on his payroll before... How long have you been sleeping, er, working for the Unicorn, Crane? Were you planted in the force?"

This got the reaction Lorne was after. Crane jumped up and tried to slap her around the face. The chief read her intention and grabbed her wrist before she made contact. "We can put cuffs on you, Crane."

"No, you can't. And you both bloody know it. You'd be violating my rights. I have a right to have my solicitor present, and I'm demanding that any interview should take place after he gets here."

"We're not interviewing you. The tape is off. We're trying to help you see sense. If you agree to be interviewed willingly and you help us catch the Unicorn, you'll be looked upon as a valued witness and, as such, will be protected at the highest level. All charges will be dropped against you," the chief said.

"I don't trust you, sir." Her tone denied the respect the title warranted. "I would rather take my chances with the Unicorn."

Lorne decided to take her on woman to woman, cat-fight fashion. She just hoped she had the chief's backing.

"So, how long have you been sleeping with the Unicorn then? Or were you... umm, too old for him? Or maybe you were just too damn ugly for him. That's it, isn't it? You weren't sleeping with him at all. You supplied information in exchange for a promise of a leg-over. You're pathetic. What? Never had a boyfriend you could take home to Mummy, eh? Oh, we know he paid you well, but he still kept you dangling with that promise didn't he, Crane?"

"Inspector..."

Lorne reeled around and looked at the chief, willing him to let her continue. He had perched himself on the edge of his chair, ready. He didn't relax back, but to her relief, he nodded his consent for her to continue.

"I bet he made you all sorts of promises. Arranged to have theatre tickets sent to you and then backed out at the last minute, made reservations at top restaurants only to call you ten minutes before the date to cancel? Go on, tell me I'm right, Crane."

Tears ran down Laura Crane's face. Her chin dropped onto her chest. She didn't say anything. She didn't have to. Lorne felt confident she was right on all counts. She softened her tone. "Why, Laura? Why let yourself be manipulated by this vile man?" Crane continued to sniffle. Compassion crept into Lorne, but was quickly swept aside when Charlie's smiling face flashed in her mind. She knew it was imperative to continue. Inhaling deeply, she asked, "Do you think your mother would've been proud of you? Did she know what you were up to?"

"Leave Mum out of this."

"Why should I, you didn't."

"It was because of Mum I did it," Crane said, her voice faltering.

"It was? Do tell, Crane. We're all ears."

"She was dying. She needed care. I wanted her to have the best treatment available. That's why I did it. I did it all for her, not for me."

"So you decided to sell your soul to the devil. Did she know? Or were you too embarrassed, or was it the shame that prevented you from telling her?"

"It just never cropped up, that's all."

"Your mother must've had an idea what salary you were on. And you're telling me she never once questioned where you got the extra money from that you lavished on her palliative treatment?"

"No. You don't understand. I lost my mother long before she died. The drugs were so strong, her brain shut down. Unless you've lived with someone dying of terminal cancer, you can't possibly know what it's like, Inspector."

"Oh, I know what it's like, Crane. You forget my mother died of cancer last year, but unlike you, I didn't make a deal with Satan to get her through it."

"Maybe that's the difference between us. I happened to love my mother."

Lorne winced. The times she'd had to cry off visiting her mother slapped her in the face. She hadn't dealt with it all yet. Thankfully, the chief intervened.

"Listen, Crane, we're running out of time. Are you going to tell us who this guy is and how we can find him or not? This is a one-time-only offer. No response now, and the deal's off."

"For the very last time, sir. *No comment.*"

Crane laughed a harrowing hysterical laugh that sent shivers up Lorne's spine.

"You know what, Crane? I reckon if we snapped you in half, you'd have desperation running through you like a stick of rock. You're one sick, desperate bitch, and that's the one thing the Unicorn cottoned onto, your bloody desperation. I just hope your mother isn't turning in her grave right now."

"That'd be difficult, Inspector. She was cremated."

"Figure of speech, Crane, but I wouldn't expect you to comprehend a simple thing like that. Oh, and by the way, if that bastard hurts my daughter, it's your hide I'm coming after. Of that you can be certain."

"So he's got your daughter, has he? Well, as you said, Inspector, he does like his girls young." Her laughter crackled again.

The chief rose and glanced at his watch. His body language told of his rage as he opened the door and barked at the young officer standing outside. "Lock her up again."

Lorne followed him out. Her hopes were dashed. Her heart felt heavier than ever.

She too looked at her watch: five thirty AM—only six and a half hours to go.

Chapter Twenty-Nine

"What have we got?"

Everyone stood to attention as Lorne and Roberts stepped into the squad room and the DCI roared out his question. Several officers scrabbled around their desks for information obtained in their absence.

"Sir, we've located the Merc. A patrol car spotted it by the river on a waste site just inside the Kent border. That's the good news. The bad news is the car was burned to a crisp," Storey announced.

Roberts raised his eyes towards the discoloured, smoky ceiling. "I suppose I half expected that. This guy does very little to make our job easy, does he? What about the inspector's phone?"

Simon shook his head. "No lead there, Chief. He used a pay-as-you-go phone to contact Inspector Simpkins. Thanks to *Crane*, he's likely to know the ins and outs of our procedures, surveillance techniques, and the way we gain information. He's bound to know a pay-as-you-go mobile is nigh impossible to trace."

"The list, Jackson—tell me you've got some good news on that front, at least?"

"I have, sir, but I thought you wanted to treat the info as sensitive."

"You're right. We'll go over it in the inspector's office afterwards. Anyone else got anything they want to contribute?"

DS Fox stepped forward. "Yes, the facial recognition file has come back from forensics. A couple of the guys are going over it now, checking with the airlines and ports, that sort of thing, sir."

"Good. Follow through with that and let me know ASAP what they come up with. Anything else come to light with regard to the bomb, Saunders?"

"Nothing yet, sir, just a lot of speculation so far. The press are putting Al Qaeda in the frame."

"Well, it makes a change for us to be ahead of the press, doesn't it? And we don't want anything of our suspicions out there yet, so let them think we agree by our silence. Right, come with us, AJ. We'll take a look at what you've managed to dig up on our fine *upstanding citizens*."

As the three of them headed towards Lorne's office, the phone on her desk rang. She quickened her pace as the two men slowed down behind her.

"We'll give the inspector a bit of space to answer it."

As soon as she knew who it was, Lorne appreciated the chief's thoughtfulness.

"Yes, Tom, I was just about to ring you. As you can imagine, things have been a tad chaotic around here—"

"What do you think *I've* been bloody going through all night, Lorne?"

"I sympathise. Honestly, I do. Look, it's hard on both of us, but I'm trying my darnedest to get Charlie back."

"Have you heard from her or the guy who has kidnapped her?"

She hesitated. She considered telling him about the photos she'd received and what she would do if she were dealing with a total stranger. *Would I tell the parents I have evidence their daughter is safe? Of course I would.* But then, she knew how Tom was likely to react. If he demanded to see the photos no matter how awful they were, he'd be well within his rights. She couldn't do that to him. *What would it accomplish anyway? Jesus, what a dilemma?*

"Lorne?"

"I'm here. Yes, the guy called. You should be here, Tom..."

"What use would that be? I would only be in the way. But, Lorne, think how it is for me, please. I know you're doing all you can. Just keep me in the loop. I can't bear it."

"Oh, Tom, I'm sorry. I will, the moment I have any news. There's such a lot going on. All I know is she's safe. He's made contact and assured me of that. I heard her voice—"

"What? What did she say? Are you sure she's all right?"

"Yes, she just called out my name."

"Okay, Lorne. I'm sorry. I know you have to keep it together. Don't forget, ring me. I'll contact your dad and let him know you've heard. Oh, God, what a bloody nightmare! It's been nearly ten hours since she was taken. What the hell are we going to do?"

"I must continue to do my job, Tom. It's all we can do. Look, try and get some rest. I have to go. And I promise I'll call you if there are any new developments."

Although she had detected some softening in his attitude, a strained atmosphere still remained between them, something she couldn't put her finger on. It was wrapped up in how he didn't feel the need to be with her. And if she were truthful, in this, their hour of real need, her desire to be with him wasn't that strong either.

"See that you do, Lorne," Tom said as they hung up.

Oh well, at least he didn't slam the phone down on me.

"Safe to come in now, Inspector?"

"Yes, sir, sorry about that. Poor Tom, it must be hell being at home wondering..."

Neither of the two men commented, and her words trailed off. Then the chief urged AJ to tell them what he had.

"I'll start with Judge Walter Winwood. We're all aware how influential he is. There's a lot of information out there about him, so I've decided to look at his case files more thoroughly later, if that's okay with you, boss? I'd like to go over what we've discovered about the other guys first."

"The ball's in your court, AJ. Fire away."

"Phillip Solly, football player in the Premier League, presently serving an eight-month ban for refusing to take a drug test. He's got a clean record as far as we're concerned. Press coverage is a regular event in his life, as he enjoys partying, women, et cetera. Paul Solomon, aide to the home secretary. He's married with two children in their late teens. My mate at the press office says there's plenty of hints suggesting he's not too fussy whom he shares a bed with, bats on both sides, so to speak, and age isn't a consideration, but nothing proven that they can go to press with yet. They think there are connections with him and his wife belonging to a swingers' club, but they're clever with it. They haven't given enough away to cause a scandal."

"I'd rather we dealt in factual events, AJ."

"It's interesting though, sir. If any of it is true, the Unicorn or Abromovski could be using the knowledge of his antics in some way, what with him being the personal aide to the home secretary. The possibilities of his usefulness to them are endless. Legalities surrounding immigrants, layout of the Houses of Parliament, who will be where at any given time..."

Lorne stretched as she spoke. Looking out of the window, she watched the sun coming up over the towering buildings of London. "Of course, if all what AJ is speculating is true, then he's a grave danger to our security, but MI6 must be on to that, surely?"

"If they are, they're not sharing."

"As is typical. Okay, what else have you managed to find out about him, AJ? Anything specific?"

"I'll keep digging, but at the moment, his public persona is exemplary, sir. There's a couple of interesting councillors in the mix, though. And these just happen to work in the planning department of Knightsbridge Council."

"Jesus Christ. Abromovski certainly is well connected, isn't he?" Lorne mumbled under her breath.

"Yes, running down the list we've got. The judge, two solicitors, Paul Solomon, two planning officers, three property developers, and the notorious footballer-"

"And, a partridge in a pear tree," Lorne added sarcastically.

"I know, Lorne, but let's keep the faith. Something's got to give."

"You're right. But if it doesn't give soon, sir—"

"I've had some cooperation from the vice guys," AJ butted in. "They're sending over a copy of the tapes. I'm going to look through them, just to check we haven't missed anyone."

"Good. Just remember, the clock is ticking, and we've only got five hours before the deadline."

"Yes, ma'am."

Roberts glanced at his watch. "Good God, where did the last hour go? In fact, for that matter, where's the whole bloody night gone?"

Chapter Thirty

"Are the vests ready, Gary?" The Unicorn asked his head minder.

He walked between trestle tables sagging with the weight of the military equipment, ammunition, and arms he'd acquired through Abromovski and other contacts. Their cost in monetary terms had been high, but he knew the outcome would far outweigh the cost, and the satisfaction would be mind-blowing.

"Yes, boss. Four vests, just like you wanted. Have you decided which girls you want to use for this little *exercise*?"

The Unicorn savoured the moment, enjoying the charged atmosphere of the room. Excitement seared his blood. After all, it wasn't every day he had the British government jumping through hoops like crazed dogs.

"I've got two in mind so far. I'm having trouble deciding on the other two, though."

"Can I ask which two you've chosen?" Gary asked.

"The copper's daughter is one. I want rid of her. She's more trouble than she's fucking worth. Can't bear to have her round me any longer. English girls are too feisty for my liking. And Sasha, yes, *darling* Sasha... It'll give me great pleasure using her. I'm bored with her. Anyway, she has it coming. I taped a conversation she had with the cop's daughter. She'll live to regret her betraying words."

A sudden irritation ran through him as the men in the room copied his sardonic laugh. Their forced loyalty didn't fool him. Trust was a dirty word.

"What about Sasha's family?"

He hadn't missed Gary's reaction to him naming Sasha as one of the girls. His question didn't surprise the Unicorn, but he wondered why Gary appeared to be in such turmoil. The Unicorn studied him closer, saw the slight reddening of his cheeks, and noted the beads of sweat glistening on his forehead.

No, it's not possible, is it? Could this fool be in love with the whore? He was used to his men thinking with their dicks, but he hadn't seen this coming, not with Gary.

"What about them?"

Gary looked even more uncomfortable. "Well I... I just wondered if you wanted me to tell our guys to set them free?"

"Do we *ever* let the families go, Gary?"

"No, but—"

"You *know* what has to be done, or do you need me to *spell* it out for you?"

He took a step closer to his head minder, wondering if Gary was trying to undermine him.

"All *four* members of the family?" Gary asked, and gulped.

"Gary. You're starting to piss me off. What the fuck's wrong with you? Not going soft on me, are you? Too busy thinking with that puny dick of yours, instead of this." He jabbed a finger at Gary's sweating brow and took another step nearer.

The two men stood toe to toe, nose to nose.

Gary backed down. "I'll get it organised straight away, boss."

"Kill the kids first. I want the parents to suffer. And make sure it's filmed. Before Sasha dies, I want her to see and understand how I treat people who betray me. I want her to see her family perishing. In fact, we'll show *all* the girls how we deal with people who go against me."

He was satisfied he'd crushed Gary's rebellion but was unhappy with what might lie behind it. "I want the girls we use to be dressed like soldiers. We'll call them 'our little soldiers of death.' Have them ready by eleven thirty. Organise the film show for eleven. If you have to knock seven bells of shit out of them to keep them in line, feel free to do so. After noon today, they'll be of no further use to me. It won't matter how *pretty* they look when they meet their maker."

He left the warehouse and headed back towards London in the chauffeur-driven stretch limo he'd *borrowed* from Abromovski.

* * *

Sasha was lying next to Charlie. Sweat glistened on her forehead. Charlie's nearness comforted her. They shared the same bed since it was the only spare bed available when she'd been shoved back in this room with the rest of the girls.

The air hung heavy with animosity. She understood. These poor girls would naturally resent the position she'd unwillingly held. If only they knew. But why? She wondered why two of the minders had grabbed her and dragged her back here.

She closed her eyes, but she didn't want to sleep again, not to dream. Her mind refused to rest. Something had been different about the dream this time. It had been more real, like a premonition.

She clenched her hands together in front of her. She hadn't prayed to God in a while. There was no point. He'd done little to help her so far. Despite these thoughts, she felt an intense obligation to pray hard for her family's safety.

As the words touched her lips, tears rolled down her face. "Be safe, Muma and Papa. Be safe, Jordi and Johan. I'll love you always and pray I'll see you again soon. And we will be together again, safe and well in Romania in our tiny flat. God bless you all, and always remember how much I love you."

Charlie woke beside her.

"Sorry, I didn't mean to wake you."

"That's all right, I was only napping. Are you okay, Sasha? You seem so sad."

Sasha felt Charlie wipe a tear from her cheek. "I'm fine, Charlie. I'm being very silly."

"It's not silly to cry. It's understandable with everything that's going on. I mean, we're being treated like convicts."

"I know, and I fear for my safety, little one. The other girls will not take kindly to my being here again. It puzzles me. Why I have been put back here? For months, I have been at *his* beck and call. Why has he discarded me like a well-used oil rag?"

"Just be thankful you're no longer up there with him. And don't worry about this lot, either. I'll make sure they don't hurt you. My mum taught me some nifty karate moves. I might not be able to use them on the goons, but I could certainly wipe the floor with this lot."

"Sssshhh." The sound came from the bunk above them.

Charlie pointed a finger upwards and mouthed. "She's first."

They giggled at this, cuddled each other, and drifted off to sleep, wrapped in each other's arms.

Chapter Thirty-One

"Simon, have you got my mobile?"

"Yes, ma'am, it's right here."

Simon handed the phone to Lorne. "You had a text message come through a little while ago. I took the liberty of seeing who it was from, ma'am."

"And?"

"I didn't read it. It's from your father. I only checked because I thought it might've been from the Unicorn, ma'am."

"Fair enough. Thanks, Simon. DS Fox, any news on that bloody facial recognition yet?"

"I've heard back from the ports. Nothing has surfaced on their wanted list, and I'm still waiting for the airport authorities to get back to me."

"I'll get on to Agent Warner, see if he can hurry things along a bit. We're spending far too much time on this and getting nowhere fast. Chief, I'd better ring Dad back. I expect Tom has been on to him."

"Of course, Inspector, your father must be worried sick about you. Send him my regards."

She grabbed a glass of water from the large water cooler in the corner en route to her office. Searching through the drawer in her desk, she located a strip of tablets. Her head thumped with pain.

"Hi, Dad. It's me."

"Lorne, what the *hell* is going on? I've tried getting in touch with a few of my old contacts, but nobody's willing or able to enlighten me on anything. Damn it, girl, I have a right to know. Charlie *is* my granddaughter, after all."

He sounded as though he were on the verge of breaking point. Guilt wrapped itself around her like an unwanted straightjacket.

"Okay, Dad, you win. Here's what we're up against. I don't have to remind you about confidentiality, do I?"

"Lorne."

His tone reminded her of how he used to warn her in her rebellious teenage years.

"I've heard from the guy who's abducted Charlie. Not to put too fine a point on it, we're dealing with the lowest of the low here." She went on to bring him up to date with all that had transpired, finishing off with the latest development. "He carried out the bombing next door to the Houses of Parliament this morning, and he's raised the stakes, Dad. Actually, he keeps raising them."

"So do you believe he's holding Charlie as some form of ransom?"

"No. I think he's holding her as an insurance of some kind. But he's given me no indication she'll be returned once the money has been paid."

"I'm confused. When I spoke to you earlier, you said that he'd already made contact with you. That was before Charlie had been taken, wasn't it? What were his demands then, apart from wanting twenty million pounds?"

In for a penny, in for a pound. She wondered if his experience as an ex-DCI might throw some light on something they'd missed.

"He told me if the government didn't pay twenty million pounds by noon today, the Houses of Parliament would be no more. That's it, Dad. The superintendent has authorised two thorough searches, but they've both come up blank."

She heard him expel a huge breath. "Twenty million doesn't sound a lot to me, Lorne. All right, it might have gone up another ten mill, but governments have been held to ransom for hundreds of millions. This is such a meagre amount. It just doesn't ring true."

"Now you've mentioned it, it does seem pretty strange. Any suggestions, Dad?"

"My instincts tell me there's a bigger picture to this lunatic's puzzle. What it is, well that, my darling, is anybody's guess. And you say no explosives were found?"

"Nothing. The superintendent believes it's an idle threat, but I'm not so sure, especially after the blast this morning."

"The superintendent's still a tosser, by the sounds of it, then. He always did talk a lot of shit. He's aware that Charlie has been abducted, is he?"

"He's aware, Dad."

"What research have you done?"

"Research? What kind of research do you mean? Hey, it's not taking long for your police brain to flicker into life. I thought you'd let the cobwebs gather and multiply for the past couple of years."

He ignored her remark. "Cast your mind back to the Bill Taylor case. Remember how he threatened to blow up the underground?

That turned out to be a goddamn diversion for the bank robbery he carried out. If it hadn't been for a couple of our guys being on their toes that day, he would've gotten away with millions. Luckily for us, they saw through his little game, caught him and his gang red-handed in the bank's vault."

"Yeah, I remember. How could I forget that? You got a commendation for arresting him."

"Yes, well. Look, would you like me to come in? I'm no use here twiddling my blasted thumbs."

"I don't know, Dad. I'm not SOI. Roberts is."

"I see. I have no grudge with Sean. We've always got on well in the past. Be a love, go and see if he has a problem with me lending a hand. I'll stay on the line."

His request evoked the child in her. Once, inside this skin, she'd been a little girl, told what to do and happy to do it. Bringing memories to the surface gave her a moment of comfort. The pressure lifted. Dad had taken charge. He hadn't ordered, but said it in much the same way he might have said to the child Lorne. "Run and tell Mummy it's raining. She has some washing on the line." If only life had remained that simple.

She ran out of the office and returned a few moments later.

"Dad, the chief didn't just say yes. He said, 'Get your backside in here ASAP'."

"I'm on my way, love."

She had mixed emotions about his involvement. On the one hand, there was no greater detective in the London area than her old man. But on the other, she knew how much Charlie meant to him, and if anything ever happened to her that he was unable to prevent, it would more than likely end up killing him.

"Hi, Tony. Any news?" Lorne asked as she rang the next person on her "to ring" list.

"We're trying our darnedest to find out why he's raised the demand. We're tracing all the calls made from Abromovski's houses, but nothing has surfaced so far. Anything on your end?"

"We think we've found a bit of a lead, but I could do with some help from MI5's database. We have the facial recognition from the CCTV image taken when he had me and Pete trapped in the alley. I thought you could run it alongside the photo you gave me. And we've had it flashed to the ports and the airports to see if their computers have picked up anything, but the response has been too slow for my liking. So if you guys could stick a rocket up their arses, that would be a help, too."

"Right, I'm in the area. I'll pop in and pick up a copy. But, on the ports et cetera—I personally think it's a waste of time. Do you know if he's had any surgery?"

"We suspect he has, but I don't know how much or how recent. A couple of years ago, we found a plastic surgeon murdered in an alley. The Unicorn's in the frame for that."

"Right, I'll tap up a favour and get one of my guys to run both sets of photos through the available databases, including Interpol. If anything flags up, you'll be the first to know. Even if they turn out to be just seventy percent accurate, I'll give you the names. You can sort through what I dig up. Something might ring a bell with you."

"That's great, Tony. I'll make sure reception gets a copy right away."

Chapter Thirty-Two

"It's great to have you on board, sir," Roberts said, smiling broadly as he shook Lorne's father's hand.

"I'm afraid the rank ceased the minute I took retirement, Chief. It's plain old Sam nowadays."

"That'll take a while to get used to. You'll have to forgive me if I slip back to my old ways." Sean Roberts struggled to disguise his shock at how his ex-boss had aged since his retirement.

Sam nodded. His attention focused on scanning the bustling room rather than exchanging small talk. His reason didn't pass by Sean.

"She's in her office, Sam. She's taking five minutes to clear her head. She might not readily admit it, but I'm sure she'll be delighted and relieved to see you."

"How's she really holding up, Chief?"

"To be honest, she's a braver person than me. She has her moments, who wouldn't? But ultimately, I'd say her mind is on the job about ninety percent of the time. Considering what she's been through in the last forty-eight hours or so, I don't think that's a bad statistic, do you?"

The pride showed on Sam's face without him expressing it.

"She's a tower of strength. I don't know what I would do without her. Especially since... Anyway, is it all right if I have a brief chat with her for five minutes or so, just to reassure myself that she is indeed bearing up okay?"

Sean knew Sam had been about to refer to the loss of his wife, but being the professional he was, he'd pulled himself back. Lorne had told him how lost he'd been since her death. In some ways, he suspected being involved with the case would be good for him.

"By all means, I'll get one of the guys to fetch you a couple of coffees from the canteen. I remember you don't go for this instant crap from the machine. And forgive me for repeating myself, si— Sam, but it's an absolute pleasure to have you onboard."

* * *

"Dad, that was quick. I thought you left your Superman powers behind you when you retired from the force. Oh, Dad…"

His arms wrapped her in comfort.

"There, there, my brave one. The quicker you let things out, the quicker we can get down to finding Charlie. You should've called me in before."

His hand stroked the back of her head, the way it had done so many times throughout her childhood. She looked up at him. He had tears in his eyes.

"Come on, sweetheart, it's good to cry, but you know what would happen if Charlie caught you doing so. She'd take the mickey out of you for months. Here, dry your eyes. Dig deep for your resolve."

As she left the comfort of his arms, someone knocked on her door.

Wiping her eyes, she backed away, smiled at her father, then called out to the person to enter. Julie Saunders walked in carrying a tray holding two cups of milky coffee and a couple of Kit Kat bars.

"This is a surprise. Thanks, Julie." She looked down at the tray, gave a brief laugh, and then burst into tears again.

"Are you all right, darling?"

"I'm being silly, Dad. Just ignore me. Kit Kats were Pete's favourites, usually the chunky variety. That's why I called him 'chunky'. God, I miss him so much. I've been like a lost soul without him."

"I know these will sound like empty words right now, but it will get easier, Lorne. Right, let's get back to what I'm here for before I start blubbing with you."

"Yes, you're right, Dad. Thanks."

"I don't suppose you've told the chief about our conversation yet?"

"Are you kidding? You said you'd be half an hour. Five minutes later, you're standing in my office. I didn't even have time to nip to the loo."

She smiled as he shrugged his shoulders. "Come on, you. Let's see what the chief makes of your suggestion."

* * *

"God, that's something I never even considered. It's certainly plausible." The chief shouted across the office to DS Fox, "John, get me a list of any major events going on in the capital today."

"Such as, Chief?"

"I don't know—rallies, demonstration marches—there must be something going on out there today, John. There's *always* something going on in London."

"Okay, sir, leave it with me."

"Good man. Hey, sorry. I didn't mean to snap. It's been a long day for us all."

DS Fox acknowledged the apology with a nod. "You can say that again, Chief."

The banter and general clattering of keyboards that had become quiet at the irritation in the chief's voice started up again.

Chapter Thirty-Three

For the next half hour, the three of them scrutinised every detail of the case. One or two things seemed to be slotting into place. But for the most part, it was as if they were trying to assemble a five-thousand-piece puzzle, and some of the major pieces had gone missing.

"So we've established that a select clientele use that particular house. Do we know how often?" Sam asked.

"No, not really. The event we staked was billed as a party, but turned out to be some kind of auction of human flesh. In my opinion, this wasn't the first time one of these events has taken place, but as to how long these parties have been going on or how often is anyone's guess."

"Maybe they've discovered a new way to market their brothels, found a niche in the market, trying it out to see how profitable it can be." Sam studied the list for a moment and then let out a long whistle.

"What is it, Dad?"

"He's bent, and him." He pointed to a couple of the names.

Lorne glanced at the sheet and gave her dad a puzzled look. "Bent as in gay, or bent as in corrupt?"

"Bent as in corrupt. The only person who doesn't fit into this scenario is this footballer lad. So what's his part?"

The chief was the first to throw a suggestion in the air. "Well, it's common knowledge how much these guys earn. He probably has a lot of money burning a big hole in his Gucci trousers. He has a reputation for partying and having a bevy of beautiful women on his arm. Could be a drug or gambling connection."

"What if Abromovski invited the footballer, hoping he'd encourage his mates to tag along next time?" Lorne said.

AJ approached at that moment, waving a piece of paper in his right hand.

"Found anything relevant, AJ?"

"I'd say something major, ma'am, but maybe that's just my take on it. Going through the tapes, I came across a face I recognised. It took me a while to figure out who the guy was. A certain Glen Waverley."

"Who?" Lorne and the chief asked in unison.

"You mean Chief Superintendent Glen Waverley of Kent Constabulary, formerly of the Met, promoted sideways instead of demoted because of—"

Lorne looked at her father. "My God!"

"Hold it right there. Chief superintendent, you say?" Roberts said.

Lorne couldn't remember when she'd seen Sean look so shocked.

"Jesus. The implications just keep multiplying in this bloody case. Sorry, Sam. You were saying?"

"It was about seven years ago, Chief. I'm surprised you didn't hear about it where you were stationed at the time. A drugs case went drastically wrong. A couple of detectives were killed, and the finger pointed in Waverley's direction. No hard proof substantiated what we all knew, and it looked like he'd get away with it, but a few good men under me were so incensed they tried resigning. Word soon got around. Quite a few high-ranking officers put their foot down, all of them ready to throw away years of pension. In the end, the powers that be shipped Waverley out. As far as I know, he hasn't put a foot wrong since."

"I just can't believe what I'm hearing. Is this all about money or what?"

"Money, power, who the hell knows, Lorne? Do you mind if I make a suggestion, Chief?" Sam asked.

"By all means, Sam."

"Because of the deadline involved, I think we should consider rounding these guys up, bring them in for questioning."

"But, Dad, we haven't got time for that." Lorne glanced at her watch. "It's almost eight o'clock."

The chief nodded his acquiescence.

Her father tutted. "Split the team up. You've got a bigger team now than I ever had, *use* them."

"But they're stretched to capacity as it is, Dad."

Her father's gaze rose to the ceiling. "Prioritise the investigation. Go with the information you have. Stop looking for things that you may never find."

"Your father's right, Lorne. What are the guys wrapped up in at the moment? They're busy searching for the Unicorn, looking in places we don't even know he's been. We *know* he was at this party.

Maybe some of the dignitaries at that party can shed some light on him. Let's face it, as things stand, we're getting nowhere fast. I agree. Let's haul them in. By the testicles if we have to," Roberts suggested.

"At this time of day, are you kidding? They won't like that."

"Tough shit. Get things organized. Lorne, I'm going to have a word with the superintendent."

"Chief, I'd hold fire on that call if I were you. We don't know how far all this goes or who's involved."

"I can't do that, Sam. I know you and the superintendent have never really seen eye to eye, but if I keep him out of the loop... well, that's unthinkable. God, my life as a DCI wouldn't be worth living if or, more likely, *when* he found out."

Chapter Thirty-Four

"What is going on, Chief Inspector? I think an explanation is warranted. Your office, now."

The superintendent marched through to the DCI's office. Roberts followed, cursing the bad timing of his appearance just as the partygoers had started to arrive with their briefs.

"Well? I'm warning you, Roberts, you'd better have a good reason for not keeping me in the loop when I specifically told you to. Why wasn't I consulted about this mass hauling in of some the most highly placed men and dignitaries in the city? Why did I have to hear about it from the commissioner?"

Roberts looked in alarm at the superintendent, who, his face purple with rage, resembled the man on the Blackcurrant Ribena TV advert.

"Sorry, sir. I know I should've contacted you, but I didn't have time."

"What? You didn't have *time* to make a thirty-second phone call? What kind of fool do you take me for, Roberts?"

A leading question. "You're aware of the time restraints we're under, sir."

"Oh, the bloody deadline. A figment of Simpkins' imagination, which hasn't been verified and hasn't an ounce of hard evidence to support it. Didn't I inform you about the Houses of Parliament having been swept and given the all clear? This Unicorn character is doing what he does best. Making a fool out of the Met and *you*. He's got no intention of carrying through this threat."

"Is that what you truly believe, sir?"

"Unless you can provide evidence to the contrary."

"Well, let's not forget the fact this man is holding Inspector Simpkins' daughter hostage as part of the deal. What do you propose we do about that?"

"I admit that is unfortunate, but you know as well as I do that it's our government's policy *never* to bargain with terrorists."

"Let me get this right, sir. You *know* there's no intention whatsoever of paying the thirty million pounds."

"That's right. Of course, that decision isn't really down to *me*, but no, there is and never has been any intention to pay out a penny.

And before you question the fact you weren't told of this, it was thought it best to leave it on a need-to-know basis."

The superintendent's distinct nervousness worried Roberts. But at this moment, keeping his anger in check to even think clearly about a reason for it wasn't easy.

"And as the leading investigator on the case, you didn't deem it necessary to tell *me?*" *Who the hell does this guy think he is? Perhaps Lorne and her father were right about him all along?*

"The right time didn't present itself. I have a busy schedule as well you know, Roberts."

"Ditto. Don't we all. You're aware of the breaking news this morning, concerning a bomb exploding in the vicinity of the Houses of Parliament, I take it? Surely, this gives some credence to our taking the Unicorn's threats seriously, or are you inclined to think *that* is a coincidence, too, sir?"

The superintendent's eyes opened wide, and his tongue slipped out, like a lizard's, to moisten his dry lips.

"A bomb…. Well… Possibly, yes. Do you have any evidence to say otherwise? Do you know who carried out the attack?"

"No, sir." *Dumb prick! What's the point in arguing with the man?* "But we did think we should act on an assumption it's connected to our investigations. It's too big an event to ignore."

"Yes, put like that, but let's get back to the reason I've come down here. Explain why on earth you have pulled in these people and on whose authority?"

After expelling an impatient breath, Roberts told him the reasons behind the questioning.

"As far as I know, DCI Roberts, it is *not* an offence to attend a party."

"As I said, sir, it may have been billed as a party, but it ended up as a despicable auction. A sale of *human flesh.* We believe illegal immigrants are involved, and we're investigating whether they're here willingly or as part of a human-trafficking ring. Not to mention the obvious connection with our ongoing case and the involvement of the same people."

"You can't suspect these people had anything to do with the core business going on, surely? Yes, they were misguided in going to such an event, and—"

"Misguided? They knew what they were up to and knew it was illegal activity. You seem overeager to protect them, if you don't mind me saying so, sir. Is there something *you're* not telling me?"

"Such as?" The superintendent shuffled his feet.

"Oh, I don't know. Like, did you *know* about this party, for instance? Or were you aware that these parties are taking place?"

"Are you interrogating me, Roberts?"

"No, sir. It just seems as if none of this has come as a shock to you. So I wondered if you were already aware of their existence." *Maybe he's a good friend of the infamous Chief Superintendent Glen Waverley?*

"I don't know why I'm entertaining you, but *no*, I had no prior knowledge of this party. Does that satisfy your curiosity, Roberts?"

It didn't. Something wasn't right, but for now, he thought it may be better to leave it and appease the superintendent. "I'm sorry, sir. Blame it on lack of sleep and overzealousness to crack the case."

"Apology accepted. However, I do think you're going about this investigation the wrong way. Carry on doing what you're doing, and you're going to piss off a lot of people in power, and for what? Information on a guy who has been on the run for eight years. What could these people possibly tell you about him that you don't already know?"

"Until I interview them, I can't say, but I do know it's important we follow every line of enquiry which presents itself, no matter how obscure it may seem. With respect, sir, I take his threat seriously, and as SOI, I'm not prepared to leave anything to chance. Now, I'm afraid I have to cut this meeting short. Sergei Abromovski is due any moment now."

Feeling uncomfortably unsure of his superintendent, Roberts led the way out of the office.

* * *

They arrived back at the squad room just as Lorne and her father were coming out of her office. A silence fell over the room. Shock registered on the superintendent's face.

"Hello, Superintendent Greenfall, how nice to see you again," Sam said, extending his hand.

Lorne held her breath. It seemed an eternity before the superintendent recovered from the surprise and found his missing voice. "Sam? Er... what brings you here?"

Whilst the two men's focus remained firmly on each other, Lorne looked at Sean and silently pleaded with him for help.

"I called him in, sir. I thought we could use his valuable experience, and of course, he's a support for DI Simpkins, as well as the fact he's the grandfather of her daughter."

"DI Simpkins should not be on the case."

"I needed to be, sir. I'm not in charge and not causing a hindrance. In fact, I'm able to contribute a great deal under the leadership of DCI Roberts." Lorne could feel her dad tensing beside her and prayed the superintendent would accept the situation. He was now a civilian who hated this man, and there was no telling what he would do if pushed.

"I hope you know what you're doing, Chief Inspector," Greenfall barked.

Sam Collin's took a step forward. "Now look here—"

Before Lorne's father could say another word, Roberts stepped in between the two men. "Sam, let me handle this."

Lorne dragged her father by the arm and led him back to her office. "That wasn't helpful, Dad."

"I'm sorry, sweetheart. That little prick just rubs me up the wrong way. He couldn't investigate a hole in his lawn, let alone a big case like this, and yet, he has the audacity to act as if *I'm* dirt under his feet. God, the little weasel makes my blood boil."

"Which reminds me, have you been taking your tablets, Dad?"

The sheepish look he offered told her he hadn't.

"Dad! You can't stop taking blood pressure tablets whenever you feel like it. I'll see if the police doctor is around and ask him to come and check you over. If he says you need your medication, then I'll get someone to take you home to get them."

"Now don't fuss, Lorne. We've got work to do."

"Who's the child around here? I'll be right back." She left her office as the chief and the superintendent were going through the swing doors out of the squad room.

"What happened, John? Did it calm down?"

"Yes. I think the superintendent came to think the chief had done the right thing."

"Where are they going now? Do you know?"

"The chief's on his way to interview Abromovski. As for the superintendent, I don't know."

"Shit." The last thing Lorne wanted was to bump into the superintendent whilst seeking out the doctor.

By the time she reached the reception, she breathed a sigh of relief. So far, so good. Sergeant Burt Harris stood behind the desk, his face etched with worry. He dropped the phone back in its cradle.

"Oh, there you are, ma'am. I was just going to contact you—"

"Right, perhaps we can help each other? I'm looking for the doc—"

"He's with Crane in Interview Room Two."

"Interview room... Crane? But why? What's happened?"

"Her brief came in to see her. He was only with her a few minutes—"

"Her brief? Oh, my God." Turning on her heel, Lorne bolted down the hallway of interview rooms.

Sergeant Harris followed. "They're in number two."

The door to Interview Room Two was wide open. The doctor was standing just inside. Laura Crane's body sprawled out on the floor at his feet. Her unseeing, half-closed eyes stared a mocking accusation at Lorne.

Chapter Thirty-Five

The blood in Lorne's veins chilled. He'd done it. And inside their so-called protective area. *My God, there's no stopping him.*

"What happened?" Her question met a wall of silence.

Sergeant Harris stood looking at her. His worried expression had turned to something akin to terror.

"Burt?

"Sorry, ma'am. I… I did everything to the book. I wasn't to know—"

"Okay, Burt, take it slowly. Tell me what happened from the beginning. No one is accusing you."

"A man came to the desk. He introduced himself as Crane's solicitor. Said he'd been called in to see her, and he needed to interview her before she went to court to face charges this morning. I didn't know him, but he had all the right papers with him, and I'd been informed earlier that she'd refused to be interviewed with the duty solicitor present but had said her own would be here this morning. I asked him to wait in this interview room. I went to tell Crane he was here. She didn't object. She came with me and greeted him as if she knew him." He stopped to take a breath. "He asked if I would be kind enough to fetch two coffees from the machine. I obliged. I mean, it wasn't an unusual request. Then I left them to it. The next thing I know, he buzzed to say they were finished. I sent WPC Sullivan to let him out and take Crane back to her cell—"

"Did Sullivan find the body? Was the solicitor still with her?"

"Sullivan came running to me shouting, 'Sergeant, Crane's not well. She's fainted'. I told her to put a call out for the doc and stay on the desk. I came down here. When the doctor arrived, I went to call you."

"And the solicitor, did he leave? Did you get his name?"

The sergeant, who had regained some of his composure as he recounted the events, drained of colour and took on the face of a frightened man again. "I don't know. I was caught up in all of this. I presume he left… I can't remember his name. I'm sorry, ma'am."

"Right, Burt, go and find WPC Sullivan. Find out if the man left the building. Check the signing-in book for his name. Run the CCTV tapes for this room and for the car park. Let's get an ID on him and his vehicle and get things in motion to trace him. Send two officers down here to protect and make the crime scene safe, and get forensics here ASAP. After that and as soon as you can, both you and Sullivan write up your reports while everything is still fresh in your minds. Dot all the i's and cross the t's. Don't leave anything out. Try to remember every word spoken, then if there's an enquiry, you'll be ready."

"Yes, ma'am."

The police doctor, a very approachable, mild-mannered kind of guy in his mid-thirties, stripped off his latex gloves. At six foot five, he towered over her. "I'm sorry, there was nothing I could do. I'd say she's been dead around twenty minutes," he said.

"Cause of death?"

"At a guess, some kind of quick-acting poison. Cyanide perhaps."

"Cyanide?"

"Yes, it's becoming quite common nowadays. Mostly linked to terrorist deaths. The post-mortem will confirm or deny."

"Yes, I'll get Jacques Arnaud to do the post. We need people we can trust on this one. It's very sensitive, Doctor, and linked to an ongoing investigation. It couldn't have passed your notice that the dead woman is a serving officer?"

"No, it didn't. I recognised her, of course. What was she doing in custody?"

"I'm afraid I can't say too much. She was caught leaking information, but the case is going to be very high profile, top secret. You know what that means? Do as I told the sergeant. Make your report as thorough and detailed as you can, and because of the security surrounding everything, do it here, and hand it in. Don't take it home to do."

The doctor left just as police officers arrived armed with tape to cordon off the room.

Lorne took a moment to catch her breath. Her robot-like actions and instructions had been driven from her. Her mind had closed to the horrors trying to undo her. But now they flooded in. This cruel, callous man seemed capable of anything, and he still held her Charlie. She leaned against the wall. Her strength drained from her.

"Are you all right, ma'am?"

She had no time to answer. The swish of air caught her body in its draught, and the ominous bang of a door left to swing back on its self-closing hinges shocked her out of her feeling of dismay.

"Ma'am, he's still here." The sergeant rushed towards her. "His name is Reynolds. Mark Reynolds. And Sullivan said he came out of the toilet as soon as I'd gone to the interview room to check on Crane. He asked her to direct him to the interview room where Abromovski was being questioned. He said he was representing him too. He's still in the bloody building."

Chapter Thirty-Six

It took minutes to cross over to the west interview rooms where the partygoers were being interviewed. Fearing for the safety of the chief or Abromovski, or both, Lorne didn't stand on ceremony, but barged straight into the room.

"Excuse me, sir. Mark Reynolds, you're under arrest for the suspected murder of Laura Crane."

The silence following her words didn't last long. The screeching of chair legs on the wooden floor and shouts of, "What the hell are you talking about?" and "For God's sake, Lorne?" almost unnerved her, but she kept it together.

"For the tape, sir. This is Inspector Lorne Simpkins. I have entered the room to arrest Mark Reynolds, whom I presume has already been identified as being present, on suspicion of murder." She directed the rest of her speech at Mark Reynolds. "I am basing my suspicion on the fact that moments after you left her, Laura Crane collapsed and died. The police doctor informs me she did *not* die of natural causes." She turned to the police officer she'd brought with her. "Take him to the cells."

"You can't do this, you fucking tart. You have no proof."

Wondering what had happened to his posh accent, Lorne sought to frighten him into submission. "You forget, we have CCTV in all of our interview rooms. A little rusty on procedures, are we?"

"But—"

"Handcuff him, Officer." Lorne leaned over the chief and picked up the phone on the desk. She buzzed the front office and requested another officer to attend. "He's to be treated as extremely dangerous," she told the officer. "Strip search him, and bag up all his clothes for forensics."

"You're foolish if you think you can pin this on me, camera or no fucking camera. One of your officers let me out. Crane was all right then. A bit distraught, but that's to be expected. She fainted, that's all. I left the policewoman taking care of her—perhaps *she* did something. From what I know, any one of you lot had more than enough reason to want revenge on her. Besides, would I still be here if I'd done that?"

As the officer moved forward, Reynolds gave in. "All right, all right, but I want a solicitor here now with my client, and I want to call one for myself, too." He turned to Abromovski. "In the meantime, Sergei, say nothing. No comment, right?"

"For the tape, I am suspending this interview for Mr. Abromovski until a new solicitor arrives. The time is nine fifty AM," a still shocked DCI Roberts said.

Reynolds bent to retrieve his briefcase.

"Leave that there, sir—it will be searched. Forensics will scan it for evidence, and if a full charge is made, it'll be logged as an exhibit."

Lorne allowed herself a glance at Abromovski. The terror on his face sunk a satisfying revenge in the pit of her stomach. She couldn't resist capitalising on it.

"Play with fire, gentlemen, and you invariably end up getting burned by it. Carry out disgusting deeds for the Unicorn, and you're the ones who end up in prison whilst he gets off scot-free. That is, unless you'd like to make your lives easier by sharing some information with us on his whereabouts and activities?"

"Of course, if you were to do that, it would help your own causes considerably," the chief added.

Abromovski's interest piqued at the veiled proposal, but Reynolds remained defiant.

"What cause? You have nothing on us, *nothing* whatsoever. And who the hell is the Unicorn?"

"I think you know who he is. And as to whether we have something on you or not, we'll see. In the meantime, bear in mind cooperation is looked upon very favourably," the chief replied.

Lorne followed the officers taking down Reynolds. As they reached the reception area, he asked to be allowed to make a phone call.

"I know my rights, Inspector."

Lorne nodded. They led him to the back office, and after releasing his cuffs, they waited whilst he used his mobile.

"That's okay, mate, take your time. There's no hurry. I've got all day."

He turned towards Lorne as he emphasised those last words. She got the message intended for her. His victorious smile further sunk any hope she had of getting the information they desperately needed. But she tried to keep that despair from her expression as he leered at her.

He mouthed at her, "Suck my dick, Inspector."

She gave him a withering look, took his mobile, handed it to one of the officers, and waited until he was safely cuffed again before she left the officers to carry out the instructions she'd given them. Part of her wished she could stick around and witness him suffering the indignity of the search. In fact, she'd gladly don the rubber gloves herself to complete his humiliation. But she knew everything had to be done by the book.

She sought out the chief. He'd remained with Abromovski. This time, she knocked on the door before entering.

"Can I have a word in private, sir?"

She told him all that had happened, as she knew it, concerning the death of Crane and about Reynolds's call to his solicitor.

"The bastard! We thought we had her protected by keeping her in. There's going to be hell to pay. You know that, don't you?"

"Yes, Chief, there's bound to be an enquiry, but I stand by what we decided. How could we know the very solicitor she herself rang would murder her?"

"She probably rang the Unicorn, and he sent Reynolds along. I feel sorry for her, though. She was bloody used. It's just a pity the poor bitch couldn't see it."

Thinking of Pete and Charlie, Lorne couldn't go along the pity line, but she didn't say so.

"Anyway, we're having none of Reynolds' delaying tactics. Time is too short. Once he's in the custody garb, we'll get the duty solicitor and start the interview. If he isn't happy, we'll give him a chance to get his own in immediately or carry on. We have no choice, and we won't give him any either."

Lorne nodded. With all they had at stake, there could be no comeback from them taking this step.

"In the meantime, Lorne, go along all the interview rooms and see how things are going, then get what you have back to me and your father. Let's make sure we keep him in the loop so he can be mulling everything over whilst we're busy with Reynolds."

The mention of her dad reminded her of her original reason for seeking out the doctor. She made a quick call to Sergeant Harris and asked him to see everything was taken care of for her in that department before she started the rounds of the interview rooms.

Frustration built as she found the interviewers were coming up against a wall of silence, until at last, she came to the room where the footballer was.

One of the officers carrying out the interview stepped out of the room to update her. "He's singing as sweetly as that pop star he's reported to be shagging, ma'am."

"Good. What have you got so far?"

Nothing of what he told her helped with regards to information about the Unicorn. Philip Solly's involvement had been as they expected—that of an overpaid prick wanting his thrills however he could get them and as a lure to others like him to indulge at a later date.

Lorne was deeply shocked as she listened to the depravity of exactly what had been going on and how young the girl she'd seen him "buy" had been. She was Charlie's age. He insisted it was his first time at the house, and he'd been appalled once he'd found out the girl's age. He stated he'd comforted the poor girl and that nothing sexual had happened. She'd told him of her plight and that of the other girls. The appalling tale of rape, drugs, violence, near starvation, and families being held hostage brought the bile to Lorne's throat and deepened her fear for Charlie.

"Everything all right, Inspector?"

The chief's voice was a welcome distraction. She motioned to the DC to return to the room and continue with the interview. She relayed the information she'd just heard to the chief.

"What the fuck are we dealing with here, Lorne? Christ, every stone we turn over is soaked in depravity and fear. They're fucking animals. Oh, sorry... I mean, well... You must be feeling like shit. We'll crack this. I promise you. We'll crack it, and Charlie will be brought home safe, and we'll see to it the Unicorn and Abromovski spend the rest of their days rotting in prison."

Lorne couldn't feel so sure or settle the swimming pit of fear in her stomach.

Chapter Thirty-Seven

"It's done."

The Unicorn, engrossed in the news coverage of his successful bombing on the TV, didn't take in the meaning of what his guard had said. Without taking his eyes off the screen, he demanded, "What's done?"

"Sasha's family. They're dead," Gary told him.

The Unicorn turned. "Problem, Gary?"

"No, boss. Just tired."

The Unicorn glared long and hard. He enjoyed the man's nervousness. It made him smile. He took great pleasure when those around him showed discomfort. It empowered him and kept his men on their toes. *Power, what a truly magical possession.*

"When this is all over, you have my permission to take off for a week. Go somewhere hot, screw a few girls, gamble away some money. You deserve it. Me? I'll be lazing on a beach in the Caribbean whilst you're on an overcrowded beach in Malaga or somewhere distasteful like that."

Was that a twitch of annoyance he'd seen around the smirk of his guard's lips?

He checked his watch: ten minutes to ten. "Have the video ready for eleven. We'll all watch it together, you, me, and the girls. Now, bring one of them to me. I fancy a bit of fun before the main event."

"Any preference, boss?"

He didn't answer immediately, but thought it over. For a moment, he considered asking for Sasha, just to confirm what he thought was going on in Gary's head and piss him off more than he could see he was already. But he held back. What he needed to do often ended in death for whoever he chose to do it to. He couldn't risk that with Sasha. He needed her intact or at least able to stand and walk. What was in store for her would be his ultimate revenge.

"Nah. Any slapper will do, except those chosen for the job we have to do, of course. I have a lot of pent-up emotion I need to take care of, if you know what I mean. And stay on hand to mop up after me."

His laughter echoed in his own ears sounded like a madman's. This further amused him, especially as he saw the effect it had on Gary.

As Gary left, the Unicorn pulled his thoughts together. They centered around Gary and the weakness he'd detected. In days gone by, he hadn't flinched if the games played with the whores ended in strangulation or a broken neck. He'd just wrapped up the body and taken it away, laughing his head off and joking about it being fish food by morning. The thoughts strengthened his resolve to keep an eye on this guard he could no longer trust.

* * *

The monotony of the last few hours had dampened Charlie's fear. Some of her pain had subsided or hovered behind the cloud inside her head, which Sasha had said was the effect of the drugs.

She remained on her bunk close to Sasha, and when they weren't dozing, they chatted about how their life had been before their capture. But for the last few minutes, they had been lying back and not talking.

The crashing sound of the doors opening catapulted them upright. Three of the guards came in. One of them she recognised as one of the men who'd been in the room when the Unicorn had injected her. Her fear erupted in her chest and tightened her throat. Her head cleared as her body went into flight mode. Sasha held her arm to keep her still.

"Get up, come on. Get up." Their shouts rendered the girls rigid with fear until slaps around the face and hair being pulled delivered the message. Then, as if they were one, those not yet punished jumped off their beds and stood, their bodies quivering as they stared at the men.

The one she recognised sauntered down the space between the beds towards them. When he reached them, he stood for a moment and gazed into Sasha's eyes. Sasha gave him a faint smile. Embarrassed, he looked away. His head motioned to the other two, and then he pointed at the girl in the bunk above Charlie and Sasha's.

The girl's hollers of distress tugged at Charlie's heart until, when dragged past them, she spat in Sasha's face.

"This is your fault, bitch. You should have stayed upstairs where you belonged, you cock-sucking whore."

Putting her arm around Sasha, Charlie allowed the change in her feelings and knew a pleasure at the girl's plight. Though unaware of what that might be, Charlie thought the girl deserved what she had coming to her for what she'd just done to Sasha.

The girl's screams filled the room. Her body twisted and turned, and her fists lashed out at the men. Some pity seeped into Charlie, but it mixed with terror for herself and Sasha as the man bent over them. The moment froze. Not even a prayer came into her blank mind. When he moved, she shrank back. Sasha remained still. After a moment, the man laid his hand over Sasha's and squeezed it.

Charlie tried to read his expression, but couldn't. Abruptly, he withdrew and left the room. The closing door blocked out the girl's screams and pitiful cries for help.

Charlie turned to Sasha and saw the shock registered in her eyes. "Are you all right, Sasha?"

"Yes, but I have no clue what that was all about. Why did he do that?"

"I don't know. It was as if he was trying to tell you something."

Lowering her voice, Sasha whispered, "Do you think he was trying to tell me everything will be okay? Is he going to help me escape? He did seem to be trying to tell me something. I am afraid. Something is going on, but what?"

Charlie couldn't even speculate. She had no understanding of the way these people worked. But Sasha, who until now had been so together and there for her, had an air of uncertainty about her, and this left her feeling bereft of support.

Chapter Thirty-Eight

Back in the squad room, after leaving Abromovski with his solicitor and Reynolds safe and seething in the cells and after giving instructions to the other interviewers to capitalise on the footballer's testimony, Lorne had been briefed on the current position and intelligence. As soon as the chief joined her with her father, who had been given the okay as far as his blood pressure was concerned, Lorne brought them up to speed.

"On the question of what's happening in London today, there are a few insignificant rallies, the usual thing, a group of pensioners moaning about their high council tax, and a bunch of students marching in protest of their outrageous student loans. However, there is a demonstration about the war in Iraq, which looks important. It doesn't appear to be a run-of-the-mill-type demo, either. There's expected to be ex-front bench members, scientists, and financial bods marching side by side with the general public. Word has it they see this march as a way of pushing the prime minister out of office."

Lorne paused to take a breath. "We also have information that the bomb which went off earlier was a small incendiary device, the type a student could've assembled in a chemistry lab at college. Maybe they had. And it isn't beyond the realms of possibility that it could be down to the students taking part in the rally today. The device had been on a timer, and it went off in the doorway of the building. Probably planted to cause as much panic as possible. My thinking, though, is that it *was* the Unicorn's work. But what point he was trying to make or what he was trying to achieve is anybody's guess."

"Right, the demonstration protesting about the Iraq War, where's it taking place?" her father asked.

"As it happens, it's due to pass the Houses of Parliament sometime between twelve and half past."

"Jesus, now you mention it, I knew about it. Damn, I should have made the connection." The chief thumped his forehead with the heel of his hand.

"Well, that's what comes from being a deskie. No, joking apart, there's no point in getting too upset about it. It's in the picture now."

"You're right, Sam. I take it there's a good police presence arranged? There usually is when the demo concerns a red-rag-to-a-bull subject, and there are plenty of fors as well as againsts in this issue."

"Yes, plenty have been drafted in. It is a well-controlled, planned event," Lorne said.

"Good. From what I remember about the briefing on it, it's due to end outside Number Ten with a petition. What's your instinct telling you, Sam?"

Lorne surprised them by saying, "I know what I'd do. My instincts tell me to get down there straight away. We should stop wasting valuable time on the likes of Abromovski and his *esteemed* clientele and find out what's going on down there at the Houses of Parliament. I know the superintendent insists they've swept the place, but I have my doubts how thoroughly it was checked over. If it had been checked properly, wouldn't they have found the device next door?"

"Not necessarily, no. We don't even know who planted the damn thing yet. However, I do think you have a point. We're simply banging our heads against a hundred-foot wall around here. I'll let the superintendent know we're going down there. I wanted to see if he's got the all clear on you carrying a gun, anyway. Give me five minutes, okay?" Roberts said.

"I'm not usually a betting woman, but I bet you a month's wages the outcome remains the same. They'll refuse point-blank. No pun intended."

"And I'd be right with him on that one, Lorne," her father piped up.

"Come off it, Dad. This is a one-off occasion. After what happened with Pete, I would be far happier and feel much safer having some form of protection. Given the circumstances, even you can understand that, surely?"

Sean Roberts left them and headed for his office. *Coward,* she thought at her boss's avoidance of the expected argument.

"So wear a vest. How many times have I told you, as a precaution, you should be wearing one every time you go out there. This Unicorn fella isn't the only dangerous criminal out there. In case you hadn't noticed, Lorne, London is a very dangerous place to police."

"That's *precisely* my point, Dad. And the vest argument doesn't hold. There's no vest to protect your head."

"It's just wrong, Lorne."

"Oh, I know. I know all the arguments against and agree with some of them, but remember, I've just lost a partner in circumstances I needn't have if we'd been armed. What were we supposed to fight back with? Pebbles?"

Forgetting where he was, he grabbed her, pulled her into his arms, and whispered, "I've lost your mother, Lorne. I couldn't bear having to grieve for you, too. My heart couldn't cope losing something so precious a second time."

Lorne looked up and saw tears welling in his old, tired, and bloodshot eyes. It was her turn to try to lighten the mood between them before she, too, broke down and cried.

"Don't be silly, old man. You've got everything to live for. Any day now, Jade's going to present you with another healthy grandchild for you to coo over in your old age."

He pushed her away by the shoulders and swallowed hard before declaring, "Before I can even consider thinking about my *new* grandchild, I'm going to do everything in my power to bring Charlie, my *first* grandchild, home safe and well."

"Let's hope we find her soon, Dad. I don't know how much longer she can survive out there by herself."

"She'll be fine, sweetheart. After all, she's her mother's daughter."

Lorne stepped into her father's loving arms again and gave him a squeeze that reaffirmed how much he meant to her, should he be in any doubt.

"Sorry to barge in, but we've been given the all clear, Lorne," the chief said.

"To carry guns?" she queried, shocked.

"Yes, the commissioner has given us both special dispensation. He wants the Unicorn off the streets as much as we do. Looks like he's finally realised what a dangerous man we're dealing with."

"If it's not too cheeky to ask, sir, can you actually fire a gun?" she asked.

"I take it you didn't see me practicing in the lane next to you down at the range, then?"

"You weren't."

"I guess that's another little mystery for you to solve, Inspector. Maybe you're not the only one with secrets around here." Roberts smiled and tilted his head.

"I'd say, watching you two, it's a bloody shame nothing further worked out for you in the life-partner department and not just the working partnership... Not that I am displeased with the one you did choose, Lorne, of course."

"Dad." Lorne cringed and didn't dare look at Sean. For a moment, what was left unsaid hung in the air charging the atmosphere.

Sean broke the tension. "What? I have enough trouble taming her *here*. Spare me even the thought of having to do so in my private life. She'd make minced meat out of me. I actually feel sorry for poor Tom."

Lorne took a swing at him, and the three broke into a laugh, which eased things, but didn't touch Lorne's heart. Instead, she thought, *Until Charlie is safe in my arms, I can't give any part of me to humour.*

Chapter Thirty-Nine

"Chief, the desk sergeant wants to know if we're charging any of that lot we hauled in or not. If not, he's asking for permission to release them, says he's being besieged by solicitors demanding one thing or the other."

"Shit. Bloody solicitors! Right, well, I'd like to say we're charging them, but we only have the hearsay evidence of our footballer, nothing concrete. Tell him he can release the shitty lot of them. Damn."

"My sentiments exactly, Chief," Lorne said.

"A waste of bloody time, Inspector. I could spit…"

"No point in dwelling on it. Look, I'll call Warner as we go, just to touch base with him, see if they have anything."

Lorne grabbed her coat with one hand and dialled with the other. "Hi, Tony. Lorne here. Anything new to tell me?" she asked, her mobile flying from one hand to the other as she wrestled into her black woollen coat.

"We're getting close to identifying just exactly who the Unicorn is. We've whittled it down to four possibilities. Just doing some final checks with Interpol before I divulge them. What about you?"

Lorne summarised what had been going on at the station.

"You're kidding? Have you any chance of getting a conviction out of your thinking the Unicorn and Abromovski are involved in Crane's murder?"

"Depends if Reynolds squeals, which he might do once he realises he's taking the whole rap for it. But at the moment, though it pains us to do so, we have to release all the suspects, including Abromovski. We've no hard evidence, well, not enough. I mean, even the tapes from the surveillance could be slaughtered by a good lawyer, and unless we can get some of the girls to testify, Phillip Solly's evidence won't stand up to much. God, something's got to give soon, surely. I can't wait for the pleasure of wiping the smug smile off Abromovski's arrogant, ugly face."

"I'll get my source at vice to keep an eye on him. I'll see if any of them are going to be in the vicinity of the demo. If they are, I might see if there's room for me in one of the vans."

"Our paths are liable to cross again soon, then. Keep me informed, Tony."

"Goes without saying, Lorne."

She flipped her phone shut and was about to tuck it into her pocket when it tinkled, announcing the arrival of a text: *Your daughter fits me like a glove.*

Lorne's strength crumbled, leaving her legs unable to hold her. DS Fox caught her as she stumbled towards his desk.

"Inspector. Are you okay?"

"Oh my God."

"Oh, Dad…" She handed the phone to her father and watched the colour drain from his face and his body sag. Then, handing the phone to the chief, her dad did as she'd expect of him: he pulled himself to full height and offered her comfort.

"He's winding you up, sweetheart. Take no notice. He's worried. He knows you're closing in on him, so he's using every tactic in the 'scumbag's handbook' to try to unnerve you. You must remain focused. *Do not* let him win, Lorne. Charlie needs you."

With her father's arm on her shoulders and seeing the massive effort he'd made, she took what she could from his strength and gulped down large amounts of air to regain her self-control and resilience. Pulling her coat around her cold body, she strode towards the door leading to the car park.

The chief shouted after her. "Lorne, are you sure you're up to this?"

"Yes, I'm up to it all right, sir. I'm more than up to it. This time, I'm going to get the *bastard*." Her hand found the gun strapped in her belt. The feel of it empowered her. She'd let nothing get in her way of finishing the Unicorn. His days, as far as she was concerned, were numbered.

Chapter Forty

"What's going on?"

To the Unicorn's amusement, Abromovski's head swivelled and bobbed like a balloon on a stick as he stepped out of his car. The Unicorn stood on the doorsteps of the Russian's home. Abromovski looked from him back to his bodyguards, who were leaning against the car, grinning sickly grins as only traitors can.

"A welcome home party, my friend. Would you expect anything less?" the Unicorn asked.

He put an arm around Abromovski's shoulder and guided him through the hallway to the kitchen of the Russian's deceptively big house-cum-business premises. Made up of several large Victorian three-storied houses knocked into one, it provided ample accommodation for the activities that went on there, besides a luxury apartment on the top floor for Sergei's own use.

"The cleaners let me in. I'm intrigued to know how your interview with the police went." He steered the trembling Russian towards the door leading to the soundproofed basement. The Unicorn unlocked the door and stood back whilst one of Sergei's ex-loyal guards swung the door open. "I think it prudent to conduct our meeting out of earshot of the staff, don't you agree?"

Sergei didn't protest, but his agitation and pleading looks to his guards gave the Unicorn intense pleasure as it dawned on Abromovski once and for all that he no longer had their protection. The promise of a good payout, coupled with the fact that none of them had any respect for the Russian, meant they had snatched at the chance to switch sides as soon as the opportunity presented itself. They had prepared things whilst they awaited the call from the police station to go collect their boss.

Once down the stairs, the guards took hold of Abromovski and steered him in the opposite direction of the offices and vaults and led him towards the dormitory where the girls were being held. They passed a grubby kitchen and turned along a passageway to the left.

Now fully aware of where he was heading, Abromovski struggled and protested. "I haven't given anything away... None of us have! I promise, nothing needs to change. You should put your attention to getting Reynolds killed. The idiot thought he could fool them by remaining after he'd seen to Crane. They arrested him for her murder. He's the one to fear. He'll squeal the moment he realises we have all been released. He's bound to."

"Shut up. That's being taken care of." The Unicorn kicked open the door of one of Sergei's own pleasure rooms, and the guards shoved him inside.

"No… There is no need for this. They know nothing…" Abromovski's eyes protruded as his fear grew.

Sheer terror registered on Sergei's face as he looked over to where his own implements of torture lay—handcuffs, nipple clips, whips, and knives, which he had used unmercifully on the girls before raping them—and saw other, more sinister items had been added to the collection. His legs buckled beneath him. The guards held him up and led him to a chair.

The Unicorn swiped his hand from left to right; the back of it connected painfully with Sergei's dumbstruck face.

"Now tell me, how did the cops know about the party?"

Sergei tilted his chair, trying to back away, but two pairs of hands gripped his shoulders, forcing the chair's front legs back onto the floor. The Russian gulped loudly. Saliva dripped from the side of his mouth. "No. Look, I don't know anything," he pleaded, his voice rising as high as a choirboy hitting a top note.

"So you don't know anything, eh?" Without warning, the Unicorn's right hand shot out and grabbed the Russian's balls, twisting them one hundred eighty degrees.

Sergei let out an agonized cry, doubled over, and vomited. Tears of pain seeped from his bloodshot eyes as he gasped for breath.

"Ugh… Get something to clean that up with."

Sergei's turncoat guard left the room and came back with a mop and bucket. Gary turned the chair the other way and over to the right so the Unicorn could avoid the pool of sick, and Sergei faced the laptop. Until now, Abromovski had only glanced at it and hadn't asked its purpose.

Still holding his crotch and wincing with pain, Sergei managed to grit his teeth and beg. "Please, I don't know. Everyone was sworn to secrecy. Maybe if you hadn't borrowed my car and led them to me, none of this would have happened."

"Don't fucking blame me. You were the one who approached me. You got me into this stupid venture of yours. But now you're going to make it up to me."

The Unicorn tapped the computer's mouse pad, and the screen lit up. "Right, what do we have here? Oh look, Sergei, it's your Cayman Islands account."

"What... How?"

"Ah, I have the means and the know-how to get hold of anything I want. Now you're going to fulfill my ultimate desire to be rich beyond dreams. You're going to transfer all the money sitting in your account into mine using an immediate transaction." He couldn't stop the triumphant smile creasing his face as he nodded to Gary, who punched a number into a mobile he held and handed it to Sergei.

"I've even got the number of your bank to hand, isn't that kind of me? All you have to do is press the little picture of a telephone."

"And if I refuse?"

"You won't, or at least, not for long. What do you think these are for?" He spread his hands towards the weapons of torture. "Not for your pleasure, I can assure you."

The room resounded with the same laughter he'd likened to a madman's. Where it came from, he didn't know, but he enjoyed possessing it and the way it emerged at times like this. It struck terror into those around him.

His laughter stopped, and he looked at Sergei. His Adam's apple jumped to the top of his neck and bounced back down again.

Sergei took the phone. "And if I do this you'll let me go?"

The Unicorn nodded. "You have my word on that."

Relief was written all over Sergei's face. He pressed the button to connect to his bank, and then, after answering several security questions, he gaped at the screen as two billion dollars flowed from his account.

Once the transaction was complete, The Unicorn took the mobile, tapped in some more numbers, and handed it back. "Right, now the Swiss bank."

"No... Why? Haven't you got enough? Leave me something, please."

The Unicorn smirked at him, typed on the keyboard of the computer, bringing up another account bulging with numbers.

"I'm sure you have more, but the billion in here will suffice for me, added to what I have already. Just do it."

Again, Sergei went through the motions. Once he was done, he went to rise, but the two heavies standing behind him forced him back down.

"But... I have done all you asked of me..."

The Unicorn shut down the computer. Then he moved towards the other end of the table. His hands counted out the objects. His voice in a sing-song rhythm, he said, "Tinker, tailor, soldier, sailor, rich man... ha, poor man, beggar man... thief. This'll do for starters."

The Unicorn's pleasure grew to exquisite heights as the Russian's screams echoed around the room. The Unicorn swung the metal hook back and then thrust it satisfyingly into Abromovski's soft flesh and tore away chunks of it, leaving a gaping hole. Stinking intestines flopped like a bundle of snakes and hung from his knees. Blood spurted, thick and bright, painting everything red. The Unicorn plunged the hook back in and dragged out the remaining life-giving organs, letting them drop to the floor. His terrible laugh verging on hysteria, he squashed what looked like the liver under his foot. The squelch brought silence to the room.

A heavy disappointment hung like dumb-bells inside the Unicorn. The death had been too quick; he'd lost control. He looked at the men. Shock registered on their faces. Sergei's man looked that way because he'd never seen anything like it, but Gary had witnessed for the first time his boss acting without cool detachment and thought.

Seeking to gain the upper hand once more and some kind of credence, he snarled at them. "If any of you even consider double-crossing me, you'll end up like that. Do you hear me?" He spoke to them both, but intentionally directed his real meaning towards Gary, the man he'd entrusted to be his right-hand man, but in whom his faith had been shaken of late.

"Yes, sir," they said together. Gary held his gaze, but to the Unicorn's amusement, didn't outstare him for long.

"See to things."

As the Unicorn walked out of the room, three other guards entered.

Ramon, who worked often with Gary and had seen what happened between them, put his hand on Gary's shoulder. "He's on

137

to you, Gary. Whatever you're planning on doing, you'd be wise to reconsider."

"I ain't planning nothing, and don't know why he thinks I am. I follow his orders to the letter..."

Yes, thought the Unicorn, who hadn't missed this exchange from where he stopped outside the room. *You do, but there is something... And it is a dangerous something, as it is tied up with your feelings for that bitch, Sasha.*

Chapter Forty-One

"What do you think this is all about?"

Sasha looked around her and shrugged. The group of girls had been gathered together with specific instructions to look their best. Now they were nervously sitting in the same room where the auction had taken place the previous evening.

The chairs were still laid out theatre style. The catwalk where some of them had paraded the night before had gone, and a huge screen now hung in front of the stage.

Sasha nudged Charlie, then motioned with her head. To Charlie's dismay, Sasha had directed her gaze across the room to where the shivering form of the girl from the bunk above them was sitting.

Pity mixed with a sick fear settled in Charlie's stomach as she saw the evidence of what the girl had been subjected to. Her eyes were swollen so badly, it was hard to imagine she could see out of them, and every visible part of her was covered in terrible bruises and raw, gaping wounds.

"Oh, God," Charlie whispered as her eyes ran the length of the tragic girl's swollen body.

"Ssh, please, Charlie, don't speak," Sasha pleaded.

Charlie heeded Sasha's warning, but found it impossible to take her eyes off the girl. Her conscience pricked, and an unexpected shame washed over her for wishing the girl harm. No one, she thought, not even her worst enemy, deserved to be treated like that. Her eyes welled up. Charlie questioned whether she could withstand such a beating. What she'd endured so far had been bad. *But how far do these men go?* Her body trembled at the truth. *They may even kill—*

The Unicorn's appearance stopped her train of thought. He came in flanked by his usual, muscle-bound entourage. He stepped onto the stage and stood alongside the screen. His evil eyes scanned the room. The hatred emanating from him radiated immense power over the girls. His stance dared them to challenge him. A cold streak of ice chilled Charlie's backbone when he looked over at her and Sasha. She sought Sasha's hand, and they held on to each other.

"You two!" he bellowed.

Charlie and Sasha looked at each other, and Charlie saw that Sasha's eyes held the same terror that gripped her. Panic told her to flee, but she couldn't move. The guards approached, their heavy footsteps resounding in the silent room. It took only seconds for the guards to reach the girls and grab them roughly by the arms. Charlie tried to resist, but it seemed the iron man himself had hold of her, and the force that dragged her forwards didn't give her a chance.

"You two." The Unicorn pointed at another two girls in the front row. "Get to the back. I want Sasha and her new playmate to have a prime position for the main event."

Something like relief momentarily crushed her fear until they passed by the Unicorn. He put his hand up to halt their progress. They stood trembling in front of him while he tweaked their nipples. But his action, though painful, didn't scare or even humiliate Charlie, if that was his intention. Instead, she had to hold back a laugh. If he thought after all he'd done to her he could get any reaction from tweaking her nipple until it hurt, he had another think coming. She didn't even flinch as the other girls did. But when Sasha nudged her, Charlie realised her defiant stand may only cause pain for the rest of the girls, so she went through the same motions they did.

As they sat down, she noticed the guard who had come into the dorm a few hours earlier. Sasha had told her he was called Gary. He stood by the door just behind the screen. He was taking deep breaths, as if to calm himself. His eyes never left Sasha. Charlie was certain the man was trying to tell Sasha something, and she felt sure his look was one of adoration for Sasha, too.

"Come, Gary. Stand by me," the Unicorn ordered.

Gary wandered slowly over, giving his boss a hate-filled look.

Once Gary was in position, the Unicorn draped an arm across his shoulders. Gary looked worried and humiliated. The Unicorn seemed to be trying to wind him up. Charlie sucked in her breath, unsure what would happen next.

Chapter Forty-Two

Sasha, too, had been reading Gary's expressions, and now his defiance; she knew the Unicorn was aware of it. His grip on Gary's shoulder held a warning. But she felt some hope as she analysed the meaning of how Gary had looked at her.

Could it be conceivable that Gary is on the turn? What could that mean? Is there a possibility of him helping me get out of this mess? She couldn't allow her hope to be raised that high, could she? *No, to do so would be foolish.*

Her attention came back to the Unicorn as he clicked his fingers. Speaking like a master of ceremonies, he announced, "Draw the curtains. We're about to see one of my favourite movies. You'll enjoy this, girls. It's a movie I shot with a specific purpose in mind."

His sickly smug smile sent a shiver through Sasha. She could feel the tension in the room. The screen lit up. Sasha gasped, "Familia mea. Mama, şi Tatăl, şi Jordi, şi Johan."

"Your family?" Charlie whispered.

Sasha nodded. Her joy at seeing them playing and laughing together was tinged with a sick worry that grew to a terror as the ball her brothers played with came to the forefront of the screen. A man's foot stopped its progress. Her heart pounded as she wondered who the foot belonged to, but it almost came to a grinding halt when she saw the apprehension written on her parents' faces as they clung together and called the boys to them.

The camera panned around, and as it circled, Sasha saw her beloved home situated in the middle of the surrounding fields she ran through as a child. In the distance were the homes of her neighbours and people she loved. Finally, the camera shot came to rest on the ugly, huge man with his foot on her brother's ball. His menacing laughter rippled through the speakers and echoed through the hushed room. When he stopped laughing, he motioned to other men standing behind him to come forward.

A tight band wrapped around Sasha's lungs and heart. Sweat beaded her body. "Nu, nu... te rog... nu."

She couldn't bear it. They were rounding up her family as if they were cattle. Again, but silently, she pleaded, *No... no... please... no!*

The Unicorn's scornful laugh penetrated her ears. She looked over at him. She started to rise, but the guard behind her held her firmly in her seat. Her head exploded with hate, and spittle ran down her chin as she snarled. "Te Urăsc, nenorocitule!"

He laughed back at her. "Yes, I am a bastard, aren't I? And, Sasha dear, you cannot hate me more than I hate you. But do keep watching. The next bit is very entertaining."

She saw Gary move as if to come to her, but the Unicorn shot him a warning look. Beside her, she felt Charlie surge forwards as if to go towards the Unicorn, but she, too, was restrained.

Her mama's screams brought Sasha's attention back to the screen. Jordi cried, "Fiul meu, nu, pleae nu-l doare. Nu, Oh Hol Maria Maica lui Dumnezeu, ajută-ne!"

Oh God. Her mama was pleading with the men who'd dragged her brother Jordi away not to hurt him and had beseeched the Holy Mother to help her.

"Oh, Sasha, Sasha..." Charlie's arm came around her.

"Silence. Hold your tongue, girl, or I promise you this, it'll be your family next."

Charlie was pulled roughly away from her, and she sat still. Sasha could feel her fear and longed to hold her hand. Loneliness and despair clogged her heart.

The scene in front of her stretched her sanity to a breaking point as her beloved brother's heart-wrenching, terrified screams pierced her soul. Two men held his writhing body as two others tied him to a pole. Once he was secured, branches were placed around him. His screams turned to pleading cries to his mama and papa to help him. "Mama, Tata, ajuta-ma... Ajuta-ma!"

Sasha couldn't cry out. Agony dried her throat. The gasps, sobs, and pleas coming from the girls around her, all using their mother tongue, held her in limbo, between here and her beloved Romania.

The screen held images so near to her heart, scenes beyond her screaming family, which transported her back. She felt as if she floated, unseen, around them. But all of it became flashing, intermingled colours as a whooshing noise prompted the camera to turn back to her brother, an eight-year-old boy, now encased in flames.

She gasped a breath of pain that took her into a black, black hole. Here, she knew no pain, no sorrow, no fear. Mama smiled at her, and Papa held her hand. Everything was going to be all right...

Ice cold water hit her face, shocking her back to reality. Vomit shot from her mouth, clogged her nose, and slimed down between her breasts. A stinging slap brought blood trickling from her nose into her mouth.

Opening her eyes, she saw the Unicorn's face swim before her. Saliva gathered around her teeth. She sucked it together and spat with all the ferocity she could manage. The red-speckled spit splattered his face.

"Stand her up."

One of the men standing behind Sasha's chair pushed her to her feet.

She couldn't brace herself against the brutal, vicious blows to her stomach. The air left her body, and she couldn't gasp it back in. Her eyes bulged. Tears, snot, and sweat mingled together and ran down her face. All the time, horrific scenes swam before her. Flames crackled, and hoarse, hollow moans groaned ever louder, ever nearer to death. Her mama's voice, thick with agony. "Sasha mea, te iubesc. Fii puternic... Live pentru noi... Slavă Tatălui şi Fiului..."

"Sasha, I love you. Live for us. Be strong... Glory be to the Father and to the Son..."

Flames licked around her body and blackened her face until her prayer died on her lips.

Mama, scumpa mea, Mama... Mama, my sweet, Mama...

Once more, the blackness took her, and she swooned against the chest of the man who held her. With her into the black hole, she took the image of her father's and Johan's burning bodies, the sobs of the girls around her, Charlie's desperate cries, and her father's last message. "Sasha, viaţa noastră trai în tine. Nimic din toate astea e vina ta. Fii tare, copilul meu. Te iubesc."

"Sasha, our lives live on in you. None of this is your fault. Be strong my child. I love you."

"She's coming to. Come on, Sasha. It's over. Come on, wake up." The words filtered to her through the imaginary dark tunnel. They were spoken in a kind, caring way. She recognised Gary's voice. She opened her eyes just as the Unicorn shoved Gary out of the way.

A huge void, cold and detached, had taken root in her where she'd once had feelings. The screen still mocked her, though no images flashed there, only large letters.

The Story of Sasha's Family
The End.

Next to her, Charlie sobbed, but they were quiet and dignified sobs. Sasha knew she wept for her, not for herself, and the tenseness of her body told Sasha that Charlie's brave spirit still held strong.

"Sasha, you wronged me. What you've seen is only part of my revenge for your deceit. I have a further punishment for you." The Unicorn now addressed Charlie, "And you, spawned of a bitch, will suffer the same fate. Now, Sasha dear, I need four girls altogether, but the last two have to be chosen by you."

She did not respond. Something in her had changed. Being void of feelings gave her a courage she'd only dreamt of before, and a sure knowledge came to her that she would escape. For the sake of the memory of her family, she would be free.

"Don't ignore me, bitch."

The blow she expected didn't materialise. The Unicorn held her face and turned her to look at him. "Choose, or they *all* die."

When she didn't respond, he said, "Very well, I'll take the two baby girls who have just joined us."

"No, choose us." Toni and Carly, two older girls who'd been imprisoned nearly as long as Sasha, stood up.

"So there is honour amongst whores after all."

"We are not whores by choice, but good Romanian girls," Sasha spat at him. "It is you and your filthy ways that have tainted us. Proxenet nenorocit."

"You call me a fucking pimp bastard. Huh! You honour me, but I am much more than that, as you'll soon find out." He laughed loudly and, after a pause, looked around furiously. Sasha guessed he was angry because his men hadn't laughed with him.

"Is something wrong?" He sneered, looking from one man to the next. Only Gary didn't respond. The others all shook their heads. The Unicorn stared at Gary. The stare shook Gary's resolve.

When the Unicorn asked again if something was wrong, Gary answered, "No, boss."

"Enough of these futile games. The clock is ticking. We only have forty minutes left. Get them ready."

Two guards came forward, carrying four sleeveless jackets. Each one bulged with explosives.

Chapter Forty-Three

It was approaching eleven twenty-five by the time Lorne and Roberts reached the gathering point for the start of the demonstration. Thousands of protesters milled around, organising themselves into groups. The atmosphere was like a carnival's. They waved the usual banners, amongst which Lorne spotted one held by the person waiting to lead the march; it depicted the late Sir Robin Cook, who'd been a staunch critic of the war in Iraq.

A quick glance around didn't give any cause for concern. She hoped they weren't making a mistake latching on to this one event.

She noticed a couple of white vans across the road and wondered if Tony was inside one of them. As if reading her mind, one of the vans, the nearest one to her, briefly flashed its headlights. She acknowledged the contact with a swift nod.

Within minutes of their arrival, the demo got under way. Lorne and the chief followed the group at a snail's pace, but soon became bored and decided to get ahead by taking a shortcut. With the chief behind the wheel, Lorne kept a constant lookout for anything suspicious.

"Anything?" asked the chief.

"Nothing out of the ordinary. Which begs the question, do you reckon we've read things right?"

"It's hard to tell, but I hope we have, as there are only thirty minutes left to the deadline."

They had just crawled past Great Peter Street when the chief said, "Look... Over there."

Lorne followed his pointing finger. A black van with blacked out windows was parked at an odd angle, which smacked of a hasty pull-in rather than a planned parking.

"Could be interesting, though it's a bit of an obvious vehicle. It practically cries out to be investigated. Can you pull over?"

As he did so, the chief said, "That could be the ploy, to be so in our face, we won't believe it. Get on to Warner. Hopefully he's in one of the surveillance vans and will be able to get a quicker check on it than our boys can."

Lorne grabbed the binoculars lying on the backseat of the chief's Lexus and focused on the number plate of the van.

"Damn, I can only see half the number. That bloody Mini is obscuring the rest."

She flipped out her phone and selected a number she'd recently put on speed dial. "Hi, Tony. Are you in one of the vans?"

"Yes, it was me who flashed the lights at you. Anything up?"

"Not sure. We have a van sticking out like a sore thumb, the type gangsters on the telly choose, but the chief thinks it's worth checking out. He thinks it's possible they'd use such a vehicle either as a decoy or with the idea, it being so visual, we would ignore it. Do me a favour and run the plate, though I've only got half a number for you."

"Fire away."

"November, Mike, oh-six, Romeo. And that's it. It's a black Ford Transit."

"Christ, you don't expect much, do you? Hold the line, Inspector. One of the guys is just searching the database…"

Lorne kept her eyes peeled on the van.

"It's coming through now, Lorne… Let's see. We've got twenty matches."

"Shit. Anything that leads back to Abromovski?" she asked.

"That's a negative. We're matching the names to the Russian's businesses and addresses and coming up blank. We're still following the crowd. Give me your location. We'll get close to it and try and pick up on any activity inside."

She gave him their location. He told her they were only a couple of streets away and would be with them in a couple of minutes. She didn't have to wait long before she spotted his van across the street from the black one.

Her phone rang, and she answered it.

Before Lorne could say her name, Tony said, "Right, we've got a full plate now, and it matches one stolen this morning."

"That puts a positive spin on things, I guess." She turned to Sean Roberts and mouthed the information to him.

"Lorne, are you still there?"

"Yeah, Tony. Why? What's up?"

"The satellite has tuned in, and we're getting some chatter coming through. Can you hear it?"

Lorne strained her ear.

"Get the girls ready." This was followed by a lot of scuffling. "I said, sit still, bitch." *Whack.*

A girl screamed, "Leave her alone." Another couple of slaps followed.

Lorne's heart sank. "That's Charlie. Tony, my *daughter's* inside that van."

"Okay, Lorne, we've got to see how this pans out. It may lead to vital information that'll enable us to locate any threat and stop it happening. Try to remain calm and objective."

"Is that what you would do if your child was in there?"

"No, I'd storm it. But I'm begging you not to. There's too much at stake, and by storming it, you may put Charlie in even more danger. At least she's alive. In a hail of bullets, she could be the victim… Lorne? Lorne, am I getting through to you?"

"Christ, it's a big ask, oh God."

"Lorne?" Tony shouted.

Sean had his hand over hers. She'd put the phone on loudspeaker, and he'd heard what had been going on and what Tony had said. He took the phone from her shaking hand.

"She'll be all right, Tony. Just give her a second. We'll call back."

"You sure you're up to this, Lorne?" Roberts asked.

Hurt and anger built up inside her. She tried to pull her hand from under his, but his grip intensified. Blowing out a breath she'd been holding on to for the past thirty seconds, she nodded. "Don't worry about me, Sean. I'll cope with whatever that bastard has to throw at me as long as I get my little girl back in one piece."

"Look, it's not too late to back out. You can go home and wait it out with Tom…"

"I *said* I'll be okay. I know my heart wants to go in all guns blazing, but I can see what Tony is saying. That way, Charlie would be in more danger than she is now."

She redialled Tony.

"Everything okay, Lorne?"

"Yes, Tony."

"Right, whilst you've been gone, an argument has started. They're still at it. I reckon one of his henchmen is on the turn."

"That sounds interesting. Tony, excuse my ignorance, but can the satellite pick up how many figures there are in the van, by infrared or something?" she asked.

"We should be able to. We're pulling another satellite around as we speak. There it is now. By my calculations, looks like seven people in the back and one sitting in the driver's seat. No, hang on a minute. He's climbing in the back with the others. Yeah, that's eight bodies all told."

"This may be asking the impossible, but can you make out how many girls are inside?"

"We can just about make out four slight figures. It's a good bet they're girls. The other four are thickset, bouncer-type physiques. Hold on. The argument has flared up again."

They sat in silence, listening to what was happening inside the van.

"I won't let you hurt her anymore."

"And tell me, Gary, what do you intend to do to stop me? Taken a fancy to her, have you?"

"That was The Unicorn's voice, Tony," Lorne broke in.

"No. I just think she's been through enough today, what with having to sit and watch the film of her family being burned to death."

"Oh, and how about your family, Gary? Tell me, do you know where they are right now?"

"Why, you sick bastard..."

What followed sounded like a tussle between the two men, then a thud before a girl with an accent said, "Are you all right, Gary? Don't! Please don't put yourself in danger for me."

"That's right, Gary, Sasha is fine. Aren't you, my dear? But let me show you just what a sick bastard I am."

A crack like a bone breaking came over the system, followed by a scream of pain.

Please, Charlie, don't get involved, Lorne thought with her eyes tightly shut as she listened to the proceedings.

Sean slammed an angry hand into his steering wheel. "Jesus Christ. It sounds to me like the Unicorn's under a lot of pressure. Close to the edge. What the hell is he planning?"

"I don't know. More to the point, how are we going to get those girls out alive?" Lorne asked.

By now, the demo had reached the van. A few of the students had started calling for the prime minister's head. With all the noise and commotion, it proved impossible to hear what was going on, until the unmistakable sound of a gunshot splintered the air.

Chapter Forty-Four

The demonstrators within earshot screamed. Someone shouted, "A gun! Someone fired a gun!"

The mob erupted into a panic of escapees looking to save their skins.

"Christ, what now?"

Lorne hadn't addressed Tony or the chief in particular, but it was Tony who answered.

"We carry on and let it pan out. You probably didn't hear, but after the shot, we heard screams and men shouting, but since then, nothing. We need to sit tight for a few seconds longer, then—"

His sentence was left dangling; they stared over as the back doors of the van flung open.

Four girls being pushed, shoved, or pulled, landed on the pavement. With AK-47 guns in their backs, forcing them to move forward, the girls were frog-marched towards the Houses of Parliament.

Lorne grabbed the binoculars from the chief and shuffled forwards in her seat for a clearer view through the manic crowd. "Oh, my God. No..."

"What? What is it, Lorne?" the chief asked, trying to wrestle the binoculars off her.

"Charlie... she... she has a suicide vest on..."

"What!?"

"Lorne... Chief... Are you there?" Tony shouted.

The chief picked up the mobile from Lorne's lap. "Tony?"

"We've obviously got a volatile situation here. I need your assurance that Lorne can handle it. If not, I suggest you get her the hell out of here. *Now.*"

"Right, Lorne... No... Shit!" Turning to Lorne, Sean found her seat empty. "Lorne, where do you think you're fucking going?" She didn't answer, and Sean pressed the phone tighter to his ear. "Tony, she's gone! I'm going after her. Stay connected."

Lorne pushed her way through the manic crowd, panic rising and threatening to choke her. Through all the noise, she could hear Roberts calling and pleading with her to stop, but she couldn't. She had to get to Charlie. Then two pairs of hands grabbed her arms and propelled her away from the direction she'd been going in.

"Lorne... Lorne, stop. Come on. You can't do this alone. We'll help..."

She looked into Tony's eyes. On the other side of her was one of the vice officers she recognised.

"Get in the van, Lorne."

She knew she had little choice. If she didn't comply, Tony would manhandle her into the vehicle. Once she was inside, Tony steered her to one of the seats. He sat opposite.

"Lorne, you said you could handle it... Oh, fuck, what am I saying? Dave, pass that flask. As he undid the lid and steam escaped, the chief's voice came over Tony's phone lying on the desk behind him.

"Tony? Tony?"

"Tony, here—"

"For God's sake, tell me that was you lot grabbing Lorne? I'm outside your van."

"We've got her. I'll let you in."

The door flew open, and Roberts climbed into the van.

"What are you fucking playing at, Lorne?" Roberts asked breathlessly, his tone coming across more as a concerned friend rather than her superior.

"I think it was a knee-jerk reaction," Tony suggested.

"It was, Tony, thanks... I'm sorry, sir. I'm okay now, I promise. Just give me a minute, lads." She spoke to the other officers. Tears of frustration and humiliation pricked as only unshed ones can, but she swallowed hard. The officers in the van swivelled their seats around and stopped staring at her. Tony handed her a cup of coffee and then cleared a space for the chief to sit down.

"Sir, please ring my dad. Put him in the picture and tell him to contact Tom and Jade. Tell him to get Tom to be with him. Whether that's at the station or at home, they should be together. With all these news cameras covering the march, this will be headline news within seconds."

As she thought of her husband and his anguish and that of the rest of her family, her strength came back, as did her focus. The chief dialled the number.

"Don't put any of them on to me. I haven't got time to cope with them. They have to console each other. And tell them my phone has to remain free—no, order them not to phone me... And you'd better give the forensics department a ring, too. Leave a message for Jacques Arnaud." In answer to the chief's astonished look, she said, "He... he's a special friend. His reaction to seeing this on the TV will be to ring me, too."

The chief said nothing. Lorne turned her attention away from the arguments she knew would go on when he made contact and looked at the monitors.

The officers focused on an intensified reaction of the crowd, which had become aware of the drama playing out in front of the protesters.

The Unicorn's men had placed the girls at regular intervals outside the Houses of Parliament's large entrance. Police battled with the crowd, trying to form a cordon and push them back.

"We've communicated with the inspector in charge of the security out there. He's called Rudgely and knows where we're up to. He's taking orders from us," Tony told them. "Obviously, his first concern is to get the crowd under control, which we've agreed with, but he won't do anything other than we instruct him to do. He's a capable bloke."

Lorne leaned forward. Her eyes concentrated on the four girls. She could see they were sobbing their hearts out.

"Sean, Tony, we have to do something."

The chief excused himself from the caller, leaving him on hold. Lorne presumed he was talking to her father.

"I know Rudgely. He's a good man, like you say. If you agree, we should take dual lead on this and run everything by each other. I think the armed response team? And what about trying to talk to the Unicorn? Have you a megaphone in here?"

"Agree. Nothing else has been implemented so far. Yes to armed response, but not sure about negotiation. I suggest the bomb-disposal team is put on stand-by."

"I think we should negotiate," Lorne said. "One thing, it will give the girls some hope. They'll know we're here, and the Unicorn will be less likely to do anything if he thinks we might cooperate or at least are taking him seriously."

"Agreed."

"But it has to be me, Chief."

"No, Lorne..." The chief, who'd allowed her father to listen in to the strategy they were taking, now said his goodbyes to him, having already instructed the desk to put the word out to everyone, including forensics, that Inspector Simpkins' phone was not to be used under any circumstances.

"Chief, you know it has to be me. It's me he's been talking to all this time. He won't talk to you. I know him. Look, I know what's at stake more than any of you. I'm not going to muck up."

She watched as he and Tony eyed each other. The chief nodded before he handed her the mobile.

Chapter Forty-Five

Charlie shivered with terror. A trickle of warm liquid ran down her leg, and tears wet her cheeks. She looked over at Sasha, who was standing still, her head held high, staring straight ahead of her. The other two girls sobbed and pleaded. She looked towards the men. The barrels of their machine guns, black and menacing, looked back at her. Then she turned towards the crowd and all the police officers.

Will none of them stop this? Will my mum be able to do anything?

"Mum, Dad, *please* come and save us. I promise I'll be a good girl in the future." This went over and over in her head. Reciting it gave her comfort. *They will come. They have to.*

"Stay strong, little one," Sasha called over.

Charlie wondered how Sasha could be so brave. She, above all of them, had felt the pain of the brutality of these men. The images of Sasha's burning family screamed horror through every bone in Charlie's body.

Her attention was drawn by a moan beside her. One of the girls who'd volunteered to be here collapsed. Sasha spoke to her. "Toni, Vă rugăm să se ridice în picioare, dragă, nu-i lasa sa vezi frica. Au curaj. Totul va fi bine."

"What are you saying? Is she all right?"

"I'm trying to tell her to have courage. They will come to save us. I know that, Charlie. Everything will work out. Look, there are television cameras. The whole world will know what is happening. Something will be done, I promise you."

The goon standing next to the girl roughly hauled her to her feet. She collapsed again, and this time, the man punished her by striking her head with the butt of his gun.

"That's enough," the Unicorn shouted. "If she wants to die on her knees, let her. This, my pretty ones, will go off in exactly two minutes. That is, if I haven't heard from your mother by then," he said, addressing Charlie. In his hand he held a small device that she guessed must be a detonator. He thrust it high above his head, making sure the crowd got a good look.

* * *

"Tony, any chance you can jam that bloody device of his?" She didn't think he could, but she was clutching at straws. Lorne's hands shook as she scrolled down through the contacts on her phone, searching for the Unicorn's number. She pressed the loudspeaker button so they could all hear his response.

"Don't think so, not without knocking out the phone network," he told her regretfully.

The Unicorn's name lit up on her screen again as she flipped her phone open. She let her finger hover over the ring button.

"Ring him, Lorne. Time's marching on," Tony urged. Picking up the binoculars around his neck, he focused them on the scene.

* * *

The agent operating the camera zoomed in on the Unicorn. His image beamed out from the monitors. A smug smile stretched across his face as he answered his phone.

"Ah. The inspector calls at last. Ringing to have a final word with your daughter, Lorne?"

The chief nudged Lorne, warning her to remain calm.

"We need more time."

"Time? Ah, such a valuable commodity, don't you think? You have exactly one minute to come up with the thirty million pounds or *BABOOM*! Bye, bye, Charlie."

His chilling laugh rippled the hair on Lorne's neck. She stared in horror as he toyed with the top of the device in his right hand. She almost dropped the phone from her shaking hand as his tormenting, callous words registered.

"Tell us what else we can do to prevent you from going through with this."

"I'm assuming you have no intention of obliging me with my request? That's a shame, Inspector, such pretty girls. Do you have any idea what damage a piece of Semtex can do? I can tell you truthfully, it ain't pretty."

"Please. I'm begging you, please let them go. They have their whole lives ahead of them."

"And what do I get in return?"

"Me. You get me."

155

"You? And what would I do with *you,* Inspector?"

The chief and Tony shook their heads in disagreement. "Don't go there, Lorne," Roberts mouthed.

"Anything you like," she said, ignoring them.

"Hmm, now there's a thought. I must say, police pussy sounds very tempting."

"No, Mum, don't do it!" Charlie cried out after hearing the Unicorn's side of the conversation.

The sound of her daughter's terrified voice drove her on. "I'm right here, about thirty metres away. If you agree, I'll walk towards you. But once you see me, you must let Charlie and the other girls go free."

"The odds aren't great, release four and get one copper as a replacement. That's hardly a good deal, Inspector, now is it?"

"It's the best I can come up with..."

Bong, bong, bong. Big Ben began to chime midday.

"Times up. Where's my thirty million pounds, Inspector?"

"We haven't got it," Lorne said, her tone flat with failure. "There must be something else we could—"

"I'm not listening." As he spoke, the Unicorn strode over to the girl on her knees, placed a handgun to her temple, and pulled the trigger.

"No! Oh God, no..."

Blood and brain matter stained the pavement. The girl's body shuddered and, for a split second, stilled and remained upright before falling forward.

Lorne tasted the bile in her throat. She looked from Tony to the chief, then back at the monitors. Chaos broke out. The calm crowd, held back at a safe distance until now, broke into a frenzy of pushing and screaming as they realised the madman they'd been watching was heading towards them. The cordon gave way under pressure. People ran in all directions. The sheer force of their momentum meant they got nearer to the scene, rather than farther away.

"I've lost him. He's vanished," Tony shouted, anxiously scanning the crowd through the binoculars.

Lorne shouted down her phone. "Don't do it! Don't do it... Please!"

Her phone went dead. She snapped it shut and spoke to the agents. "If you can do it, block that signal *now.*"

"It's no good, we can't do..."

Lorne never heard the last bit. She was out of the van, running like she'd never run before. Seconds later, the chief and Tony joined her. In the black van, the Unicorn was nowhere to be seen. Tony wrenched open the doors. Sprawled inside was the body of an executed man in his thirties.

Tony radioed through to Inspector Rudgely and instructed him to send some officers over to protect the crime scene.

"We've lost him. Fuck, what's he playing at? Why did he take off? Was it me saying I was close by? Why hasn't he detonated the vest? The bastard is unfathomable. Look, I'm going over to Charlie. I have to reach her. Whatever's going to happen, I'm going to be with her when it does."

"Absolutely not, Lorne. I forbid you to go near her until the bomb-disposal team has done their job. They're standing by. Let's go back to the van to see what's happening, see if it's possible to give them the go-ahead. Maybe the henchmen have left, too... Did anyone see if they had?"

"Yes," Tony said. "The Unicorn turned to them, indicated something with his gun, and they followed him. As he disappeared, my heart was in my mouth. I thought they'd start shooting, either at the girls or into the police cordon, but as that had broken up, they didn't have to."

"In that case, Lorne, if the police have the crowd back and under control, you can go near enough so Charlie can see you. Talk to her and the girls. Try to keep them calm and explain about what the bomb squad will do. I think if he was going to detonate the bombs, he would've done it by now. My idea is that he's been playing with you again, Lorne. Let's hope that's the case anyway."

"Thanks, Chief. I'm inclined to believe you. He uses decoys all the time. What are your intentions?"

"I'll set up road, airport, and seaport alerts. Every major getaway will be blocked to him. We've got a good image of his face now, so that'll be circulated. And I'll get some of the police not needed in the cordon to try and find out which direction he set off in. He can't have got far, not in this lot, and someone would've seen him leave."

As Lorne set off, Tony's radio burst into life. Inspector Rudgely's voice came over.

"We have a problem. A big problem. I'm with a crowd now. They're telling me one of the protesters was taken by force by your man."

"A hostage, you mean? Bloody hell, didn't he have enough with the girls?" Tony asked.

"This wasn't just *any* hostage. This was none other than the prime minister's son, Simon Clovelly…"

Chapter Forty-Six

"Mum... Oh, Mum..."

Lorne fought against the urge to run forwards and gather her sobbing, terrified child in her arms, but she had to follow the orders of the officers in charge of the scene and remain ten metres back. It felt like the worst possible child abuse ever.

"Help me, Mum. Help me. I'm scared... I don't want to die."

Charlie's cries tugged at Lorne's thundering heart.

"Don't worry, darling. It'll be all right. We have men coming over to you. Bomb disposal men. They'll make you all safe, and then I can come to you. I'm ringing your dad. He'll be here soon."

"Tom, it's me. Oh, Tom... Are you watching the television? Can you see us? Get over here, Tom—"

"Lorne... Oh, thank God. Is she going to be all right? Can I come? I need to be with you both. Please tell me she's going to be all right."

His sobs almost undid her.

"Your father called... I could do nothing... I've been watching it all unfold. It's been hell...Oh, Lorne."

"I know, love. There was nothing I could do to lighten it for you. But now I need you. I need you to be here."

"How? The crowds, the chaos, what's it like there? It looks as though everything for miles around is at a standstill. They have a helicopter circling, and the traffic is all jammed up..."

"I'll get the chief to get a police escort for you. Just get ready. A motorbike will pick you up. It'll be quicker."

"Okay, Lorne, but don't go, not yet. Tell me what the chances are of the devices exploding."

"Truthfully? I don't know. It's a case of keeping our fingers and toes crossed, and if you're going to ask me if the Unicorn has a backup plan, I can't answer that either. All we can do is hope and pray. At the moment, we have to assume that Charlie is safe."

"Oh..."

"Don't give up hope, Tom."

"It's not easy. Look, tell Charlie I love her and that I'll be there soon."

"I will, love. See you soon." She was just about to flip her phone shut when he shouted something else at her.

"Sorry, what was that, Tom?"

"*I said*, I love you too. And I'm sorry for being a bastard ninety percent of the time. It's not easy living with an independent, wilful woman who takes in her stride what life has to throw at her."

It was hard for her not to smile at his unexpected admission and the way he still rebounded the fault back at her. Tears misted her eyes, and she whispered back, "I love you, too, Tom. I promise, when all this is over, we'll have a good talk. Now get your arse down here!"

She put in a quick request to the chief; he granted it immediately.

With Tom en route, she turned her attention back to her only child. "Hi, sweetie, how you doing? Daddy's on his way."

"When, Mum? How long will he take? Will I die before he comes?"

"You're not going to die, darling. Look, the bomb squad is on its way over to you. Hey, why don't you introduce me to your friends?"

Her strategy worked. Charlie became animated and visibly brightened.

"This is Sasha. She's from Romania. She's only here because she tried to help me. He broke her arm, Mum."

Sasha interrupted her, "No, it is not your fault I am here. It is mine that you are. I became careless. I tried to comfort her when I thought we were alone. I should know the Unicorn listens in to everything. I am pleased to meet you, Charlie's Mum."

Lorne smiled at Sasha. "There's no blame to be attached to any of you. I know that. There's only one person responsible for all this."

Her heart bled for the girls, just two of them, now. They were skin and bone. Their cheeks were hollow and their eyes sunk deep into their sockets, signs of hunger and a lot of suffering.

She wanted to ask Sasha questions, give her something to think about too, but she didn't dare ask about her family. Sasha could be the one Lorne had overheard from the black van conversation and whose family had been killed.

"I'm pleased to meet you too, Sasha. And who is this next to you?"

"This is Carly. She and Toni…" Sasha indicated with her head towards the dead girl. "They volunteered to be a part of this. Not that they knew what was in store for us, but he was going to choose two of the younger girls…"

"That was very brave of you, Carly. I'm sorry about what happened to Toni. It won't happen to you. I promise you, none of you are going to die."

"Mum, Sasha… her family… Oh, Mum…"

"I know. We heard what went on in the van. I'm so sorry, Sasha."

"He forced us all to watch a video of it this morning, Mum. It… Oh, Mum, how could anyone do such a ghastly thing?"

Lorne listened to her daughter's sobs and knew what she would get back wasn't a rebellious, aggravating, wind-up of a teen, but a damaged little girl. There was a long journey of recovery ahead.

"There are wicked, evil people in the world, Charlie. We cannot know how their minds work, but we won't let them win. Sasha, we'll do our best to help you—"

"Yeah, she can come live with us, can't she, Mum?"

"We'll see, sweetheart. We'll see."

The chatter carried on, back and forth. To her right, Lorne could see the bomb squad. *What the hell are they doing? Why are they taking so long to move in?*

Her mobile rang. "Lorne, how are you doing?"

"Not bad, considering, Chief. What's happening? Haven't you given the go-ahead for the bomb disposal yet?"

"Any minute now. We've had some intelligence in. Abromovski is dead. Murdered. And not very pleasantly, you'll be glad to hear."

"Oh, that's what you call good and bad news. With him dead, he can't be made to squeal. I'll get the details later, but, Chief, why is there a delay? I want my daughter safe—"

A hand touched her shoulder. She whizzed around, straight into Tom's arms.

"Is she all right?"

"She's okay whilst I'm talking to her, love." He held her tightly to him. Warmth seeped through her. "I'm so glad you're here, Tom."

"What are we going to do?"

"Keep her talking, love. Keep her spirits up. I'm just getting an update from Roberts."

Tom turned and called over to Charlie. "I'm here, sweetheart. Everything's going to be okay."

"Chief?"

"It will happen. They're ready to move... Look, there are things going on." He told her about the abduction of the prime minister's son.

"Is that what all this is about?"

"We don't know. But we have some details of how the Unicorn got away. He hijacked a car. The driver is still unconscious. Everything possible is being done to trace the car and, Lorne—"

A crack startled everyone into silence. Charlie slumped to the ground.

Chapter Forty-Seven

Lorne ducked under the tape and rushed towards Charlie, but an officer grabbed her arm.

"You can't go over there, ma'am."

She fished out her ID card and flashed it. The officer stood aside. A disorientated voice called out to her. She looked around, then realised it was coming from her phone.

"Lorne, we can see what's happened. Tell us Charlie's not…"

Her life stood still. She didn't have an answer for herself, let alone for Sean.

"Lorne…"

She closed the lid. She couldn't deal with anything or anyone other than Charlie at that moment.

"I'm here, my darling. Mum's here."

She lifted Charlie's injured head and placed it gently in her lap and began to rock her back and forth, just like she had when Charlie was a babe in arms. Her hand skimmed over her child's wound. She could hear her own voice, trembling, saying her daughter's name over and over. Above her, the distraught voices of the other girls were calling out for help. All of them, sitting targets.

Charlie still had a strong pulse. Lorne assessed the wound and came to the conclusion it was superficial. She couldn't deal with another shooting with the same outcome as the previous one.

"Lorne?" Tom's voice, hollow and full of anguish, came to her from way off. His face reflected the same trauma she felt. He stood like a statue. She knew shock had taken hold of him and worried about the effect it could have on him. She called over to one of the nearby officers and asked him to check on Tom.

"Charlie, sweetheart, can you hear me?" As she spoke, Lorne saw the officer taking care of Tom. Someone had produced a fold-up chair for him to sit on, and he had a glass of water in his hand. He lifted his other hand in an effort to let her know he was okay.

Her mobile buzzed again; she flipped the lid to hear Sean's traumatised voice. "Lorne? Lorne, is Charlie all right?"

"She's been shot… Oh, Sean, help me get the bomb squad into action, please…"

"Oh my God. I'm coming back."

"*No*. You have to stay on the *bastard's* tail, Sean. Get the *maniac* who did this to my little girl."

"Lorne? Is she… is she dead?"

She could tell from his tone how painful the words had been to voice.

"No, I think it's just a graze. She has a pulse, but the paramedics can't come near. She's still trussed up in this fucking vest."

"Are you with her? Tell me, Lorne, have you gone beyond the cordon?"

"Yes, she's lying in my lap, like a little angel. Oh God, please don't take her to be one just yet."

"All right… Now, keep calm. I want you to hang up the phone. I need to speak with someone, okay?"

Without replying, she hung up.

* * *

Roberts pulled over to the side of the road and rang the incident room. "It's Chief Roberts. Put Sam Collins on the phone immediately." His fingers drummed on the steering wheel.

"Chief, hi. How's it going?"

Roberts detected a note of caution in Sam's voice and wondered how to proceed.

"I take it you haven't seen the latest news?"

"I've just walked back into the office. I've been observing the interviews, why?"

"Oh God, Sam, where the fuck do I begin? Look, you need to follow what's happening. Put the TV on, but first, Sam, I… well, I can't dress it up. Things have taken a horrific turn. Charlie's in danger. She's a human bomb outside Parliament with three… two other girls. She's been shot… Lorne's with her."

"What? Christ, couldn't someone have told me? How bad is it? Is she—"

"No, she's injured, not dead. I've spoken to Lorne on her mobile. She says the bullet grazed Charlie. It sounds like he's playing games." A noise like a sigh holding a moan registered through Sean's earpiece. "Sam… Sam, you okay, Sam?"

"Yes, I had to sit down. Oh dear God. Tell me everything is under control, Sean. Tell me you're going to bring this to a good conclusion."

"You know the answer, Sam. You know me, and you know Lorne."

"Yes, I do— wait a minute. The news is coming on. The breaking news banner says someone has kidnapped the prime minister's son. Is that true?"

"It's true all right. I'm tracking the vehicle now. At least I was, but there are plenty of squad cars mobilised. Sam, I need your help. Do you have a visual on-screen of Lorne?"

"Yes. God, Sean, she's behind the cordon."

"I know. I need you to talk her out of there, Sam."

"I'll be wasting my time. Put yourself in her position. If that was your child in there, you'd do everything possible to comfort them, wouldn't you?"

The chief hesitated, but only for a second. "You're probably right, Sam. Can you at least try? A sniper, probably one of his henchmen, hit Charlie. They could take a potshot at Lorne, too."

"We're talking about a very stubborn woman here, Sean."

"I know. You don't have to bloody tell me how stubborn she can be."

"I'll see what I can do. I take it there's no danger in ringing her mobile? Is that *Tom* sitting on the edge of the cordon?"

"Yes, Lorne called him for moral support. The aim was to help keep Charlie's mind off the vest and no, no danger. I checked with the bomb squad before I rang her."

"Good, what are our chances here, Sean? I mean, is there a possibility of the vests exploding?"

"We think the vests were decoys. We tried to block the frequency, but couldn't. Knowing the Unicorn, he's bound to have some kind of backup plan. He's already used one of them, the sniper. That's why I'm urging you to help me get your daughter out of there."

"I understand, Sean, leave it with me. I'll get back to you in a while. We've been gathering some intriguing facts from the interviews."

"Great. I'll give it another half an hour out here, and then I'll return to base. Thanks for your help, Sam. Do your best, eh?"

Chapter Forty-Eight

"Why are you doing this to me?"

Simon Clovelly's voice, muffled by the canvas hood covering his head, irritated the Unicorn. He couldn't take the kid's constant whining.

"Didn't they teach you anything at that posh school of yours? You're what's known in the trade as a valuable bargaining tool."

"It won't work. My father never bargains with kidnappers or terrorists."

"If you think I believe that bullshit, then you're a bigger fool than I first took you for. Does *Daddy* know that you were involved in the rally today?"

"Of course he does. I never do anything without him knowing."

"Just who the fuck do you think you're trying to kid, eh? So you're telling me he knows about all the visits you've made to prostitutes recently, you and that little gang of toffs you hang around with? Oh, and don't waste your breath denying it either. I have the proof. I've got it all on tape."

He laughed at the sound of Simon swallowing hard.

"He's not concerned about me and what I get up to. All he's worried about is destroying this country," Clovelly bluffed.

"At least that's one thing we agree on. Although, I can't see him not caring about his son cavorting with whores. Anyway, we'll find out soon enough. Should be fun, hey boys?"

His faithful followers laughed.

"Where are you taking me?"

"Inquisitive little shit, aren't you? You'll find out soon enough. Now shut the fuck up." The Unicorn landed a slap across the covered head and smiled at the frightened whimpering noise that followed. "A word of warning, we're not the snivelling little gang who took you last time. There's no good outcome for you unless we have cooperation, get it?"

Pleased he'd managed to shut up the annoying little fuck, the Unicorn turned his attention to how much longer they had to travel and asked his driver for an ETA as he looked out of the window. The urban landscape had turned into widespread, green Kent countryside.

"Another thirty minutes or so, boss," Ramon told him. "Why don't you grab forty winks. I'll wake you up when we get there."

Ramon's manner smacked of someone trying to get into his good books. The Unicorn hated creeps. He locked eyes with Ramon in the rearview mirror, glaring at him as if he were the enemy.

"Let's get one thing straight, shall we? And this goes for both of you. I'm the *boss*. I sleep when *I* want to sleep. I eat when *I* want to eat. I shag when *I* want to shag. I don't have to remind you how Gary ended up, do I? Right, and another thing, don't think any of you are going to be promoted any time soon, either. You all work for me, and *I'm* in charge. I've decided I don't need a head honcho anymore. If anyone wants to leave, let me know now, and I'll personally see to it that you get a good send-off, if you know what I mean." He liked that. *Yes, quite funny.* His laughter filled the car and reverberated back to him, sounding sinister and unreal.

Chapter Forty-Nine

Sam replaced the phone, put his elbows on his daughter's desk, and let his head drop into his hands in a gesture of despair.

"Everything all right, sir?"

"Not exactly, DS Fox. My daughter and granddaughter are in danger of losing their lives at any second, and I can't do anything about it. I've just come off the phone with Lorne, and try as I might to get her at least to safety, I couldn't persuade her. Not that I expected to... Or if the truth be known, want her to. In fact, I don't want her to obey me. Charlie needs her. Am I making sense?"

"No, sir, as I don't know what it is you were trying to get Lorne to do. What I do know is that Pete always said it was her *determination* he admired most, God rest his soul. That's why he loved being her partner."

"In this case, it isn't her determination she's displaying, but her courage and love for her only child. No man can talk sense into a woman in that mode." Sam explained to Fox where Lorne was and why.

"All I can say, sir, is put yourself in her shoes. Wouldn't you be reacting the same way?"

"Yes, I would, but it still doesn't make it right, does it? One life at risk is bad enough. Now we have two, and both of them are very dear to me."

"I'm sorry, sir," Fox said, looking at the ground in front of him.

"Thanks. Look, give me some good news. Has anything else come to light yet?"

"There is something, sir. One of the uniformed guys let it slip, pretending not to know who was in earshot, that Abromovski's *body* has been discovered at his house."

Intrigued, Sam Collins asked, "And who *was* within earshot?"

"Mark Reynolds, Abromovski's brief. Apparently, the look on his face was priceless. Running round like an excited puppy, he was, demanding they lock him in a cell and give him police protection. Reckons he'll be next on the Unicorn's to-kill list. Anyway, Sergeant Harris pulled a blinder and asked him what it was worth. He said he'd tell us everything he knows about the Unicorn, warts and all, if only we save him."

"Good work. I'd better let the chief know right away. Thanks, John. This could be the breakthrough we've been waiting for. Oh, by the way, who discovered the Russian's body and how?"

Amused, Fox replied, "Vice left some cameras in the house. One of the guys went back, pretending they'd left some equipment behind. He followed the path the Unicorn and the Russian took on the camera, and bingo. Looks like he suffered a long, drawn-out death, and the result is far from pretty. The word barbaric even cropped up in the description."

"Right, Fox, tell them downstairs, no interview until the all clear to do so comes from the chief. Keep Reynolds guessing as to whether or not we can grant his request and to what extent—you know, depending on the quality of his info, that sort of thing. I'll contact the chief."

Sam picked up the phone and rang the chief.

"Hi, Sean. On the Lorne front, no go, but I can't be angry with her, though I'm desperately afraid for them both. It's just that I wouldn't expect anything less of Lorne and in the end realised we have to ride this out her way. It's agony to do so, but you know, if I was there, I would be behind the cordon, too."

"I know, Sam, but we had to try."

"Have you made any progress?"

Roberts slammed the heel of his hand into the steering wheel of his Lexus for the umpteenth time that day. "No, I lost his tail when I pulled up to ring you— not that it mattered. The snatch car turned into a fucking red herring. The helicopter surveillance reported they had it in sight, but when the squad picked up the trail and stopped the vehicle, the only occupant was a well-known petty criminal on the biggest earner of his life, without a clue he'd been set up. It appears after the snatch, the kidnappers drove the vehicle inside the back of a waiting lorry with ramps and everything in place. We've probably caught the manoeuvre on camera, when we can get hold of the CCTV of the area concerned."

Sean scanned the nearby roads. "The lorry then drove off, dropped the car, minus the PM's son and his kidnappers and with our petty driving it. He had a wad of notes on him and thought he had to deliver the car, which he believed stolen, to a garage just off the M25. His instructions were to avoid the police at all costs, but a stinger got him as soon as he left the motorway. The officers attending said they almost felt sorry for him. He knew nothing about what was going on or who had hired him and thought the lad he'd seen with the heavies had taken drugs, as he seemed out of it. In the meantime, the kidnap gang could have gone miles in the lorry or, most likely, just picked up another car a few miles away and went on their merry way, undetected."

"Whew, a pretty elaborate plan, but one that was used before. You remember the Ferry gang? That lot we busted before your promotion?"

"Yes, I thought of them straight away. They got away with a lot of high-class cars by using the lorry method, shipping them over to Ireland within a couple of hours of the theft. All by driving them into a lorry and getting them off the streets in minutes, so they couldn't be tailed. In fact, I might rake over the case again, see if there could be a link with the organisers. Most will be out of jail by now, not that it would help us much if we did establish a link. I tell you, Sam, the bastard's like a fucking slippery eel. How I'm going to tell Lorne we've lost him, I don't know. Anyhow, as soon as I heard we'd been duped, I thought about going back to the scene, but there are enough officers there to take care of things, so I've decided to come back in."

"Well, when you hear what I have for you, you would have made that decision anyway." He recounted what DS Fox had just told him.

"Right, there in five. By the way, the bomb squad's on scene and given the all-clear to proceed. I'm sure Lorne and Charlie will be okay, Sam."

Sam sat back and thought through what Sean had said and knew a sinking feeling in his heart. The bomb squad on scene didn't mean they were home and dry, as much as he wanted to hope it did. Any number of things could go wrong. What if the sniper still had his sights trained, ready for the madman's orders?

Chapter Fifty

The disposal team officer stood next to Lorne. Relief eased through her. She surveyed the scene. She was surrounded by members of the bomb squad, looking like aliens dressed in their protective gear. Two paramedics were waiting a few yards beyond them, unable to attend to Charlie until they received the all clear. To her left was a sea of blue and red flashing lights, and ahead, Tom was still sitting with a look of despair on his face, one of the medics by his side. The other girls had stopped screaming and stood, as if frozen in time, just looking at her. She gave them both an encouraging smile.

"Everything will be okay now, girls. These men are experts. They'll decommission the bombs, and you'll be safe. Just hang in there."

Sasha, her voice strong once more, related in her own language what was happening.

What a nice girl, always thinking of others.

"Ma'am, I'm going to have to ask you to leave now," the sergeant said.

She shook her head. "I can't leave her. Please don't ask that of me. This is my child. How can I leave her?"

"I'm not asking, ma'am. I'm *ordering* you. Your presence is hindering our work. If you refuse to leave, you'll be putting your daughter's life in further danger. Do you understand?"

"Oh God! Make her safe, please."

"We'll do all we can, ma'am. The best thing you can do to help us and your daughter is the hardest thing of all. I know, and believe me I wouldn't order you to do it if it wasn't necessary."

"How far must I go?"

"Our duty is to protect all members of the public. We can only protect you fully if you're far enough away from the scene, so I have to ask you to go back behind the cordon, ma'am."

Lorne knew she had to obey, though it tore her jagged to do so. Delaying further wouldn't help Charlie. As carefully as she could, she eased Charlie's body off her lap and stood up. Looking towards the other girls, she told them to stay still and have faith.

"Look, I so believe in these guys I'm leaving my own daughter to their care. You have nothing to worry about now."

Both girls rewarded her with a smile.

From behind the cordon and in the comfort of Tom's arms, Lorne watched the activity, prayers like mantras on her lips.

The officer she'd spoken with examined Charlie's vest. The man had instilled faith in her with his calm insistence and caring attitude. Seconds seemed like hours as she waited, unable to speak, giving comfort and taking it, her whole life out there, just metres away from her. She knew if she lost Charlie, her world would end.

The bomb disposal squad consisted of four men. Whilst two of them concentrated their efforts getting Charlie out of her vest, the other two men crouched down beside the dead girl, Toni. She imagined they proceeded this way for two reasons. One, it must be easier to release the vests from unresisting bodies, and two, once they'd achieved it, the other two girls would be reassured it was possible without setting off the explosives and would cooperate more.

A strange silence born out of fear and trepidation covered the area. The two teams worked in synchronisation. The officer in charge issued instructions, and the other team followed his lead. A three-two-one countdown completed the task.

Lorne and Tom clung to each other, breaths sucked in as they watched the team's intricate rescue plan unfurl. The whole procedure took no more than two minutes to complete, but to Lorne and Tom, it felt like a lifetime had passed. They gulped down simultaneous doses of air the second Charlie and the dead girl were disrobed of their explosive garments.

With the first two jackets safely disabled, the teams placed the vests on the ground and moved on to the last two girls. The officer talked to them the whole time, asking their names and telling them how important it was to remain calm and still at all times.

The girls nodded. Lorne knew the tactic of releasing the others first had worked.

Five minutes later, all four girls were free of their wretched garments. The team carried the vests over to their specially adapted vehicle and disposed of them one by one. As the vehicle rocked violently on its wheels, the crowd gasped in awe. After the last vest had blown, a rapturous applause rifled through the air. The team did a thorough final sweep of the area, after which, the paramedics moved in to attend to the victims. The covering of Toni's dead body swept a wave of sympathy through the crowd.

Lorne and Tom surged forwards as the stretcher carrying their only child came towards them. They followed her to the ambulance.

"Her life is not in any danger. Everything is functioning as it should," the paramedic told them. "Her condition otherwise is poor, and she has many injuries. She's not well and has some way to go, poor little mite."

"Thank you. Do you think she'll come round soon?" Lorne asked.

"No, she did start to, which is a good sign, but we've sedated her, and I imagine that'll be the procedure for the next twelve hours or so. There's a danger of her body going into shock, so we needed to minimise that. As we make the journey to the hospital, we'll work on the open wounds, clean them and try to alleviate the risk of infection, but she won't feel anything. The main thing is all her vital signs are normal."

"Thank you." Lorne bent over and kissed Charlie's forehead.

"Are you coming to the hospital with us?" Tom asked. Then he surprised her by adding, "I understand, if not. I'll stay with her and keep you informed of any change."

She could tell by the love evident in his eyes that this time, he really could understand her eagerness to return to work. He pulled her into his arms and kissed her lips, not a lingering kiss, but a gentle one that sealed his love. "And don't come home till you've either killed the bastard or have him locked up behind bars. Do you hear me? Then, with a rare show of humour, he turned her one hundred eighty degrees and gently pushed her towards the nearby white van housing the vice team.

"Thanks for understanding, Tom. I love you and tell *Miss* that I love her, too, when she finally comes round. Let me know the moment that happens, and I'll be there."

"I will," he said.

Tony opened the van door to her. "How is she? I take it she's out of danger?"

"Yes, thank God..."

"Sit down, Lorne. You're shaking. Here, I have some of my coffee left. It's a bit cold, but strong and sweet. Get it down you."

"Thanks." Trying to keep her voice steady, she told him about Charlie's condition. "It isn't the visible wounds that worry me. She's been through hell, Tony. They'll keep her sedated, and Tom'll be by her side, but the minute she comes round, I want to be there for her. In the meantime, we have a certain bastard to nail and one I personally want to kick in the balls."

"Join the queue. I'm sorry about everything, Lorne, and you know, I'd advise you to get Charlie counselling as soon as she's well enough."

"What like you do, you mean, when a mission goes wrong?" She smiled and raised an inquisitive eyebrow.

"Hmm… You got me." Tony waved a chastising finger at her.

"It's good advice, though. Thanks. How are things progressing?"

"Initially, we thought we had the vehicle and the gang, but we were fed a red herring." He explained to her about the switch of vehicles.

"Shit, what is it with him? He has everything at his fingertips. It beggars belief how he slips through the net like he does."

"He's a very dangerous man, as you know, Lorne. There are a lot of people afraid of him, and when you see what he's capable of, you can see why. We just have to up our game and put all these possibilities into the equation as he does."

"So where does that leave us now?"

"Have you heard about Abromovski's death?"

"No, but guess I don't have to ask who killed him."

"No, you could win a Blue Peter badge easily with that one. Let's just say it confirms what a sick SOB this guy is. Young Charlie had an extremely lucky escape."

"Christ, I better get back to the station. Any chance of a lift?"

"I think we can arrange that, eh, boys?"

The officers nodded; one of them hopped between the seats to start the engine.

Chapter Fifty-One

The cheers and whoops of joy meeting Lorne as she entered the incident room took her by surprise. Embarrassed at the open affection shown by her colleagues, she made a quick update speech.

"Hey, guys, thanks. I'll catch up with you in a mo. I hear things have moved on a bit and you've all worked your socks off. Charlie's not out of the woods yet. But she's stable, and Tom's by her side. I don't have to tell you we have to keep the pressure on. I want this man caught ASAP."

They all nodded their agreement.

In her office, the chief and her dad greeted Lorne. It felt good to be in her father's arms. His support for her action meant a lot to her. When he released her, Sean took her elbow. His look spoke volumes, and she had a moment's impression that he too was going to take her and hug her, but he guided her to a chair, leaving her thinking she'd imagined the tenderness in his expression.

The tension clawing at her shoulders subsided. Charlie was safe, really safe. The only task left for them now was to catch the man who overnight had single-handedly turned their lives upside down and inside out. She answered their questions concerning Charlie and then got down to the job in hand.

"Tony gave me a lift back. He's filled me in regarding the chase down the M25, and he tells me Abromovski's been reduced to a stiff on a slab in the mortuary."

"Yes, and as soon as his brief heard, he demanded to be locked up, fearing for his own safety. He's ready to talk when we are. And as regards the PM's son, there's still no news there," Roberts told her.

"You say Reynolds is ready to talk? You mean about everything, names and places and Laura Crane's murder?"

"We're working on it. He's asking for a deal. We're dangling a carrot. He knows what sort of deal he gets depends on what he gives in return. I'm going to question him soon. In the meantime, I'd like you to look at the information the team has discovered. DS Fox seems to think it would be worthwhile talking to Judge Walter Winwood again."

"About anything in particular?" Lorne asked.

"Not really. He appeared a bit cagey during his interview. Have a word with AJ. See if he can enlighten you further."

"Will do. Anything else I should know?"

Roberts let out an exaggerated sigh. "Only that I'm handing the case back over to you, Inspector. You seem surprised by my decision?"

"Gobsmacked would be more appropriate, sir." Lorne looked over at her father, who shrugged and smiled at her.

"I'm a man of my word, Lorne. I told you that once Charlie was back safe and well, you'd be free to take up the reins again. Of course, that's if you feel you can handle it—"

"Yes, I do. And thank you, sir, for your confidence in me." She could have kissed him, but thought better of it. She felt like a kid in a toy shop.

"Well, that's a smile we've been waiting to see. Okay, Lorne, any problems, my door is always open. Understood?"

"Yes, sir." She gave a mock salute and skipped her way out of the office, but before she closed the door, she heard the exchange between her boss and her dad and their laughter.

"That daughter of yours, Sam, is crazy."

"That she is, Chief. It's good to see the old Lorne back, huh?"

Chapter Fifty-Two

"Pull up. I've changed my mind," the Unicorn told Ramon.

Ramon slammed on the brakes. The wheels skidded in the dry dust of the lane leading to the Kent hideaway. "But, boss, we're nearly there—"

"I can see that. But I'd rather go somewhere else. Do you have a problem with that?"

"No, no, of course not, sir. It's just that you surprised me. There's no problem."

"Good. Keep it that way. I'm sure witnessing the demise of your colleague, you wouldn't want the same to happen to you? Just remember, he came to his end because he started questioning my decisions."

Ramon visibly shook. The Unicorn allowed himself a small smile. He'd done the right thing by getting rid of Gary. Apart from the enjoyment it had given him, it served well in keeping the others on their toes. "Take me to Judge Walter Winwood's house."

"Right, it's about thirty minutes from here."

"Make it twenty."

"Excuse me, but before we move off, I need to go to the toilet," Simon Clovelly whimpered.

"Tough. I'll take your hood off, and you can do it out the window as we're driving along. Bet they didn't teach you how to do that at public school, huh?"

"I'd rather not, thank you."

"Your choice, sonny. Now shut up. I have a call to make."

The Unicorn opened his mobile and pressed number one. "Inspector, so nice to hear your voice again—"

"You bastard!"

The Unicorn laughed into the mouthpiece. He had her rattled good and proper this time. He revelled in that.

"You needn't smirk, you creep. We foiled your vile plan. It did not succeed. Do you hear me?"

"Au contraire, Inspector, I think it worked perfectly. Do you really believe those girls were worth anything to me, or even blowing up the House? No. I kept you occupied whilst I took what I really wanted. Say hello to the smart-mouthed detective, Simon."

He prodded the young man in the ribs.

"Help me. Please help me."

"It's all right, Simon. We're going to get you out of this."

"Ha, you missed your vocation, Inspector. You should've been on the stage, as a *comedienne*. You and your daughter would make a good double act. You make *me* fucking laugh, anyway."

"We'll see who gets the last laugh, shall we, Mr....?"

His laugh intensified. "Mr. Unicorn will do. I see you haven't found out my true name yet. Would you like a hint? Shall I give you my initials? Would that help, Mrs. Inspector?"

"That won't be necessary, thank you. Our endeavours have uncovered some interesting information concerning you and your plans. It's only a matter of time before we catch up with you. You can't run forever. Oh, and by the way, all the airports and ports have been notified that you're on our wanted list."

"Oh, Inspector, you disappoint me. I thought you had some brains. Obviously, I was wrong. Do you really think I'd try and get out of the country by public transport? Tut, tut. Guess you're not the great detective I've been hearing so much about, after all."

"Is there a point to this call?"

"Just keeping you on your toes, Inspector. My guess is you're close to being dead on your feet by now."

"Far from it, actually. How naive of you to believe that. You really have no concept of what motivates a good detective to see a case through to its conclusion."

"*Actually*, that's true, because I've yet to meet a *good* detective. Oh, before I go, how is Charlie? Ha. If she ever recovers, she'd do well in the sex trade, make a lot of money, that one." He closed his mobile and sat back. *Another round to me, I think.*

* * *

Lorne slammed down her receiver, blinked away the tears of agony that burned her sockets, and pressed the speed dial for Tony Warner. When she heard his voice, she picked up again.

After their conversation, she sat mulling over what he'd told her. She'd been surprised to learn he'd needed to obtain special clearance from a higher governing body before he could even start to delve into the backgrounds of the people on the list of who the Unicorn might be. But he'd explained two of them were SAS officers turned criminals, and the Army wanted to avoid this becoming public knowledge at all costs. He'd indicated which of the men he thought most likely to be the Unicorn and suggested she try out the names the next time she spoke to him to see his reaction.

She thought over the names: Robert Baldwin, Bobby Baldwin or Bob Baldwin, William Matthews, Bill Matthews. Whichever way she said them, both names sounded more like solicitors or TV weathermen than cunning members of the criminal fraternity. She decided to go with Tony's suggestion the next time the Unicorn made contact. In the meantime, she'd catch up with the chief's interview.

* * *

Standing in the observation room, she was overwhelmed with smugness as she watched through the two-way mirror. Mark Reynolds stuttered with fear and stumbled over his words, giving what she hoped would turn out to be vital information.

The door opened behind her, and her father stepped into the room. "Hi, Dad, what are you still doing here?"

"Sean asked me to stick around for a while. Is that all right with you, love? Of course, I wouldn't want to step on your toes or anything."

"That's great! Why on earth should I mind? It would be an absolute honour and privilege to work alongside you. The opportunity has never cropped up before. In my eyes, you retired far too early, anyway."

"As long as we get one thing straight."

"What's that?"

"I'm wise enough to realise what a fine detective you are and that you're still in charge. You'll have to forgive me if sometimes I cross the line. However, you have my permission to rein me in if I do, okay?"

Lorne nodded and extended her hand. Her father shook it just like he used to during her teen years when they shared secret pacts. She remembered the time he'd arranged a secret holiday to Florida for all the family and had taken her into his confidence and elicited her help. Jade tried several attempts of bribery, but didn't have any success in getting the secret from her, even right up until the time they sat in the departure lounge, awaiting their flight at Gatwick airport. Her father had told her how proud he'd been of her, and she had learnt at a very young age how important keeping the "nice" secrets in life can be.

"What's he come up with so far?" she asked, referring to Reynolds.

"He's singing as loud as the proverbial canary. So far, he's given a whole list of names and probable addresses where the Unicorn might be hiding out."

Her father's mobile interrupted them.

Lorne wasn't paying attention to his conversation, and he startled her when he tugged her arm. "Lorne, listen to me."

The unmistakable urgency in his voice sent a shock wave of fear through her. "I'm listening, Dad. It's Charlie, isn't it?"

"No, it's Jade. She's gone into premature labour. She's on her way to hospital now."

"What? How come? Oh, no, she must've been watching the television, and I didn't contact her. Is it the shock? Oh, I feel so awful, poor Jade…"

"Now, Lorne, you mustn't blame yourself. If anything, I should've rung Luigi, warned him to keep Jade away from the TV. He's hardly the sharpest knife in the drawer, is he?"

"He was probably at work, Dad."

She thought the world of Jade's dishy husband and hated the way her father always appeared to find some fault with him. She knew how busy he was trying to build his new export business in order to make a better life for Jade and their new arrival. Luigi went out of his way to protect her. He loved her and treated her like a princess. And his pleasure that she was carrying his heir, a little boy at that, had intensified his cosseting of her.

Jade's pregnancy had been a rough time for her, not that she'd helped matters. Her sister had foolishly carried on riding her horses, despite falling off one in the early months of her pregnancy. "My life's not going to change just because I'm pregnant," she'd blasted at anyone lining up to chastise her.

Sam broke into Lorne's thoughts. "I'll have to leave, Lorne. I need to go to the hospital. Your sister might need me. It'll give me the opportunity to drop by and see how Charlie is doing, too."

"Of course, I wouldn't have it any other way, Dad. You get off. Give her a kiss from me, and tell her I'll be thinking of her. And, Dad, whatever you find out about Charlie, let me know. My stomach keeps going over and over, and my heart is like a piece of lead. I can't help thinking Tom might not ring me if there's any change. She should still be sedated, but in case they've found something, you know, internal injuries that need attention or something like that, you will let me know?"

"I promise. Try not to worry. I'll call you later if I have any news."

As her father headed towards the door, Lorne had an overwhelming urge to take responsibility for everything. "Dad, tell her I'm sorry. Everything that's happened today has been my fault. Even Pete's death…"

Before she knew it, his arms came around her. She needed a release from the heavy knot within her, but she couldn't cry. Her tear ducts had dried up. It'd been a tear-draining day. Instead, she took strength from him, felt it passing between their linked bodies.

"Lorne, if you keep thinking that way, you'll never track down the Unicorn."

"I know, Dad, self-pity never got anyone anywhere, right?"

He smiled as she recited a saying he'd used countless times to keep her on the right track through her days at Hendon. Her police training days had been tough going. Maybe the instructors had given her a harder time because of her father's rank. She'd rung home in tears many times when things hadn't gone her way.

"That's my girl. I'll call you later. Keep focused. Charlie and Jade are in safe hands. Remember that, darling, do you hear me?"

"I hear you, Dad, loud and clear."

She watched him walk from the room as she took on board what he'd said and spoke sternly to herself.

"No more self-pity, Lorne. Focus on catching the bastard that has succeeded in turning your whole life upside down and hurting all those you love."

Chapter Fifty-Three

Lorne pulled out her notebook and began scribbling down a to-do list, which grew as she listened to 'the singing canary'. The shrill of her mobile made her jump.

"*Chérie*, how are you?"

Jacques Arnaud's sexy accent made her smile, and unexpected butterflies took flight in her stomach. "I'm fine, Jacques."

"You always say that even when you are not. Never kid a kidder, Lorne. Is that how the saying you English have goes?"

"It is. But has anybody ever told you, in England it's the women who have the reputation for being nags?"

"Nag? What is this? Are you calling me a horse?"

When she heard his voice, all thoughts of Tom left her mind. Her words to Tom had been about the circumstances and not her true feelings…

She laughed and shook her head in dismay. "Never, Jacques. Let's just say that there are two meanings to the word. Call it English homework, and go look it up in the dictionary."

"I will do that, don't you worry. And if I find out it is derogatory, then I'll be straight down there to sort you out, you little tinker."

"Promises, promises." She closed her eyes, fearing his response, as the candid words caught her off guard. He didn't always understand the subtleties of harmless flirting.

"I've told you before, Lorne, it would be an absolute honour to *sort* you out. There's nothing I would like more than to tame a woman with a spirited nature."

Her pulse quickened, his accent, which he emphasised, knowing how it affected her, even at a moment like this, had her legs wobbling. She backed onto the nearest chair, covered the mouthpiece, and drew in three deep breaths, ordering her heart to calm down. "Sex, that's all you *Frogs* think about."

"It is difficult not to think of sex, when we *Frogs* are surrounded by such beautiful women, non?"

"Come on, Frenchie, back to business. Why are you calling me? I know you're not ringing *just* to annoy me."

"Aha, you give up so easily. Yet another round to me, I think."

"Get on with it, you irritating piece of—"

"Now, now, *chérie*, no need to get aggressive. That's a sign of being a bad loser, and you wouldn't want that tag hanging around your pretty little neck now, would you?"

"Jacques."

"Okay, okay. I can see I'm trying too hard to make you laugh. I am just kidding, you know. Still, I have two things to tell you. Actually, there are three. First, I have released Pete's body to the funeral home, and second, Laura Crane. I've just finished the post-mortem. Death is attributed to poisoning, but I found no suggestion of a struggle."

"By that, I take it you mean her death points to suicide?"

"It looks that way to me, yes. If she had been forced to take it, she would have had marks on her neck or her wrist as she would have struggled very hard. The body suffers terribly when cyanide is ingested."

"Still, she was obviously terrified to have resorted to it. Probably weighed up what lay ahead of her and felt she had no alternative. Was there something else, Jacques?"

"I'm genuinely concerned about you, as a colleague, I mean. No funny business."

"I know you are, Jacques. That's very sweet of you, and I appreciate your concern, but there's no need. Did you see what happened on TV?"

"No, thank God. I learned of it afterwards as I was in the middle of the Crane post at the time. How is sweet Charlie?"

She brought him up to date on the injury and how she worried more for Charlie's mental health.

"She's strong, just like her mother. She comes from a family with spirit and determination. She has that to help her pull through."

"I hope so, but my problems don't end with Charlie. Now my sister has gone into premature labour. It may have been the shock of seeing everything as it unfolded on the TV. Dad's on his way to see her now. Tom's with Charlie. I feel bad because I can't be there with them. I never thought I'd say this, as it doesn't seem right to do so at such a time, but my priorities lie here at the moment. It's imperative I find the bastard who has caused my family unit to implode."

"*Mon dieu!* How far gone is Jade?"

"She's only just reached eight months. I hope the little guy will be okay."

She wiped away another bout of tears. He had such an easy-going nature, and the kind tone to his voice gave the impression he felt everything she did. It was easy for her to open up to him. He had become her confidant, her shoulder to cry on. Pete had misunderstood their relationship, or had he? Had he seen something neither she nor Jacques had ever bargained on?

Well she had work to do and no time to waste speculating. She brought the conversation to an end, promising to keep him informed of how Jade and Charlie progressed.

* * *

Having dispatched their captive to the boot, Ramon pulled up outside an enormous white mansion set deep in the heart of the Kent countryside. Speaking into the intercom on the wall, he gave their identity and requested entrance to see the judge.

"His honour, Judge Winwood, is not at home at present." A tinny voice responded.

"Then we'll come in and wait until he is. You know your instructions are to give my boss access whenever he wants it. Now open up."

The gate swung open.

They drove through at a normal pace, but as they encountered the guard, Clovelly banged and kicked, making a racket that would disturb anyone's peace. Ramon put his foot down, sending pebbles flying, and the guard leapt back onto the grass verge. The car screeched to a halt under the covered columned entrance to the house.

* * *

Simon lay still. His head ached. He needed to think. At uni, the other students relied on his genius, and many a time, he'd brought off successful excursions without any detection from night security. He'd even perfected lock-picking, not that it helped in his present predicament. At least they'd left him in the car, which gave him time to sort something out. The noise he'd made had obviously caused them to make a quick sprint up the driveway. He wondered if the guard had heard and if he would come to his aid.

His anxiety shortened his breath. The air inside the hood stifled him. His throat dried. Fear loosened his bowels. He clenched his buttocks. *Christ, I can't shit myself... the humiliation.*

Enough time had passed since the car doors had slammed to assure him they'd all gone inside the house. There hadn't been a sound for some time to indicate any of them had remained outside to guard him.

He heard crunching feet on the pebbled drive. He listened to the rhythm. The sound indicated only one person was coming, not from ahead, but towards the back of the car.

The journey from the gate ran through his mind. The car hadn't turned around, so he assumed they'd pulled up outside the house with the boot facing the way from which they had come. When the men left the car, they hadn't walked past the boot but away from it in a forward direction, and not many steps, at that. Which meant the house was probably very near.

The footsteps sounded louder. It must be the guard. Anyone else would have driven up the drive. *Can I chance it? What if I yell, will the men inside the house hear?* He had to take the risk.

"Help... Help! I'm inside the boot. Hey, is that the guard? Help me."

The steps became louder and more hurried. Please, God, don't let it be one of the gang members. Whoever it was, they'd heard him. The catch clicked. A draft wafted through his hood.

"What the...?"

"Quick, check the house. Make sure no one's watching."

"There's no one watching. Mrs. Winwood most likely has them shown into the sitting room, which faces the grounds on the other side of the house. What's going on? Who are you?"

The guard undid the bonds and helped Simon out of the boot as he listened to his tale.

"My God, kidnapped. What can I do to help, sir?"

Simon guessed the man used to be in the services from his whole demeanour and the way he'd addressed him as sir. *Good, that means he'll be used to taking orders and will probably have a few tricks up his sleeve.*

"First, I need a hiding place. And, second, I need to use a telephone, you know, so I can call my father."

"Right, I'll get you into my office near the gate. I have a phone in there with an outside line."

"No mobile?"

"I'm Greg Scrivens, by the way. No, sorry, sir, no mobile. Does it matter?"

"Well, a mobile would be better, that way I can erase the number from its memory. Dad won't be pleased, even if it did mean saving my life, to know his retrievable private number sat on an unknown phone."

"Don't worry about that, sir. Someone will fix it. I'm sure that'll be the least of his worries. Knowing you're all right would be his priority. Now, let's get going before someone comes out to check on you."

Chapter Fifty-Four

The well-dressed woman held her coiffed head high as she stood near the fireplace of the elegant room. In a stilted voice, she introduced herself as Sondra Winwood and told them she didn't expect her husband would be long.

"I take it he wasn't expecting a visit from you?" she asked. Then, not waiting for an answer, posed another question, "Can I get anyone a drink? Tea, or coffee, perhaps?"

Her false smile didn't fool the Unicorn; her attitude annoyed him. She did little to hide the fact they weren't welcome. He stared at her, letting his eyes take in her youthful figure with curves that were not generous, but in all the right places. Her face looked taut as if it had been lifted or was full of Botox, giving her an appearance of being in her forties, but he guessed her age to be ten to fifteen years older than that. He enjoyed her nervous reaction to his invading her space.

"Scotch, ice, no water for me. Boys, tell the nice *lady* what you want to drink."

"We'll have the same," Ramon stammered. The Unicorn knew Ramon was still terrified and mystified about what he planned to do next.

"They'll have tea. Earl Grey if you have it? My boys have very refined tastes."

He kept his eyes on Sondra Winwood, his look as cold as steel, then grinned when she shuddered involuntarily.

She turned to her maid. "Okay, Sara, and I'll have a coffee."

The maid almost ran from the room. The Unicorn motioned for Ramon to follow her.

Sondra wandered over to the inglenook fireplace, where the fire in full glow sent crackles of flames up the chimney. She settled herself into the Queen Anne winged chair standing to one side of it. The Unicorn followed her. He rested a nonchalant arm on the huge oak mantelpiece and locked eyes with the woman again.

"Tell me, Mrs. Winwood, how do you know your husband won't be long?" He took in her long shapely legs. *Not in bad nick for an old bird.*

"I rang him as soon as you arrived."

"How very astute of you. My, what I'd give to have a woman like you to look after my *every* need." He laughed when he noticed her shiver again and her hands tremble. "I see that idea doesn't appeal to you, Mrs. Winwood."

"I'm sure I don't know what you're referring to. I find it very chilly today, that's all."

"Perhaps we can think of a way to warm her up, eh, Giorgio?"

Sondra gasped and sat back further in her chair as he inched his way towards her.

"Tell me, Mrs. Winwood, *when* was the last time a *real* man satisfied you?"

"Why, I can't—"

"What? Can't remember? That's what I thought. You know, I usually like my women wrinkle free with firm breasts, but I'm not averse to servicing women who are clearly unsatisfied by ungrateful, pre-occupied husbands."

She shrieked as he stepped forward. He tormented her further by crouching down in front of her. His hand shot out, and he stroked her trousered thigh.

His face inches from hers, he could see her struggling to remain calm and unperturbed. Her cheeks flushed, the colour rising upwards from her slim, elegant neck. He stroked his index finger down her cheek, coursing his way towards her inadequate, much hated cleavage. She sucked in and held her breath. A bead of sweat trickled down her forehead, leaving a visible line through her makeup.

The return of the maid and Ramon's presence stopped him pursuing his game for the time being. As the maid put the tray on a table near to the sofa, the Unicorn asked, "Did you bring one for yourself, Sara?" The glance she gave her mistress angered him.

Before the maid had time to react, the Unicorn stood up, marched over to her, and grabbed her around her neck. Twisting his arm, he threw her to the floor. She landed with the hem of her black dress around her waist, exposing her slim legs and black lacy underwear.

"What's the matter, Sara, cat got your tongue? You look at *me* when I ask a question, bitch. Do you hear me? When I'm in the room, I'm the only one in charge, have you got that?"

"Please don't hurt her." Sondra Winwood jumped out of her chair.

The Unicorn shot her a warning look that sent her scrambling for her seat again.

In one fluid movement, he yanked the maid to her feet and faced her towards her mistress. Holding the maid's chin, the Unicorn jerked her head one way, then the other. A sickening crack cut through the silence before the maid's lifeless body sank to the floor.

"Now where were we?" The murder had heightened the whole experience for him. He needed to stop playing and act. He took up his previous position in front of the terrified Sondra Winwood and once again placed his hand on her leg.

He liked the fear she displayed in the way her type would, stiff and unyielding, as if to show courage. He toyed with the button at the top of her linen trousers. Releasing the button, he watched her squeeze her eyes shut tightly as his hand played with the zipper, up and down. Tired of the game, he moved away. Her eyes shot open.

Motioning to Giorgio, the Unicorn took the DVD case Giorgio held out to him and removed the disk. Surprised and impressed by the latest technology he found at his disposal, the Unicorn inserted the disk. He'd always thought of Winwood as a stick in the mud who was way behind the times. He pressed a button and shouted, "Let the party begin."

As the DVD started, he rushed back to Sondra. "Stand up." He yanked her right arm. Then, taking her place in the chair, he pulled her down to sit on his lap.

"Really!"

He snuggled into the nape of her neck. The wonderful smell of Chanel lingered there. "Umm, it would be nice to have a piece of posh totty for a change."

She struggled to break free, but his arms encircled her, gripping her like a vice. "Now, now, Sondra, play nice. You wouldn't want to end up like Sara over there, would you?"

Shaking, she glanced at her maid's lifeless body lying in the centre of the room and shook her head. The quiver of her body registered on his sensitive penis. He liked the feel and knew she could feel the strength of it pressing into her back.

"Good. Now I have a surprise for you. I hope you like movies. Although I must warn you, it's a little on the raunchy side. Can you handle that?"

She nodded. The large ultra-modern widescreen sprung to life.

"What? When? Who is that with…?"

"Oh, Sondra, you're so funny. Did you believe your husband to be a monogamist? I hate to disillusion you, but I've yet to meet a man who could ever live up to being one of those."

"But, that... that girl... she can only be about fourteen or fifteen."

Pain and humiliation swam in her tearful eyes. She turned away from him and stared at the screen.

The Unicorn watched, too, sickened not by what Winwood did but by the sight of the man's old body thrusting his less-than-adequate manhood into the girl's every orifice and his sweating and grunting. *Ugh.*

"Please stop it... Please, I've seen enough. What do you want from me?"

Whilst he ripped open her blouse, the Unicorn laughed at the way Sondra Winwood tried to fight him and cover her modesty.

"I thought we'd show your husband how filthy *you* can be. Has he ever seen you naked before? Or do you do it with the lights off? Ramon, Giorgio, make the lady comfortable whilst I get myself ready to teach her a few new tricks to try out on her husband so he won't want to stray in the future." He pushed her away from him. She ran towards the door, but Ramon blocked her path.

"Please, I have money. *Please* don't let him do this to me."

Ramon shrugged at the woman and steered her back into the room, towards the white leather sofa positioned in front of the French windows, overlooking the large, immaculate garden.

Chapter Fifty-Five

Simon followed the guard.

"We'll go through the gate. Stick to the edge here, as the security cameras are covering the grounds. He's bound to have put one of his men in the observation room," Greg said.

Sweat poured from Simon, and the old injury he'd picked up playing rugby objected to his crouched position.

They only needed to skirt the back of the small gatehouse that held the office, and they'd be home and dry.

A blood curdling scream stopped them. They threw themselves to the ground and froze.

"That's the mistress. I'll have to go, sir. Stay down."

"No, no… Greg…" *Fuck. Damn and blast.* Simon watched in despair as the stupid man raced in full sight back towards the house.

* * *

The Unicorn stood, arms folded, a smile playing around his mouth. *The fucking guard, look at him edging his way across the French windows.*

The Unicorn's smile broadened as the guard caught sight of him and stopped dead. He watched the man's eyes light up in horror and his mouth drop open, then noticed the guard's eyes focus on the two bodies lying on the floor.

His henchmen grabbed the guard, opened the doors, and dragged the snivelling, shaking wreck of a man inside.

"What's your name?" the Unicorn asked with contempt.

"Greg," he replied, his voice trembling.

"All right, Greg, well this hasn't been your lucky day so far, has it? But I've got a treat for you to make up for it. Strip off your clothes."

"What?"

"You heard me. You seem an intelligent kind of guy, Greg. Do it."

"Don't… Please don't kill me."

The guard's snot mingled with his tears as he undressed.

"Pull yourself together, man. I have something I want you to do. Ramon, fetch the camcorder from the car."

Ramon didn't move. Instead, he looked at his boss and raised an eyebrow.

"Do it, numbskull. Stop wasting bloody time."

Ramon left the room and returned with a camcorder a couple of minutes later. "Boss, something's happened. I need to see you in the hallway."

"What is it? Spit it out. I don't have time for your infantile guessing games."

"The kid's gone."

"What? What the hell do you mean *he's gone*? Escaped, you mean?" He shot the guard an angry look. "You fucking let him out, didn't you?" Before the guard could react, the Unicorn grabbed his testicles, then let them go as he quickly changed his mind. "Count yourself lucky. You're going to need them. Otherwise, I'd have twisted them off and stuffed them into your cowardly mouth. But don't underestimate me, Greg. I'll give you to the count of five to tell me where the boy is. One… two… three… four…"

"All right, all right. He's in the garden near the gatehouse. Have you any idea whose son he is?"

"You useless bag of shit! Why the fuck do you think we have him? I've had enough of you. I haven't got time for this crap. Get down on your knees."

Greg surprised him by refusing to comply with the instruction, appearing to have found some guts from somewhere. Either that, or he'd accepted his fate.

The Unicorn flicked a finger, and Ramon and Giorgio stepped forwards to force the man to his knees.

"Start wanking."

"*What?*"

"Is that the only word in your vocabulary? Now don't tell me you've never had a wank before, Greg? Get on with it."

The guard played with his dick until it sprang to life.

"That's enough. Now move over to your boss." The Unicorn clicked his fingers. "Ramon, start filming. Go on, Greg, do it, or I'll kill you right now."

The guard hesitated, but then decided to obey.

"Now fuck her. Go on, bang her like your life depended on it, which by the way, Greg, it does."

Greg positioned himself behind the woman. The Unicorn held back a laugh as he watched the guard struggle to lift the body on to its knees and then try to insert his almost drooping penis inside the dead vagina.

"Right, now pump. Open your eyes, Greg, at least look as if you're enjoying it. Don't tell me you've never wanted to screw your mistress before. Go, Greg, pump her hard. Pump her like there's no tomorrow. Does she feel good, Greg, warm and welcoming or cold and hostile like your Mrs?"

Greg remained quiet, his rhythm slow and deliberate.

"Go on, Greg, ride her. Ride her as if you were the leading jockey in the Grand National."

He laughed at the man's inept effort, but stopped when Greg vomited over Sondra Winwood's torso. The guard pulled himself out and collapsed in a heap. Sobs wracked his body, making his words sound like a child's. "Go on, kill me, you bastard. Get it over with. I won't do what you want anymore."

The Unicorn was disappointed and barked at his henchmen, "Go and find that fucking boy." Then he pulled out his gun.

Chapter Fifty-Six

The lock would give. He knew it would. It just proved harder to pick than any he'd tackled before. Simon tried again, twisting the bit of metal he'd found in the gravel this way and that. God, if only he could stop shaking. A shot stopped him in his tracks.

He slumped to his knees. Terror clawed his insides, and sadness filled him as he realised the final bullet probably had Greg's name on it. He'd never felt so alone. The click of the front door echoed towards him, pulling him out of his reverie. He glanced along the drive and saw two men.

Shit, where's the boss? He had no time to speculate; the men were heading his way. Simon figured that the guard had probably divulged his whereabouts before being shot.

He looked all around him. Behind him, a clump of trees offered him his only option. The branches of the pine trees were joined together and formed a dark tunnel beneath them. He scrambled into it, but once the men arrived, he knew this would be the first place they'd look. Going as fast as he could in his bent position, he made his way through. Sweat trickled into his eyes, and his mouth felt as dry as cardboard.

Brushing the branches aside, he emerged into a clearing. A three metre-high wall bordered the ground to his left. Ahead lay an ornate, well-kept garden. To his right, around two hundred metres away, stood the imposing house. In between him and the house and a little way off centre, he saw what might be his salvation. A maze.

A rustle behind him signalled that his pursuers were close. A yell told him they'd seen him. Urged into action, he ran across the lawn at a speed worthy of a gold medallist, making it to the dense green hedges in seconds. He rushed in and immersed himself into its concealing depths. Having negotiated several passageways, Simon stood still. He could hear the men on the edge of the maze, debating what they should do.

"Should we follow him in there, or should we head back and tell the boss?"

"Are you insane? You heard what he said. We can't go back without him. Come on, he couldn't have got far."

Simon swallowed, willing himself not to move. He tried to judge which way they were heading.

Their feet crunched the pebbled path, but then stopped. They didn't speak, but Simon knew by the change in sound that they had separated.

Once more, his small frame helped him. Sticking to the narrow grass path near the hedges roots, he continued around the maze until he spotted a flaw in the otherwise perfectly symmetrical hedge. Some of it had been hacked away, probably diseased, but whatever, it gave him the option to climb up and search for an exit.

Once on top, he planned his route. A couple of right turns, and he'd be there.

A few seconds later, he was outside. He listened for a moment, trying to judge the men's progress. He heard them call out to each other; their voices sounded anguished.

"Ramon, where are you?"

"How the fuck should I know?"

"Christ. He'll kill us for this. We're dead men."

Simon chuckled. *Dumb pieces of shit.*

He made his way over to the Volvo, hoping the keys would still be in the ignition. But the third man, whom he guessed to be the boss, was leaning against the bonnet. *Thank God, he hasn't noticed me.* Simon changed direction and skirted the back of the house. *Fuck! What the hell do I do now?*

Then he spotted the open French windows, ran towards them, and leapt inside. He backed across the room, his hands out behind him, feeling for any obstructions. Suddenly, his feet hit something. He stumbled and landed on his back, the object he'd fallen over cushioning his fall. Turning his head, he looked into the bloody mess of Greg's dead face. With vomit caught in his throat and threatening to choke him, Simon pushed himself up and spat out the vile-tasting liquid.

The horror of three dead bodies surrounding him caused him to snivel like a baby, and his fear turned to despair. But then a new courage took hold. He decided this may indeed turn out to be his last day on earth, but he'd give these guys a good fight. Struggling to his feet, he ordered himself to think logically.

First, he must slow them down in their pursuit of him and lock every door possible behind him. He rushed through to the hall. The adjoining door had a key dangling from an old-fashioned brass lock.

He shut and locked it. Looking around, he saw a door at the end of the hall, which had to be the main entrance.

Simon knew the car and the boss were just outside. He needed to lock the main entrance, but not with the key. That would make too much noise. And as it wasn't in the lock, locating the key would take too much time. He pushed the bolts across, trying hard not to make a noise. Turning back the way he'd come, he looked around for a phone and saw one on a carved table halfway along the hall, but changed his mind about using it. *If they got in through the French windows, how long would it take them to break down the inner door?* He glanced up at the stairs. *There would be phones up there, surely?* He ran up the stairs, taking two steps at a time.

* * *

"Right, listen up."

DCI Roberts silenced the room. Lorne straightened herself. She had finished her briefing, giving the team all the new information gleaned from Reynolds and they'd worked out strategies as to their next moves. She had a feeling it was all to no avail.

Roberts looked around the room as he spoke. "We have a definite on where our hostage is. Somehow, the lad managed to escape his captors, but still remains in grave danger. However, he found a phone and called his father. Told him he's being held at the house of Judge Winwood."

In answer to her gasp and that of most of the others, he said, "Yes, I know. The implications are wider, given that we released the judge half an hour ago, and he's probably making his way home and almost there by now. We've tried contacting him on the mobile number he gave us, but he's not answering. I had it scanned, and he received and answered a call just after he left here. The call came from his wife. Therefore, I'm assuming he already knows he has guests. I've circulated his plates to all units, and we can only hope one of them intercepts him. Also, I've activated an ART, and they're en route to the house."

"Have we missed something? Is the judge more involved in this than we thought?" Lorne asked.

"Could be, or he owes a few favours. Nothing in his interview suggested he had any deeper involvement, other than using the services offered to satisfy his lust for sex with young girls. But there's something else. The Unicorn hasn't just called in favours and holed up at the judge's home. Simon Clovelly reported three murders." Roberts outlined the supposed identities of the victims. "At this moment in time, we don't know how safe Simon is. He might've found a possible hiding place. If they've caught him, let's hope they think of him as a ticket out of that place."

"Sounds like you have it all under control, sir." Lorne hoped her tone admonished him; he'd put a lot in place before briefing her. Roberts had the good grace to look shamefaced, but then she regretted the inference she'd made. "Why hasn't the case been taken off us? Surely MI5 would be the PM's first port of call for help?"

Roberts looked relieved. It was enough for Lorne that he realised he'd stepped on her toes and made her feel like a team member rather than the lead of the investigation. "Maybe the superintendent put in a good word for you, for us. Who knows?"

"Yeah right, is that a pig flying past your window? All you ever hear from him is 'you've been chasing this criminal for eight years, and you haven't even got within striking distance of arresting him.' Anyway," she addressed the whole room, "the case is still ours, so let's take up this new challenge. We've dug deep into the judge's background, as with the others involved in the party. Then, it looked like he was a bit player. His profile in the game just lifted, so I want everything we have on him mapping out. Don't miss a thing. Look into his recent cases, his lifestyle, his bank accounts, anything. The information is all there. Go through it with a fine toothcomb and highlight the smallest thing if you think it has relevance." She stopped and looked around.

Bleary, bloodshot eyes looked back at her.

"We're on the final lap, guys. I can feel it. We know where the Unicorn is, and within minutes now, thanks to the DCI's prompt action, we'll have him trapped in a small, enclosed area. Just one more push, eh?"

The room buzzed into life. Energised officers scrambled for computers and files. They had the same fire in their belly she had. And the same objective: to nail the bastard, once and for all.

"There is something worth noting," AJ shouted as he sifted through a file. "Judge Winwood recently presided over a high-profile terrorist case—that of one Abdul Mansaud, the man behind the attempted bombing of an American Airline passenger jet departing from Heathrow heading for the States in May of last year. Despite a good dossier of evidence, the case against Mansaud wasn't proven, and he was set free."

"Yes, I vaguely remember the case. It's got to be the connection we've been looking for."

"It does sound significant, and is why I flagged it, but I haven't a clue why it should be," AJ said.

"Right, let's analyse it. What if the judge was at the party, but not to take part?" Lorne moved over to the board and wrote: Judge – Interested Party.

One of the young officers at the back of the room chirped up. "But he joined in the auction and paid to have sex with that young girl."

"Right, which may suggest only the Unicorn knew of his interest and he had to look as though he was just a guest." She followed her thoughts through and noted the bullet points on the board. "One: The Unicorn pays money back to the judge. Two: The judge gets a cut of the profits from the auctions. Three: In return, the terrorist goes free. Four: The judge is now vulnerable to blackmail."

"But what about the jury?" AJ asked.

"Well, he took a chance, granted, but a judge of his calibre can influence any jury."

Everyone agreed Lorne had something in her theory.

"Good thinking, Lorne," DCI Roberts said. "So, if you're right, the judge is in this up to his neck and is now a pawn for the Unicorn to use as and when he wants to, and that time is now."

"Blimey, you'd have to be a devious geezer to think of this little scam." The voice of the young rookie who'd posed the first question piped up.

"And that's exactly what we're dealing with," Lorne told him. "A man with a list of hideous crimes as long as your arm and with his finger in many pies. But for the time being, focus your minds on the fact he killed one of your own and the terrible things he did to my daughter. Make it personal, leave no stone unturned. This scenario," she pointed to the board, "escaped us. Don't let anything else do that." Lorne turned to the DCI. "Sir, I think we should take a ride over to the judge's residence."

Chapter Fifty-Seven

The Unicorn watched through an upstairs window as the judge swung his car into the drive and looked around for his guard. There seemed nothing hurried about the way he drove up to the house and parked. When he climbed out of his car, Judge Winwood looked around again, then at his watch. Any minute now, he'd be through the door, which was now unbolted and which reminded him that fucking little arsehole Clovelly still roamed free. Although seething at the way the lad had outwitted him, the Unicorn couldn't help letting in a small strain of admiration for him. He played a good cat-and-mouse game and hadn't wasted time locking the French windows, which would not have taken a second to get through, anyway, but where the little shit was holed up still remained a mystery.

"Sondra? Sondra... Where the hell is everyone?"

"I'm here. Can I help you?"

Winwood's face as he looked up at the Unicorn leaning over the banister and into the barrel of his gun was priceless. "Surely you expected to find me here? Your beautiful, sexy wife told me she'd phoned you."

"Ye... yes, but..." Winwood's head twisted around as he spoke.

"I hope you're not looking for your guard? Oh, I've had him occupied, gave him the treat of his life before I sent him to his maker."

"Where's Sondra?"

"Oh, she's okay. She's... resting. Yes, she needed her rest. She didn't really enjoy the film show of you and that tart, but it made her randy, and now she's having a long sleep."

"What have you done?"

"Oh, suddenly the caring husband, are we? Not the one planning to get the hell out of here and abandon her, after all? What happened? Find you couldn't go off to Brazil and leave her and all this behind?"

"If you've hurt her—"

"I always hurt my women, but they love it. Yes, I would think despite the pain, she had the best fuck she's ever had. Ha, or going to have."

"But—"

"Shut up. I've had enough bantering words with you. I've got something to show you." The Unicorn sprinted down the last of the stairs, keeping his gun trained on the judge, and motioned towards his study. "In there, everything's set up."

Once they were inside the office, the Unicorn pushed Winwood into an armchair.

"I hear you've been down the cop shop."

"That's right."

"Well, don't keep me in suspenders, judge. I'm dying to know what you told them."

"What we agreed. I told them what we agreed. I didn't renege on our plan."

"I'm glad to hear it. What's up? Why are you acting so nervous, Walter?"

"Wouldn't you be if you had a gun pointed at you?"

"I've never found myself in such a tedious position, so I can't really answer that. Anyway, let's get on." The Unicorn moved over to the television set and switched it on before flicking a button on the camcorder he'd set up on a stool next to it. The screen flickered into life.

The sickening image of Sondra's naked, dead body made the judge gasp.

"Oh, suddenly found some feeling for the bitch, have we? I thought you told me you despised her. Well, that's just after I gave her the fucking of her life, so she died happy. But wait, I have a further treat for you."

The film showed the guard moving towards the body; his penis was erect, but losing its hardness with every move. What followed made the judge vomit and clutch his stomach.

The Unicorn laughed out loud. Then catching the judge off guard, the Unicorn grabbed his head in a vice-like grip and again forced him to watch the TV. Walter cried out in pain and the sick dribbled from the side of his mouth. He choked on his own vomit as he watched a naked Greg Scrivens pumping Sondra.

"No, please. Stop. I can't watch anymore."

Simon Clovelly crept down the stairs and listened in the hallway. He only needed to take a couple more steps to reach the front door. The sound of a man pleading stopped him. Through the crack in the door, he could see the man who'd captured him brandishing a gun in the face of an older man. Simon hesitated, wondering if there might be something he could do to help the older man, but after seeing the evidence of what the Unicorn was capable of, he knew any attempt of help he could muster would be hopeless.

From his hiding place in an Ali Baba wash basket in the corner of a bathroom at the top of the stairs, where smelly underwear and dirty gardening clothes formed his camouflage, he'd heard the exchange between the boss man and the man in the chair, whom he assumed to be the judge and owner of the house. He'd heard the boss man's footsteps going down the stairs, and then, after all had gone quiet, Simon had decided it was safe to make his escape. That escape seemed all the more probable after peeping through the landing window and seeing the activity building up outside the gate. Relief had spurred him on. He couldn't jeopardise his freedom now.

He turned sharply and walked into a marble pedestal, sending the bust of some old wag resembling Shakespeare crashing to the ground. *Shit!*

He bolted for the door.

"Stay right where you are, arsehole."

Simon turned, thinking the words were aimed at him, but the boss man hadn't come out of the room. Making one last effort, he grabbed the door, flung himself through it, and banged it shut behind him.

"Get down now! Spread your arms and feet."

"It's me, Simon Clovelly, the prime minister's s—"

A searing pain grated through the bones of his shoulder, and his body hit the ground. "Oh God."

* * *

After reaching through the smashed window to shoot Clovelly, the Unicorn pulled his arm back and quickly hit the floor as a hail of bullets shattered the rest of the frame.

When the barrage stopped, he looked over at the judge, cowering in a heap of misery under a desk. Bullet holes sprouting tufts of horsehair peppered the back of the chair where the judge had been sitting.

Ha. I bet that's the quickest that fucker's ever moved. The hateful laughter threatened. He swallowed it down.

"You'll have to give yourself up. These guys are well trained, and you're done for, *Mr. Unicorn.*"

"Don't make me laugh, Winwood. These guys aren't the elite. I was one of the elite. These guys aren't even fit enough to wipe my old squad's arses. So don't try and play mind games with me, do you hear me? Now get up." He yanked the man by the scruff and pushed him into the lounge. The sight of the bodies lying on the floor caused the judge to be sick again.

"Funny, I felt like doing the same thing when I saw her naked."

"You bastard!"

The Unicorn ignored his comment and threw him onto the sofa. Then he took his mobile from his pocket, pushed the number for his pilot, and yelled into the mouthpiece. "Where the hell are you? I don't care! Get here ASAP. We've got company. There's a pool at the rear. Pick me up there." He flipped the phone shut and started pacing up and down.

He looked over at the judge and was amused by the devastation etched on his face.

The man mumbled, "Sondra, forgive me for getting us into this bloody mess." Then he moaned and rubbed his left arm.

Bloody fool's having a heart attack.

Chapter Fifty-Eight

"Inspector Tyler," Lorne spoke to the officer in charge of operations. "There haven't been any shots for a while. Can't you deploy two officers to get the lad out of there? He's injured, and we don't know how badly."

Tyler looked up from the plans of the house the three of them had been studying.

"It's too risky. I'd be sending my men into a death trap."

"Don't forget who he is, Inspector. I think the PM would not rate your men over his son…"

"Well, I do," he snapped back at her.

"For fuck's sake," Lorne said under her breath.

"Lorne…" Roberts warned.

She turned to the DCI. "I don't give a damn for your bloody politics. One child has had her life ruined already today by that bastard. And I don't have to remind you how I view that as the child's parent or how I'd view those who could have saved her and didn't. So I think I have a right to speak up on the PM's behalf—"

"All right, all right. I understand your emotions are running high, DI Simpkins, but you have to think rationally about this."

"There is no rationality, Inspector Tyler, where the Unicorn is concerned. There's plenty of cover around the gatehouse, and you could set up a couple of shooters to keep a barrage of shots firing off towards the house to make sure the bastard has to keep his head down. It would take seconds to get the boy out on a stretcher."

"You're right." Mark Tyler snapped out his orders to his men.

Several men fired shots into the front of the house while two other men dragged Clovelly away from the scene. The paramedics took charge of Simon, and word filtered back to them that his shoulder bone had splintered, but he would make it and was a lad of courage. He had a lot of useful information and thought that more important than the pain, refusing pain killing injections until he'd told them what he knew.

The DCI pulled her to one side. "Lorne, you allowed your emotions to intervene there and undermine a man with twelve years' experience. Any more stunts like that, and I'll relieve you of your duties again. You're showing signs of not having the clear-cut thinking skills needed to bring this case to a conclusion."

Mortified, Lorne gave him a look that would kill at ten paces and muttered, "Yes, sir."

"Right, everyone, the lad told my men this Unicorn geezer has the judge held captive in the study. That's here." Tyler tapped the plan with his pen and circled the study window. "This is also where the shots came from, but of course, he could've left the area by now. This," he circled another window, "is the lounge, where a number of bodies are, and it's the room where our lad gained access to the house, through these French windows here."

The forefinger on his left hand tapped as he expressed his thoughts. His eyes darted around the plan. Seeking out the entrances and exits available to them on the ground floor, he circled each one as he went and pointed them out with his pen aimed at the house. "There's just too many for us to cover. But…" He shouted orders to members of his team and dispatched them around the perimeter with instructions to cover what they could. "There's more backup on the way. Keep your eyes peeled and your ears tuned in to your radios. Don't wait for the order to shoot, but make sure of your target. You all know what Judge Winwood looks like, so don't let me have to report back that he's taken a hit from one of my men."

"Not wishing to tell you your job, Inspector, but if I was the Unicorn, I'd move to the rear of the property," Lorne said. "So wouldn't it be wise to put more men back there?"

Tyler stood upright, taking in the surrounding grounds of the mansion. He was about fifty, greying slightly, but in tiptop shape for a man of his age. A determined look stretched across his otherwise expressionless face.

"You're right. And the lounge does overlook the back of the property, here. But there's another complication to consider. Here is a maze, which overlooks the side of the house, and in there, the lad tells us are two of the Unicorn's henchmen. Both armed and I should imagine very frustrated as it seems they've gone round and round for nigh on half an hour, now."

Lorne's mobile buzzed. One look at the caller ID, and her palm broke out in sweat. "Chief, it's him. Do I answer it?"

"Yes, play it cool, Lorne. Keep his attention. Maybe we can gain entry whilst he's distracted. What do you reckon, Inspector?"

Tyler nodded. "Worth a try. See what he has to say. Can you put it on speaker phone?"

She could but didn't want to. "Not really. I'm afraid it's a bit tinny when on speaker. Leave it to me. Hello?"

"Ah, Inspector. Why the delay? Getting instructions on how to play things, were you?"

This was the opportunity she'd been waiting for. She decided to try out the names Tony had given her.

"I wondered when you'd ring again, Bill."

"Nice try, Inspector, but you're so wrong on that." His sickening, contemptible laugh mocked her.

"Right then, if Bill Matthews isn't your name, then Robert Baldwin definitely is. Am I right, Bob?" The brief silence confirmed her suspicion.

"You're a smart cookie. You should get a promotion out of this case, Inspector." His tone told her he wasn't best pleased, but he recovered and attacked once more. "By the way, how's that little minx of yours? Boy, did I teach her a thing or two. She might've only been with me a short time, but..."

Lorne burned with anger, but a glance from Roberts told her to keep calm. She covered her phone with her hand and drew in three deep breaths. She smiled, hoping this would transfer to her voice. "Charlie's fine, safe and well. I'm sorry to disappoint you, but so are all the other girls, too."

"Well not all of them, hey, Inspector? And to add to the toll, you'll find another three dead bodies in here, too.

"Who are they?"

"Ah, that'd be telling. Where would the surprise be? I wouldn't want to spoil things for you. You're the detective. I'll let you detect who they are."

"Just answer me one question?"

"Shoot."

"Is the judge still alive?"

"What kind of idiot do you take me for, Inspector? I thought you had more brains than that. He's my escape route out of here. I'm not likely to kill him now, am I? Well, not yet."

"So you think you're going to get out of here alive, do you? We have this place surrounded," she said.

A movement caught her eye. The two men instructed to make their way to the house whilst she kept the Unicorn talking had reached the maze. The sound of an approaching helicopter sent them diving for cover. *Shit!*

"Ah, I think you're wrong there, Inspector. I see my transport has arrived." The Unicorn laughed as the red chopper hovered into view and prepared to land in the judge's expansive rear garden.

Lorne had to think fast. "Leave the judge here, and you can be assured of a clear getaway, Baldwin."

His derisory laugh erupted in her ear. "When are you going to start showing me some respect, *lady*?"

"I'd respect you if you gave yourself up. If you try escaping now, our guys will be left with no alternative. They'll have to shoot you down."

"And there was I giving you credit for having brains, Simpkins. How fucking wrong I was. The judge is going with me, and no, I don't think you'll shoot us down." The line went dead.

"What did he say?" Roberts asked.

"He's got it all worked out. He thinks we won't try and stop him whilst he's got the judge as a hostage. Inspector, is there any way we can try and disable the chopper?"

Tyler shook his head. "Like you just said, Inspector, not whilst he's holding a gun to the judge's head. I'm afraid he's bloody got us by the short and curlies."

"What do you suggest?" Roberts asked.

"I'll call for backup. A Met chopper can be here within a matter of minutes. I'll issue them with orders to follow this guy, see where he lands. We'll take it from there."

"He's bound to pull some kind of stunt. He won't put up with that scenario. I know him," Lorne said. Her eyes darted between the house and the men beside her.

"It's the only option left open to us. He's aware of that fact, too. Looking on the bright side, if we hadn't turned up here, the odds are the judge would've probably been killed by now. As it is, the Unicorn will keep him alive until he's outlived his usefulness. When that's likely to be is anyone's guess. But for now, the judge is worth more to him alive," Roberts said.

"Let me deal with the situation in hand first. We'll figure out the rest when he's under way. For now, I intend on making his escape as difficult as can be."

"What do you have in mind, Inspector Tyler?"

"I suggest my men take up the search for his two guys, to prevent them from escaping the area and giving him back-up. And I'll instruct the men covering the back of the house to hinder his escape. Let's see how his nerve holds up."

"I think you should call his bluff. We can't let him escape. If that means the judge gets in the way, well, so be it. This is the most wanted criminal in the country, and the judge is no angel, either," Lorne said.

"Right, and set up enquiries into our handling of the situation? Sounds good, sacrificing a man's life, don't you think? Whether he's a criminal or not, I think, Inspector Simpkins, you should bow out and let me work this my way. This isn't the first time we've had our backs against the wall with a guy like this."

His condescending tone and the gross feeling of helplessness she felt made Lorne snap. "I realise that, Inspector, but I can guarantee you this. You've *never* had to deal with a *worse* individual than this. This guy could've shown Saddam Hussein and his vile sons a trick or two."

The inspector brushed her aside with an outstretched arm, his determination to draw the situation to a close all too obvious. "Like I said, leave it to me, Inspector."

"Look, if your men flush out the two in the maze, the Unicorn will shoot them dead. Let me get over to them. You cover me with a hail of bullets. Aim them just below the copter and at the house. I can then negotiate with the men, offer them a deal, and get information about the Unicorn's likely destination. That way, we're armed with knowledge of his next move."

"No, Inspector, that's crazy. Besides, why should they listen to you?"

"I have no doubt they've heard of me. Part of the Unicorn's tactic has been to keep me informed every step of the way. I'm the only one they would believe. I could speak to them, convince them they're dead men if they come outside the maze, which is what they probably are once the helicopter gets into the air from where the Unicorn can pick them off. We need the info they have before that happens. Like I said, I know him, and he shows no signs of taking them with him, does he?"

"Lorne's right. I know it's dangerous, but she can handle it. And I am authorising you to arm her. She has clearance for missions such as this."

"If you say so, Chief. But I must strongly register my objection to the plan."

Lorne sighed with relief. She had to have information on the next planned step. She couldn't lose the Unicorn now, and for a moment, that had looked very likely.

Chapter Fifty-Nine

Lorne checked her bullet-proof and then fastened on her gun holster. Her heart was thumping. The Unicorn would love to take her out; she knew that. She prayed the bullets would keep him crouched down so he wouldn't see her approaching his men.

With sweat dripping down her face and her blouse sticking to her, she emerged from the thicket. She signalled to the men on the wall. The firing began. The noise reminded her of the stinking alley. *Christ, Pete. Did that only happened two days ago? Stay with me, mate, I'm counting on you.*

Running like a sprinting cheetah, she reached the maze and fell on her stomach, rolling the last few yards towards the men of the armed response team. She took her gun out of the holster. "Right, officers, I'm Inspector Simpkins. My plan is to negotiate with the two men inside the maze. For me to stand any chance with them, I'll need to keep them trapped inside. I have to create a no-win situation for them to make them cooperate. I want one of you to cover the entrance and the other to make your way around the other side, get as near to the exit as you can, but keep out of view of the house."

They both nodded and took up their positions.

Lorne lay still and listened. She heard voices from inside the maze.

"Christ. It sounds like the fucking army's here. How're we gonna get out, Ramon? The boss won't wait for us, you know that. We've got to do something."

"We have to find the exit. The shooters have to be around the perimeter of the grounds, which means they can only half-cover our path to the house. Look, you're the lightest. I'll give you a heave up to look over the hedge, see where the exit is."

"I wouldn't do that if I were you," Lorne shouted.

"Who the fuck?"

"Inspector Lorne Simpkins. I think you've probably heard of me."

"Where are you?"

"I'm very near, and I have armed officers covering both exits with instructions to kill on sight. But then if they don't, Mr. Unicorn Baldwin will, so I'd say you're fucking up the creek, boys."

For a moment, only the leaves rustling in the breeze broke the silence. Then one of the men answered her.

"I don't think so. He needs us. But nice try, you fucking bitch. Don't ever think you can outsmart our boss. He knows your every move and most likely has a gun trained on you at this very moment."

"Needs *you*? Come off it, you're as dispensable as a fattened up turkey at Christmas. The Unicorn doesn't *need* anyone, least of all a couple of jerks who can't find their way out of a maze a young kid managed to get out of half an hour ago."

"She's right, Ramon."

"Shut the fuck up, Giorgio, or I'll fucking kill you meself, you arsehole."

"I *am* right, Giorgio, and I'll tell you another thing. You've had it, even if you sit tight until your boss takes off, because the first thing he'll do is hover over here and eliminate you both. After all, you know where he's heading, and he can't leave it to chance that you'll keep quiet about that, can he?"

"You know she's right, Ramon. He killed Gary didn't he? He don't give a flying fuck about us."

"All right, all right, so what the fuck do you propose we do? Come on, you know so much, so you figure it out. You're saying if we stay in here, the rotten filth of a boss we have'll kill us, and if we get out, the cops'll kill us, so what's your plan, eh?"

"We have information. Stuff that'll nail him once and for all. That must be worth something—"

"It's worth us having an early passage to hell. Christ, that's what *she's* saying, you idiot. It's what we *know* that's going to be the death of us."

Lorne jumped at the opportunity to intervene. "I can change that. Yes, you're dead if you try to escape, but if you give me information that leads to his capture, you're not only safe, but can live your lives out somewhere where no one knows you. Have a fresh start. All I need in the first instance is what his intended destination is. Then once you're out, everything you know and a signed statement, an appearance as witnesses for the Crown, and that's it. Throughout all of it, you'll have protection, and when it's over, you get a one-way ticket to wherever and a new life."

"How do we know you'll stick to your word?"

"You don't, but as I see it, you have no other choice. Who would you rather trust, me or your boss?" Lorne asked.

"I'm up for it, Ramon. Come on, mate, you hate him. You know you do."

"Yeah, okay, but fucking get on with it. He'll be leaving any minute…"

"Right, where's he heading?" Lorne held her breath. She had seconds to get this info; she knew that. The helicopter had already started up.

"You get us out first. You're not catching us with that one."

"And you're not catching me with your tricks, either. No information, no deal. I'd say you have minutes left to live, unless you cooperate. So where's he heading?" She didn't pray often, but now she sent up a quick request. *I can't lose him now. Not now…*

"He's—"

"Shut the fuck up, or I'll blast you, you dumb idiot. We want out of here and *now*."

"No deal. Have a good afterlife. We have a helicopter on its way. We can follow him, but with prior knowledge, we could beat him there and take him out. Just remember, if he takes off now, you die, but it won't end there. If we fail to nab him, then he'll go after your families. But before your womenfolk die, you know what the sick bastard will do to them, right? Even your grandmas and kids—"

"Portsmouth, he's headed for Portsmouth. Abromovski's boat is moored there. It has a helipad onboard. He's planning on going to Europe, setting off from Monaco. That's all we know, now—"

Lorne had a déjà vu moment as the helicopter blades drowned out the last of Giorgio's sentence. The machine soared into the air, bathing them in its shadow. Lorne looked around. Behind her stood a summer house, but she'd have to sprint twenty metres to reach it. "Back off. Back off. Head for cover!" Jumping up, she scrambled towards the wooden building. *Please don't be locked.*

Her ears hurt with the noise of the throbbing blades and the hollers of the desperate men in the maze. Bullets chopped twigs and leaves, sending them spinning into the air. Her only chance to reach cover was whilst he remained focused on taking out his henchmen.

Her gasps for air burned her lungs. She looked over her shoulder. The armed response officers were close behind her. One called out, and they both fell on their backs, firing rounds off skyward.

No, no! Christ, they're making themselves sitting ducks to save me.

She hurled herself at the door. The helicopter swirled around. She had seconds before it circled back towards her. The door resisted. There was no way she could force her way in. Lorne looked back towards the officers. They were up on their feet and running towards her. Shielding her eyes, she saw the helicopter had turned and was now swooping towards them. She could see him. His mouth was open, and his body shook.

The bastard's laughing at us.

Lorne braced herself, knowing her time had come. She thought of Charlie. Poor Charlie. And the saddest of things was she'd never know how much she was loved. She won't know there had been no choice. *She'll see me as an uncaring mother who put her work before her family, and Tom will fuel that fire because he's made it clear that's how he feels.*

Chapter Sixty

"Oh my God. Do something, Tyler. For Christ's sake, do something," the chief begged.

"I warned you, sir. I warned this would happen. What can I do? If I bring the chopper down, they'll all die. And I can't take him out, because the pilot keeps swirling round. I've given the order to shoot to kill, but only if there's a clear chance of doing so. That bloody machine can turn on a sixpence."

"Why isn't he shooting? He could kill her, kill them all. I don't understand. What game is he playing?"

"He could be playing a game, making her suffer," Tyler said in a resigned tone.

"The men have reached her. Please God, they can break that door down in time."

"If anyone can, they can. Overton's built like a brick shithouse, and Wheatley's not much smaller."

Chief Sean Roberts held his breath until his lungs hurt. He couldn't bear it. His feelings for Lorne rushed to his heart. He couldn't watch her die. He knew the pain would slice him in two. Closing his eyes, he waited for the sound of more shots. Nothing. The noise of the helicopter receded. He opened his eyes, looked towards the summer house, and saw a gaping hole.

Thank God she's safe. At this moment, he couldn't care less what happened to the Unicorn. His body shook with emotion he fought to control. He knew he had to resist running forwards and gathering her into his arms.

A strange quiet settled around him. The tail of the helicopter disappeared into the horizon. A bird started to sing, and another answered as if this were just another day. He exhaled and made a conscious effort to turn the key on his feelings once more.

"Sir… Sir?"

"Oh, sorry, what? Is everything okay. Is sh— Are they safe?"

"Yes, sir, Overton just radioed in. He's shaken. He said the helicopter came near enough for the Unicorn to blast them to kingdom come, but instead he laughed at them. Overton couldn't hear him, but the sight of him sent a shiver down his spine like he'd never felt before. I guess we'll never know what the reason for her or any of them being spared is, but he says she's okay."

"Right, I'll take the lead now. Thank you, Tyler. I need your men to sweep the area, make sure there's no further threat. Tell them to be mindful of disturbing evidence. I have forensics standing by. Once you give the all clear, they can go in. The locals are on hand to do the legwork of the grounds, cordon off the scene, and take care of the bodies, et cetera. So again, once you're happy, mobilise them. I'm going over to Lo— Inspector Simpkins. I'll give you my next move as and when I have it, which depends if we have the info we need or not."

"I still have the chopper en route. Might I suggest they land? Then if you know where he's heading, they can pick you up."

"Good thinking. Yes, organise that. If it changes, I'll radio you, and you can direct them to pick up the trail of that bastard and tell them to do whatever it takes."

"Right, sir."

* * *

"A close call, sir," Lorne said the minute she laid eyes on her boss.

"Fucking hell, Lorne..." He thumped his clenched fist against his thigh.

"I know. But you agreed the plan, so it's no use blowing a fuse. Anyway, I have what we need. And I don't care if you sack me, I'm going after him, Chief. I can't give up now."

"Don't you think I know that? Come on, the chopper should land any moment. Where're we going?"

Lorne told him what she knew. "I suppose the guys in the maze copped it?"

"It's all being swept as we speak. Tyler will update as and when. I've taken the lead to get things moving in the right direction, but he's staying on scene even after he hands over to the locals"

"Any news on Simon Clovelly?"

"Yes, he's stable. I sent a message to him to consider a job with us lot when he's out of uni. Ideal candidate if you ask me."

"Yeah right, I'm sure he's thinking about his future at this very moment. You're incorrigible, Chief."

"Just thinking of everything and anything other than the fright we've had, I suppose. Are you all right, Lorne? God, I thought I'd… I mean, like you say, that was a close call." His anger appeared to seep away, and he smiled with relief.

"Yes, Sean. I'm okay. Look, just give me a mo to phone my dad, will you? I need to know how Charlie is more than anything. And, of course, have an update on Jade.

"Hi, Dad, where are you? I'm desperate for news on Charlie and, of course, Jade."

"Not to worry, love. Charlie's awake, and she understands what you have to do. In fact, she's told Tom off a couple of times for berating the fact you aren't here. And she said to me, 'One day I'm going to be a policewoman, Granddad, or rather a detective like you and Mum. I want to catch evil men and stop them doing the things I've had done to me. Tell Mum, I'm proud of her.'"

"Oh, Dad! Oh God, I don't know what to say. I feel vindicated, and it's a sign she's going to be all right, isn't it? I mean, if she's thinking of the future?"

"Yes, she hasn't told us all about what happened to her, not yet, but she does have some horrific injuries, mostly bruising and tearing. Lorne… well, I think she has been ra—"

"I know, Dad. Don't say it. I know." A pain shot through her heart. Her little girl…

"A bloke turned up, a friend of yours, a Frenchman. He had a colleague with him, a psychiatrist. Nice woman. She had fifteen minutes or so with Charlie, said she wanted to help, but today would just be about feeling the water, introduce herself, and see if she thought Charlie would work with her. They hit it off, so I think that bodes well for the future if you and Tom decide to go down that route. I think you should, love, for her sake."

"Yes, of course. I just can't think at the moment. I'm just so relieved. Look, Dad, let me bring you up to speed. I only have about a minute." She told him what had transpired.

"Thank God, you're okay, love. What a day. Both my daughters fighting different battles and my granddaughter in such a state."

"How's Jade?"

"Oh, she's okay, a little sore, well you know, but there's a concern over the baby. They think he's got a heart condition…"

"No. Oh, poor little mite. What are they saying?"

Lorne's father told her all he knew about the position with Jade and the baby. Lorne detected tiredness in his voice, and guilt wrapped around her for what seemed like the tenth time today. "And you? How are you holding up, Dad?"

"Me? I'm hanging on in there, girl." His tone sounded more upbeat and in turn lifted her spirits. "This Frenchman whatever his name is…"

"Dr. Arnaud, Jacques Arnaud. He's a pathologist."

"Oh, right. He seemed very concerned. I haven't come across him in your circle of friends before. Far too good-looking for my liking, just how *good* a friend is he, Lorne?"

Ever the detective. "A good friend, Dad, that's all you need to know."

A blush crept up her neck. She felt grateful her father couldn't see her reaction. She coughed to clear the lump clogging her throat as memories of being held in Jacques' arms flooded her fatigued mind. *Get a grip, woman.*

"Anyway, like I say, his colleague, pretty woman, will be a big help. She warned we'll have to be careful when Charlie comes home. These things have a knack of catching up with a victim when they least expect it."

Lorne winced. *Victim— will Charlie always have that tag?* She damn well hoped not. She knew Charlie would detest any form of sympathy towards her. She'd make sure she pulled out all the stops to prevent that from happening. After all, that was her role in life, wasn't it? To deal with impossible tasks at home and at work. She had a feeling that her daughter's recuperation would be a doddle compared to capturing the man who had disrupted her family's lives so much.

Chapter Sixty-One

The helicopter had taken off. Lorne opened her eyes, but still clutched her erupting stomach and swallowed hard. She looked over at the chief; he looked pensive. She wondered if he was still battling with his feelings or if he too had an aversion to heights.

"Is Charlie all right, Lorne?

She brought him up to date on Charlie and then told him about Jade.

"Jesus, no wonder you look so glum. I'm so sorry, Lorne." He rested a comforting hand on her shoulder.

"Don't start being nice to me, Sean. I'm liable to break down and cry."

"This day just doesn't get any better for you and yours though, does it?" His eyes brimmed with concern.

"In a way, it has. I mean, I never expected to have my daughter back on my side. I thought she'd hate me. What is it in me that would risk that?"

"Well, whatever it is, Charlie has it, so I wouldn't worry. God, I'm glad I'll be long retired before she hits the department. Two of *you* would be the death of me," he said, giving a brief laugh.

She managed a smile. "Right, ETA is set at around forty minutes, and he has a head start on us of around fifteen. Is the pilot trying for clearance to fly a shorter route?"

"Yes, and we've fixed it so no other aircraft gets the same clearance. So we could catch up at least ten minutes."

The chief's phone buzzed. His conversation intrigued Lorne. He closed his phone.

"Well, it seems Ramon, one of the henchmen, survived. Hit in the legs only. He's had his rights read because he's blurting out loads of stuff, which he might think better of once he has time to think things through. But I've told them not to interview him, just get him seen to. I want one of us in on any interrogation. Also, as we thought, three bodies, horrific scene, as you'd expect. And in the office, from where the Unicorn shot Clovelly, a DVD was showing disgusting activity with Sondra Winwood's dead body. Presumably the sick bastard was taking delight in playing the recording to Winwood when all hell broke out."

They each took to their own thoughts for a time and sat back. The pilot gave them a new ETA of twenty minutes before they next spoke.

"Lorne, I know I took over back there, but let's work this as a partnership from now on. Is that okay with you?"

"For now, but when we're on the ground, you know how that can muddle things. Especially when we're dealing with officers we don't know and who haven't a clue about us. I'll take on second command, then. Leave the pecking order in place so as not to cause any confusion amongst the lower ranks."

"Agreed. I'll get on to Portsmouth. They should locate the boat for us, give us a landing location, and have an escort ready for us. Also, I think I'll tell them to get an ART holed up somewhere nearby, so they're ready to back us up. I'll use the code name Unicorn, okay? Oh, by the way, have you still got the gun?"

"Yes, and yes."

"Good. I ran it by the powers that be at headquarters whilst you were getting in position, and I haven't retracted it yet. I'm armed, too. But, Lorne, well I know I shouldn't have to, but I do feel the need to warn you. Don't let your personal involvement get in the way of your better judgment. I want a clean arrest, or if he meets his end, no comeback."

"Noted, boss. Whilst you contact Portsmouth, I'll touch base with Tony to keep him in the picture."

The screen of her phone showed she'd missed a call. She was about to tap into the menu to see who it was when it rang.

"*Allo, chérie*, how are things going?"

"Hi, Jacques, not a good line. I'm up in a helicopter."

"And you are not alone, I take it?"

"That's right. Listen, thanks for helping Charlie. Dad said your friend's visit has made all the difference. It was very thoughtful of you."

"*C'est rien*, it is nothing, *chérie*. It was my pleasure. It is what she needed, *non*?"

"Yes. Look, I can't talk now. Things are starting to come together." Just hearing his voice had made her emotions bubble to the surface. *What kind of hold has he got over me?*

"Okay, I just want you to be aware of one thing, *chérie*. You are never far from my thoughts. God be with you." He ended the call by blowing a kiss down the phone.

She closed her phone. Why did life suck so much? In another time and place, she would be knocking down his bedroom door. If her marriage were stronger, she wouldn't be having these foolish thoughts. Recently she'd asked herself a simple question: did her heart race when Tom spoke to her the way it did when Jacques engaged her in conversation? The answer, categorically, was no. *But, then again, do I have the courage to rectify the situation? Could the grass be greener on the other side?*

The chief brought her out of her reverie. "Right, all is in place in Portsmouth. The pilot has contact with their base, so they're directing him. "You all right, Lorne?"

"Huh? Oh, yes, good. Now, Warner..."

Lorne could tell she hadn't convinced the chief one iota, because he insisted on probing further. "Is there something I should know about? I mean, is there something going on between you and Jacques?"

Is that jealousy I detect in his tone? "Such as?"

"Are you two having an affair?"

"Sorry? Since we took to the air, have you changed your vocation? Have you declared yourself to be my marriage counsellor or something?"

"You're right, your private life is your own concern. I consider myself suitably reprimanded, Inspector. How about we get back to business?"

"Suits me." She pressed the number allocated to Warner and brought him up to speed. "Do you know anything about what we can expect to face at Portsmouth?"

"Well, we haven't a full reconnaissance on the boat. You're correct with its mooring. Have the coastguard police been mobilised?" Tony asked.

"No, not yet, but it might be an idea."

"That way you could stop him landing. Get the boat impounded. I should do that now. You only have ten minutes or so," Tony suggested.

Why the hell hadn't we thought of that? "Good idea. Anything else you can help us with? Oh, by the way, our man is Baldwin. I'm positive of it."

"Right. I'll give you a rundown on anything you need to know about him. First, he was one of the elite SAS. What he doesn't know about escape isn't worth knowing. He's the best of the best, which explains a lot. Obviously, he's built up a catalogue of contacts all over the world. Some have gone bad, like him, so may be coming into play now. You have to think like him, Lorne. This isn't your ordinary criminal. Look, I'll run everything through again, try to get a layout for the boat in case you're not in time to stop him landing on it and everything I can dig up on him. I'll get back to you."

Feeling like an idiot for just accepting the Unicorn was going to land on a boat and not having a plan to stop him, she told the chief what Tony had said.

"It's all in hand. The Portsmouth lot said they would get on to it. Don't worry, Lorne, we're going to get him, and we don't need Tony to tell us how to do our job."

She called her team to put them in the picture. They could tell her nothing more than Warner had. "Oh, by the way, AJ, you'd better let the superintendent know what's going on."

"I would if he were here, ma'am. One minute, he was here keeping a watchful eye on things. The next second, he told me he had an appointment with someone. When I asked how I could contact him, he said he'd be in touch with us soon."

"Did he say who the appointment was with?"

"That's a negative, ma'am. Look…"

AJ went quiet for so long, Lorne called out to him and then took the phone from her ear to check the connection.

"Sorry, ma'am. I feel a bit of an idiot saying this, so I've come into another room. It's just that… well, the superintendent seemed kind of odd, sort of shifty. I don't mean to be disrespectful, ma'am, but it worried me."

"Okay, AJ, keep me informed." She closed the phone and turned to her boss. A quizzical eyebrow rose high into the fringe of her hair.

"What's that look for?"

Conscious she needed to phrase her response carefully, she looked down at the green fields full of grazing cows speeding past beneath the helicopter. "AJ just informed me the superintendent's taken off somewhere."

Her words hung in the air for a good few minutes before Roberts picked up on her unspoken meaning.

"You think he's involved in this somehow?"

She shrugged and remained quiet, watching Roberts mull over the idea. His facial expression changed constantly.

Chapter Sixty-Two

As they approached the marina, they both peered down on the scene below. The beauty of the mooring site, with boats of all sizes bobbing on the gentle lapping waves of the turquoise sea, took Lorne's breath away. The quayside posed a contrasting picture and brought her back to reality. Here, several squad cars and ambulances with flashing lights formed a cordon around the area. As they lost height, she ignored the rumbling of her innards and peered down at the boats. One yacht stood out from the rest—a huge white monster of extravagance with a helicopter sitting on a landing pad at the back end of it. Her heart sank. *The eagle has landed, so to speak.*

The chief spotted it at the same time and asked the pilot how far away they had to land.

"It seems we have clearance for that dock over there. Can you see it, that wide expanse of concrete?" the pilot said.

"Yes, that's brilliant. It means we'll be within metres of him and the squad. I take it the armed response have been activated?" Lorne said.

"I'll check. Are you ready for this? I mean, we look like we're going to be flung into the thick of it, whereas I'd hoped the boat had been impounded and we'd deal with him on land, which would've been easier," the chief replied.

"Me, too. But, yes, as long as we nail the bastard, and surely with the resources we have in place, he's going nowhere this time. With the coastguard police at sea and our lot on land, we have him surrounded. And if he takes to the air again, we'll be on his tail. I think we've got him, Chief. I just hope we bring this to a conclusion without suffering any further losses."

"Right, the ART are getting into position. In the first instance, Lorne, I think we should get as near as possible, then you try to talk him into giving himself up. How does that sit with you?" the chief asked.

"Yeah, if we must, though, I don't give much for my chances. Personally, I'd like to shoot him on sight, but then again, I'd have a nice life knowing we have him holed up in a secure prison in solitary. Don't think he's planned for that somehow."

A dip in their height stopped the conversation. Lorne swallowed hard and shut her eyes, trying to fight back the queasy feeling.

Once the helicopter was down, an officer met Lorne and Roberts and took them to join the squad. The helicopter took off. The pilot had instructions to wait in a nearby airfield. They couldn't risk the Unicorn firing at it and putting it out of action.

Once safely shielded behind the cordon, Lorne realised she couldn't use the megaphone to make contact. The sheer size of the boat meant it had moored farther out at sea than the impression they'd gained from their view in the air.

"Chief, I'm going to have to go out in a boat. I've no chance of talking to him from here unless he rings me, which is a possibility, of course, as he probably saw us land."

"I don't like that idea, Lorne. Look, let's give him a moment or two. Like you say, he knows we're here. I'm sure of it."

No sooner had the chief finished speaking than Lorne's phone rang. The private number displayed had become a trademark for the Unicorn's calls.

She went for his jugular. "Baldwin, we've got you surrounded. I think you know the game is up. You can play this whichever way you want, but as I see it, you have two options. Either give yourself up, or end up dead."

"Ha, how did you become so delusional? I expect more from you, Inspector. Let's rewind, shall we? Not two hours ago, you had me surrounded, but that didn't do you any good, did it? I soon had you cowering like an animal in a doorway—"

"Yeah, but you chickened out. You could've taken me out, but the madness inside you took over. It beat you—"

"Shut up, bitch. I chose to leave you. *Me*, do you hear? I took out who I needed to, but for you, I have an end planned I can't deny myself. You deserve more. You've never given up, but I intend making you. You're on my list, on the very top of it. And when the time is right, I won't just blow your head off. Oh no, nothing as quick as that—"

"You'll never get the chance. Who's being delusional now? By the way, you failed on the score of taking them out. Ramon survived, and he's squealing. Add what he gives us to what Reynolds has spilled, and you're an open book. Your identity is confirmed, your bank accounts, your skills, your friends, everything. You won't be able to take a shit without us knowing about it. You're one fucked arsehole."

"Lorne," Roberts reprimanded.

She put her hand over the mouthpiece. "Leave this to me, Chief. I know him. I need to get him rattled—"

She was interrupted by Baldwin bellowing down the phone at her.

"You think you're so clever. I used to enjoy playing cat and mouse with you, but now you're nothing. You have the intelligence displayed by a dog when it chases its tail. Reynolds and Ramon know nothing. They had their uses, but what they think they know cannot harm me. I'm my own universe. I have power all over the world. I've played with you. You've been no more than an amusing toy. I've controlled you. Made you weep. Made you despair. Made you grieve. Frustrated and devastated you. Got you into trouble and ruined your marriage. Raped your daughter and took out people you were close to. You're my puppet. Your destiny is in my hands. Do you hear me? *I own you.*"

Lorne couldn't speak. The truth of his words iced the blood in her veins.

"So, the penny has dropped, has it? About time, too. Well, let me tell you how we're going to play this, shall I? You're going to log onto a computer, which has a webcam attached. You'll find one at the local pub, The Anchor. The key to the pub door is under the flower tub on the right of the entrance, and when you get in, the landlord will be tied to a chair. Ha. Just a little amateur touch for you, much more in your league, hidden keys and men tied up. Anyway, enjoy the connection with your father. Oh, by the way, I have left you a box of chocolates to help you enjoy the experience. Not that you deserve them. One more thing, before you leave, give orders to these idiots around me to behave. You've some here who should be fishermen. They don't know how to play it with a criminal of high intelligence. They're more used to pirates and smugglers. We don't want any slip-ups, do we?"

The phone went dead.

"Lorne, Lorne, what is it? What did he say? Lorne?"

"Christ, Sean. I think he's got my dad."

"What? Lorne, you're not making any sense. Tell me what he said."

"I'll tell you on the way. We have to hurry." She turned to the local chief inspector, who was squatting on her left. "Sir, I have to get to The Anchor Pub. Nothing must happen here whilst I'm away. He's going nowhere, but he has fixed up something for me, something involving my father. I have to find out what it is before anything can move on the current situation. Leave all your men in place, but whatever happens, make sure none of them play the hero. I know this man. He's likely to come out on deck to smoke a cigarette in full view, looking like he's a sitting target, but nothing is simple with him. It's a game. There'll be terrible consequences if one of your men even thinks they can take him out and have a go. And tell them all to keep under cover. Don't put themselves into vulnerable situations. We're dealing with a madman, a man who has no feelings other than for himself and his own ambitions."

"Right, Inspector. Don't worry. I'll keep my team in check. None of them will breathe unless I tell them to."

He spoke into his radio. Then he told her to walk back the way they'd come, and in a hundred metres or so, they would come to some steps leading to the promenade. An officer would meet them there and take them to the pub.

As they made their way, Lorne relayed word for word the conversation she'd had with the Unicorn to the chief."

"Christ, Lorne…"

"How has he done this, Sean? How has he set up yet another hostage? It's like we're dealing with God himself. And do you know something? I do feel like a puppet. I'm scared, Sean. I'm more scared than I've ever been in my life. No one is safe around me. No one I love is safe."

Sean spoke volumes with his silence. She knew he agreed. His helplessness conveyed itself to her. The Unicorn had stripped them of their power. They were nothing.

Chapter Sixty-Three

The screen lit up; Lorne connected with Skype and typed in the address. Her fingers felt like wooden pegs. Her exhausted mind prevented her from thinking about what to expect whilst her body was ravaged with pain as though someone had thrown it into a furnace.

The dial tone unique to Skype beeped on. Then a picture emerged. "Dad... No... no..."

Petrol is a beautiful colour. Funny that thought registered. The light caught the rainbow effect as the figure, clad in fire-protective gear, poured the liquid over her father's head from a great height. He was sitting bolt upright, his whole body bound to a chair with thick rope. Looking straight ahead, he neither flinched nor protested.

Sean put his arm around her. She shrugged it off. If her father could display such courage, she could match it.

A voice came through the computer speaker. Her boss took out his pad and took notes.

"The judge is dead. He died en route, probably from a heart attack. Therefore, as you can appreciate, a dead hostage is a *no* hostage. I threw him out of the helicopter somewhere in the countryside between London and Portsmouth."

This wasn't the Unicorn's voice, but someone reading from a script.

"My demands are that I'm allowed to leave the port and to sail without anyone following or tracking me on radar. I must be allowed to do this within the next hour. If not, the petrol will be set alight, and your dear father will burn to death."

Everything inside her drained away. She found it impossible to swallow; her chest tightened, restricting her breath.

"You're to return to the quayside to give the order. In twenty-four hours, providing you've kept to your half of the bargain, I will contact you, telling you where your father can be found. If there's one hitch to my plan, your father will get it. My man has instructions that I'll keep in touch with him on the hour of every hour. If I miss one contact, your father will be killed. Now your father will speak."

The camera zoomed in on her father's face. He didn't utter a word. His courage shone from him, but then a vicious blow sent his head reeling.

"No… Dad. Oh, God. I'm sorry, Dad."

"None of this is your fault, Lorne. You do what you have to do, girl. I love you."

The screen went back to the Skype home page.

The heavy silence clawed at her. Even to move felt like she had to wade through jelly.

"I'll handle this, Lorne. You stay here and rest. You're exhausted."

"No. I have to do it. He may not respond unless I'm there. You heard the message. '*You* must return to the quayside and give the order.' Me, Sean. It has to be me."

"It's like you said before, Lorne, it's as though we're dealing with God."

"I'm going to request something, and I'm pleading with you to back me up. I want an armed guard on all of my family and my closest friends. Use Tony. He'll know exactly who every one of them is and where they live or are at this very moment. I don't doubt with my involvement in all of this that they haven't a complete dossier on me. Some things he said intimated that to be the case. Get in touch with him, and demand they use it as a template of who to protect. There can't be anymore. *No* more, Sean."

Before leaving the pub, they ordered the landlord to stay where he was. They had removed his restraints and blindfold to make him more comfortable and stressed the need not to disturb anything. They instructed the officer outside to remain on guard. They'd send others up to help him and a medical team to attend the shocked landlord, and forensics would give the place the once over.

Once she was back on the quayside, Lorne's phone rang. She opened it, placed it to her ear, and said nothing.

"Well, well, this is a first. I expected some choice words, Inspector. Got the message, have we? Good. Now call everyone off, and quick. The clock is about to strike the hour."

Her phone went dead.

"Sir, give the order. And give it now. No ifs or buts. We have less than a minute for him to see a withdrawal of the boats surrounding him and our men to leave."

Chief Inspector Roberts gave the order. His counterpart looked astonished.

"Now wait just a minute."

"Call off the coastguard, and do it immediately. I'm in charge here. I'll take any comeback for my decision. You just follow my orders," Roberts said.

Lorne could have hugged Sean for standing by her. She watched as the boats returned to shore. She felt numb inside. In a way, it comforted her and cushioned the pain.

Her phone rang. Once again, she didn't speak.

"I see you really do get it. Well done, and see you around some time..."

Lorne and the chief remained on the quay. All units had pulled back so they were no longer visible. It took a good thirty minutes for the boat to up anchor and manoeuvre out of the dock. Lorne watched its every move. One hour later, it had become a serene picture, a modern sleek-designed yacht, sailing against a backdrop of a blue sky and an even darker blue, calm sea.

Lulled into a calm place by the sight, Lorne jumped when her phone rang. Warner's name displayed on her screen. *Fuck off, Warner. I'm not going to fight you over the security of my family.* This thought psyched her up to answer him.

"Lorne, God, sorry to hear about your dad, but something's come up. I don't know how to tell you this but, Lorne, it could jeopardise your dad's life..."

"No, Tony, don't say that, please. We've done everything by the letter."

"I know, but we've just found out something. It seems Abromovski put into place a revenge strategy. He knew what Baldwin was planning. He did all he could to protect himself. He put measures in place to destroy Baldwin."

"What? What can a man do from his grave?"

"A Russian contacted a solicitor who then contacted us. The Russian said there's a bomb aboard the yacht, and he had instructions that the moment the yacht left the harbour with Baldwin aboard, he had to detonate it. In return, there's an account in his name, activation of this account depends on the story appearing in the papers of the explosion and the death of Baldwin. We have no address, no name, nothing. This could happen any moment, Lorne."

"Oh, Tony. What can we do? I can't bear it… And, why has he made contact? Was there a reason?"

"We think it's because, like in a terrorist threat, he's warning us to make sure the area is clear of other traffic. We've contacted the coastguard. Look, Lorne, you shouldn't be there."

"But Baldwin pulls all the strings. I had to be here, he demanded it."

"I know. And though it's like shutting the gate after the horse has bolted, we've carried out your request. The rest of your family and friends are safe, and we're doing everything in our power to save your dad. Several teams are scouring that area of London, following his last-known movements. We know your dad left the hospital and went home. That was just before you called him. A neighbour said he left home around half an hour after he got in. He didn't seem in any hurry. He got in his car and drove off. She even knew the direction he took. We've checked the local shops, and it seems he stopped, bought a paper, some chocolates and flowers, and a women's magazine. From that we can deduce he intended to visit the hospital again. From there, we have him on a couple of CCTVs heading that way. Then we lose him. Now you took under an hour to get where you are, so the time lapse from his known activity to his capture and you linking up with him can only be twenty minutes at most. That places him within a thirty to forty miles radius of his home. I have every resource working on tracking him down, Lorne."

"Thank you."

She'd hardly uttered the words when a massive explosion at sea rocked her world.

Chapter Sixty-Four

She could hear a moan, but couldn't tell where it had come from.

"Lorne... Christ, Lorne, don't break now, not now..."

She looked at Sean. His arms opened. Her resistance weakened, and she collapsed against him. He stroked her hair.

"Shush, shush, baby..."

The words shocked her. No, she didn't want this. She wanted a friend. A hug from a friend, that's all. She pulled away.

"I'm sorry... I..."

"It's okay, Sean. I needed a hug, and you obliged, that's all that happened. You'd be some kind of shit if you hadn't."

He laughed and the tension lifted.

"What now?" she asked.

"Well, tell me what Tony said first. The second hour deadline passed five minutes before the explosion, so we can assume Baldwin phoned in. I think he meant to keep that promise. So that means we have just under an hour to find your dad. What's been done so far?"

She passed on what Tony had told her.

"Well that's good. Presumably, Tony has covered quite a lot of ground already. Look, I know at this moment you don't give a shit, but there's one thing to hang on to. Baldwin—the fucking Unicorn—is dead."

"Is he?"

"Now, come on, Lorne, we just witnessed him being blown to kingdom come. And he didn't expect that, did he?"

"It'll take me a long time to believe it. I want every inch of that wreckage salvaged and gone over with a fine toothcomb for DNA," she said, staring out to sea.

"That goes without saying, but have we got any to match it to? No, at least not that we know is his for sure."

"But that was before we knew who he was. There are records of him now. Military records, dental records, medical records. The SAS surely didn't leave a stone unturned in cataloguing their men."

"I hope you're right. But we know they wanted him taken off their files as if he'd never been part of their outfit, which might have meant destroying any trace of him. You have to prepare yourself for that. You should do the logical thing. The *only* logical thing and accept he's gone. Your life will change now, Lorne. Your family is safe. You're safe. The Unicorn *has gone*. Look at that blaze. No one could survive that."

A lingering doubt swept through her, but then she should expect that. The bastard had played so many tricks in his time. She'd accept it for the moment. She had to. She needed to concentrate on finding her dad. The alternative didn't bear thinking about.

"Okay, Sean, Tony has mobilised some units on the ground to carry out foot enquiries. Is there anything else we can do?"

"First thing is to inform your team what's happened and knock them all off duty. They need a rest and can't contribute in any way to this part of the investigation."

"Of course. Tell them 'thank you' from me. I can't believe we've all been on duty..." She checked her watch. "Over forty-eight hours now. Christ, the worst forty-eight hours of my life."

"I know. After I make that call, I'll contact the pilot to pick us up. The local boys can finish up here and file a report. And when we get back, you have to get some rest. I don't like to remind you, but it's Pete's funeral tomorrow."

Resting her head back, once more trying not to vomit as the helicopter took to the skies, Lorne's thoughts circled a turmoil of problems. Questions she didn't want to address popped in and out of her sleepy mind. Uppermost, with her recent feelings for Jacques escalating was her need to think about her marriage. She wondered if she and Tom could salvage it. It'd seemed when they were last together they could talk. She had felt a love for him, but she wasn't sure she loved him wholeheartedly. Deep down, she couldn't answer yes.

And what about Charlie? Are we capable as a couple of giving her all she needs and deserves? Or will our differences get in the way again, and instead of helping her to rebuild her life, will they become a further destructive device?

Lorne wondered about her future career. With Pete gone, and if proof beyond doubt showed Baldwin—alias the Unicorn—was dead, she wasn't sure she really wanted to continue in the force.

"Lorne, are you okay? You were moaning. God, Lorne, this is all too much. No human being can cope with what you have on your plate. You're to take no part in trying to find your father, no part whatsoever."

"Oh, Sean, don't start again." She closed her eyes against the anger that surged through her. *Just let me get on with my frigging job, will you?* "Stop wrapping me in cotton wool. I'm as capable as I've ever been."

"I'm having no argument this time. I gave in before because nailing the Unicorn couldn't go on without you, but this can. After you've had a rest, you go to your family. And that's an order. You're off the case."

Her face screwed up as though she'd sucked on a lemon. She pulled her arms around her as if to protect herself as Sean continued. "You're too involved. And you're full of anger and tiredness."

Anger. Too bloody right I'm angry. Wouldn't he be? In the last forty-eight hours, her whole life had been turned upside down and pulled inside out, she had a God-given *right* to be angry. And it's not over yet. *How would he feel if his dad sat somewhere doused in petrol with just a flick of a lighter needed to burn him to death? Or if his partner had passed away in his arms? Or if it had been his daughter subjected to violence and repeatedly raped and left to die wrapped in a suicide vest? And to crown it all, how would he be feeling if his nephew had been born into this shitty world with a heart defect?* Too right she was fucking angry.

"Anger is what keeps me chasing bastards like that." She pointed down towards the massive blaze at sea. "It keeps me from going under, and I think I'm entitled to be eaten up with it right now. I *can* function in my job whilst I remain angry at the injustice of it all and want to put it all right."

"Point taken, I guess," he admitted.

"Thank you. You know, a thought has just occurred to me. I still have that Skype number. What if we tried that again?"

"I doubt it'll work now. I'd say Baldwin deleted it the moment the call finished."

"You may be right, but it has to be worth a try," she said.

"I wouldn't advise it, Lorne. Let's think it through. Just supposing the boat hadn't blown up. You wouldn't ring then. You'd have no need to. You'd just play a waiting game, knowing in a few hours you'd know where your father is. The man with your father doesn't know the boat has blown up. If you get through, he'll think it strange and might become agitated. This'll be a new twist for him. Something he doesn't know how to handle. I doubt he had a contact line to his boss, so he wouldn't be able to turn to him for advice. No,

I think he'd cut and run but before he did. He may carry out the job in hand."

She could see the logic in all of this and told herself she needed to think through her ideas before voicing them. Her phone buzzed in her lap.

"Ma'am, it's AJ. I'm on my way home, but although it might be irrelevant now, I thought I'd let you know I did some digging on the make-up of the yacht. I contacted the builders, De Vries, and got her spec, in case we needed it."

"Good thinking, AJ, it might have been useful. Was there a reason you thought you should tell me this now?"

"Well, in a way. I just can't believe *he's* gone, and one specific piece of information keeps niggling at me. The yacht had a full-sized garage."

"I don't understand? What difference does that make?" she asked.

"Well, I keep thinking of all the things which would facilitate an escape which could be stored in it."

Lorne sat up. "What sort of things?"

"Jet skis, dinghies and… well, it's a bit James Bondish, but a miniature submarine even."

"But he didn't know about the bomb, so he'd hardly be prepared to evacuate, unless he'd already decided to do so, but no, he couldn't have. He had a plan in place. We'd agreed… But then, would he, could he trust us? The boat blowing up could've been a bonus for him, one he didn't expect, but a welcome one, all the same… Look, thanks, AJ. Leave it with me. I'll run it all past Tony Warner. You've done a good job, AJ. Thank you. Now go home and get some rest, and I'll see you tomorrow."

Both Tony and the chief found gaping holes in the theory and told her she had to accept the truth. If she didn't, she'd never find peace of mind. She knew it would be a long time before she could, but she would try. She had to.

Chapter Sixty-five

At the hospital, she found a different Charlie than she'd ever dealt with. A girl who'd turned into a woman overnight. This hurt a little as the thought of what had escalated this process sickened her, but Charlie's newfound maturity helped them both.

"Mum. Oh, Mum, you're safe. What's happened?"

"He's gone, darling. The Unicorn is dead. You have nothing to fear from him ever again." She hoped she sounded convincing. "Where's your dad?"

"He popped down the corridor to get a coffee. He's only been gone a minute. He's suffering, Mum. And you know, I want to say I'm sorry. Sorry that I've put you both through hell, but I'm going to change, Mum, I promise."

"Oh, darling. I wish I could hug you, but I'm afraid of hurting you. I don't want you taking the blame. Yes, you were a handful, but nothing more than any other teenager. Your dad and I didn't handle you well, especially me with my job—"

"But I understand now. I didn't before. I was pigheaded and kicked against your discipline. But now… well… Mum, I wanted to tell you how proud I am of you. Proud of the long hours you do to make this a better world for young people to live in. You fight the evil I didn't even know existed. And I've made up my mind that not only am I going to support you in your work by behaving and helping around the house, but I'm also going to join the police. So I can carry on where you'll have to leave off soon."

"Cheeky, madam, I may seem it and feel it, but I'm not near retirement yet, you know."

They both laughed. Tom came through the door at that moment. Lorne's relief in the way Charlie was coping with everything sent Lorne into his arms. All doubts dispelled for the moment. After a welcome hug, she felt a pang of guilt. Her father still faced grave danger, and she needed to be out there helping to find him, but she couldn't tell Charlie that. She sensed Charlie's newfound strength was held together by a fragile resolve and could be easily shattered. She decided to make light of her imminent departure.

"Right, first thing you need to know about this glamorous career you're thinking of emulating is there's always mountains of paperwork to do, and it has to be done as soon as the job is in the bag so nothing is missed in recording the events. Otherwise, when your case comes to court, you could lose it on something you didn't note down. This means I have to leave and get that part of the job done. But after that, I'm taking a holiday and can devote myself to you, darling. I promise."

"Okay, Mum. I hear ya. I hope you mean it about the holiday. It would be great to go away somewhere. I want to talk to you... I mean, well, I know I'll have that counsellor woman, but I want to talk to *you*. I need you to put some things right for me... Oh, I can't explain, but—"

"There's no need for you to explain, love. I know what happened. And, yes we'll talk all you want to. I'll be here for you. Perhaps a cruise in the sunshine would be the ideal holiday for us, what do you think?"

"Mum. I might've grown up, but I'm not ancient. Those things are for the blue-rinse brigade."

Lorne laughed. "No, they're not. There are a lot of young people on them, and they offer a peaceful surrounding as well as lots of girlie stuff like body massages, facials, saunas, and nails, even meditation... And sunbathing around the pool... Oh, it sounds wonderful, my idea of heaven."

"Umm, put like that... I never thought of those things. I'll allow you to look into it."

Lorne smiled and gently kissed her daughter's swollen cheek. "I love you, darling. See you soon, eh? Tom, would you walk me out to my car? You'll be all right for a moment won't you, darling?"

"Yes, Mum, now I've seen you, I think I could go to sleep again. A proper sleep this time though, not one involving drugs. Oh, by the way, Mum, will you find out how Sasha is, and think about what I said before, you know when... Well, about taking care of her in the future?"

"Yes and yes. In fact, the second request goes without saying. Perhaps we'll take her on that holiday with us, but that's up to you. If you want it to be just the two of us, then that's how it'll be. See you soon." She blew a kiss to Charlie and left with Tom.

Once out of earshot, she told Tom what was happening. Shocked speechless, he took her in his arms. It felt good. She hugged him back and forced the doubts from her mind. If she had to make this work, she would. She would at least give it as much effort as she'd given to tracking down the Unicorn. *Surely that will be enough, won't it?*

* * *

A check-in with Tony gave Lorne fresh hope. He had a strong lead. A young person had belatedly reported to his parents seeing a car swerving in front of another one, bringing it to a halt. He'd told them two men got out of the front car and forced the second driver into their car before one of them drove the man's car away. He said they drove at great speed down Tottenham Court Road.

CCTV showed the last sighting of Lorne's father's car, which led Tony's team to believe the kidnappers must have garaged it not far from the scene as it hadn't shown up on the camera along that road. And Tony had managed to locate the car in a lock-up, thanks to another witness coming forward. Forensics were on their way. But best of all, it seemed the Unicorn picked a bunch of idiots to do the work for him, as a full description of the second car, including a patchy number plate reading, had enabled them to pick up the vehicle on CCTV and track its journey. So unless a swap had taken place between sightings, they had the area of where her father was. An armed cordon had formed around the location. They stayed out of sight and didn't use sirens, because they didn't want to trigger an adverse reaction. Once they managed to identify the exact building, then they hoped to start negotiations.

Lorne's heart pumped mixed emotions around her body. She was elated by the progress made, but she still feared for her father's safe deliverance.

"Right, where are we up to?" Lorne asked.

"Still not sure of the building, I'm afraid. There's the car over there by the third lamp post on the left."

Lorne took the binoculars from Tony and pointed them in the direction he'd indicated.

"Obviously, we think our target must be the closest building to it. Otherwise, they would have exposed themselves and their activities for too long to possible witnesses. A door-to-door of that building by plainclothes is in progress. They're posing as Bible-pushing Jehovah's. So we're playing the waiting game."

"Wait a minute." Tony had taken the binoculars back and had them trained on the building. "Someone's coming out. Christ, there're two of them, and they're going towards the car." He grabbed the radio from his belt. "Contact Harvey. See if he saw which apartment those two left, and get a tail on them, now."

The information came back as a positive. Through a third party, Tony directed the team to proceed with extreme caution and to knock on that door next.

Lorne held her breath. *Please, please let him come out of this alive.*

Tony established a direct contact to the officer.

"There's no response, sir, but we can hear something. It's like a muffled sound you'd hear from someone trying to speak through a gag."

"Right, I'll get a team up there to break in. Just carry on as you were. We don't want to arouse suspicions, and I want the best profile you can glean from the immediate neighbours."

Lorne felt a reassuring grip on her arm. She hadn't realised she'd shut her eyes.

"Do you want to go up there?"

The question showed the confidence Tony felt in her.

"Yes. Yes, I do. Where's the team coming from?"

"They'll come by us. We'll join them as they pass."

"I'll come too, Tony."

Tony nodded at Sean. "Of course, Chief. No problem. But I'll be directing operations."

The team used the lift. That way, they had less chance of being seen once they were in its confines, and luckily, the door to the apartment in question stood right next to the lobby where the lift stopped.

Lorne took the steps with Tony and Sean. They walked as if they were ordinary visitors, chatting about this and that and laughing over trivial things.

Nothing untoward happened. Like a demolition gang at work, the sound of the battering ram hammering the door echoed along the corridor as they turned the corner of the third floor. Lorne rushed forward, but Tony and Sean restrained her. The noise brought neighbours onto the landing. Officers ushered them back inside.

At last, the door gave. Uniformed men disappeared inside the apartment. The seconds ticked by. No smoke wafted through the gaping hole, and thankfully, there was no smell of burning flesh, either.

A figure appeared and gave the all-clear. Lorne broke away from Tony and Sean. Petrol fumes choked her, and a cautionary arm stopped her progress.

"He's okay, ma'am. We're just stripping him and making the area safe. He'll be out in a moment. We can't take any chances, one spark and—"

"Okay, officer, thank you."

Stepping back into the corridor, she joined Tony and Sean.

"He's all right," she told them.

"That's good news. But why did they leave him? Were they called off, and if so, by whom? And don't say the Unicorn, Lorne. Even if he was alive, which he isn't, he hasn't got that much compassion. He'd delight in burning your father alive, and you know it."

Lorne shrugged. "I know him better than you think, Chief. This is typical of him. Take me to the edge. Make me think I've won, but he'll have the last laugh, not me. You haven't seen me laugh at his supposed demise yet, have you? I would say it's another part of some elaborate subterfuge to have you all doubt my sanity."

Roberts thrust his arms out to the side and then slapped them against his thighs. "Lorne, for Christ's sake, give in, will you? If you go on, you're only going to make me doubt whether or not you're losing it. Just accept he's gone. There could be any number of reasons for the men leaving. They could've chickened out, anything. Maybe your dad'll know, but act and think logically and stop hanging on to a dead man. You sound paranoid."

"Fuck you, Sean."

"Inspector," he warned.

An officer came through the gap, followed by Lorne's father. Looking like someone who'd been dunked in a tub, her father looked back at her before rushing towards her.

"Dad!"

"Are you, all right, Lorne? Are Charlie and Jade safe?"

"Yes, and it's you we're worried about. Oh, Dad, it must've been awful. Come here."

As she hugged his dripping-wet body to her own, traces of petrol fumes mixed with that of soap tinged her nostrils.

"I'm all right. I've just been bathed by two burly officers." His laughter resounded down the corridor. The three of them joined in.

Lorne introduced her father to Tony.

"Can you tell us anything, sir? I don't have to tell you speed is our greatest asset at the moment, so any knowledge you have will help."

"As to why they didn't carry out their intentions, you mean?" Sam asked.

"Anything, sir. You know how important any little detail can be in the greater picture."

"Well, you know, of course, who set this up. I can give you a good description of the two who captured me. Other than that, they received two calls on the hour, as arranged. After the second one, they started to get agitated. One of them seemed to want to pack it all in. The other wasn't so sure. I couldn't understand what'd spooked them. Suddenly, they agreed, and off they went. Not much to go on, but it's all I have. Nothing in what they said in front of me indicated a reason why, but they did carry out a few discussions in another room out of earshot. I got the impression they weren't happy with whatever new instruction had come from the second call. That's it, I'm afraid."

"Could be they were told to carry out the deed and lost the nerve for it. It happens."

"Or, Chief, the Unicorn called them off."

"The Unicorn. Haven't you got him, then? Has he sailed away? Surely, you can get him now. He hasn't got any hostages or any reason to stop you going after him, has he?"

Lorne told her father about the explosion.

"And we can't convince your stubborn daughter that he's gone. I'm worried to death about her. She's showing signs of paranoia," the chief said.

"And Sean's turned in to a fucking psychiatrist. Dad, I'll tell you my thinking later. Let's get you home. I need a bed. Tom's staying at the hospital. He's been given a room next to Charlie. They both have an armed guard. We wanted to keep Charlie confident that she's okay."

"An armed guard?"

"Yes, and I take it, Tony, you won't call off any of the security on my family, not yet. Not until we have physical proof Baldwin died on that boat?"

"No, I'll keep them in place, don't worry, Lorne."

"But…" the chief looked frustrated.

"Chief, I understand where you're coming from, but though I've only known Lorne for a short time, I've learnt to trust her instincts. And I don't see anything paranoid in following police procedure and not jumping to conclusions. Everything must have proven evidence before it becomes a truth. Textbook stuff, sir, don't you agree?"

Sean had the good grace to blush and agree. Lorne could've hugged Tony. She'd begun to doubt her own sanity.

Chapter Sixty-Six

Henry, Lorne's border collie, threw himself at her the minute she stepped into the hallway. "Hi, sweetpea. Been dying for a wee, have you?"

He whimpered, turned, and bounded towards the back door that led out to her beloved, yet neglected garden. Not having the heart or the energy to chastise him, Lorne watched the dog relieve himself over her fragrant lavender plant. She leaned her head against the doorframe, and her eyes drifted up to heaven.

She picked out the brightest star twinkling against the black backdrop. As tears trickled down her cheeks, she started talking to her best friend. "I'll miss you, big guy. I hope you're going to watch over me in troubled times. I look forward to being partners with you again one day, not too soon, though, eh?"

She gasped as a shooting star whizzed downwards, and questioned if it was a sign from Pete, letting her know he was still around. *I hope so.*

A few minutes later, Henry decided he'd had enough of relieving himself and wanted the warmth of the house again. He nuzzled her hand. She felt a strange reluctance to leave the stars.

Relaxing with the remains of her glass of Chardonnay after finishing a thrown-together omelette, she sat back, too tired to sleep and with her mind probing her like an interrogator. *Is Baldwin dead? And even though the signs were good, how will Charlie really be when all this is over? Will Tom and I ever be happy again?* Lorne reached for her mobile.

He answered on the first ring. "*Allo, chérie.* I was so worried about you. *Ca va?*"

"I'm okay, Jacques. I just needed to hear a friendly voice."

"Where are you?"

She told him she was at home and how Tom had stayed at the hospital. "I need to talk to you, Jacques. I'm very confused."

Her throat constricted, making it hard to swallow. *I'm like a bloody dog begging for something I think is better than I've got.* This thought stopped her blurting out how she felt.

"Jacques... I need to see you." The husky words came out before she could stop them. His silence unnerved her. "Jacques?"

"When?" he whispered.

She cleared her clogged throat. "I'll see you at Pete's funeral tomorrow?" At his quiet yes, she said, "I thought perhaps after… I'll go back with Tom to the hospital and leave there around seven-ish. I know a little pub—it's on the other side of Hyde Park. Could we both get a cab and meet up at Speakers Corner?"

"*Mais oui*… Of course, but I will walk through the park. I love it there, and by then, the fresh air will do me good."

"Okay, the pub's only a couple of streets from there, so we can walk to it. I'll see you then, Jacques."

"But, *chérie*, what is this all about?"

"I can't discuss it now. Like I say, I'm confused. It's about my future… I need advice, or maybe, my mind making up? Oh, I don't know… I may have read the signs wrong, and you're shocked…"

"No, you may be confused, but you have not misread the signs, *ma chérie*, if the signs you have read are about how I feel about you."

"Oh, Jacques…"

"You sound so tired, *ma chérie*, you must try to get some sleep. Until tomorrow then, *Bonne nuit, chérie*, sleep well. *Je t'aime, chérie, je t'aime.*"

Closing her phone, she had a rush of embarrassment that she'd dared to contact him and make clear how she felt and a feeling of sadness and guilt over Tom. But overriding both of these was a wonderful happiness that filled her at the words he'd whispered when he said goodbye.

* * *

Standing outside the crematorium, waiting for Pete's coffin, Lorne had a weird sensation of being somewhere else. She looked at her team; all turned out smartly and standing to attention, some had the designated duty of bearing the coffin into the chapel. All had wanted to do the honours, but the decision on who carried out the task had, in the end, been dependent on height. She tried to run through her eulogy, but gave up after she couldn't get further than the third line. She'd have to play it by ear. *I've enough material to write a book on you, Pete, so I don't think a few words will be a problem, love.*

A cough by her side brought her attention back. John Fox was standing next to her. "Everything all right, ma'am?"

Her eyes welled up. "As well as can be expected, John, on a day like today. How're you bearing up?"

"So, so, ma'am. It really hadn't sunk in until today how much he's going to be missed. There's one good thing, at least the vending machine won't run out of chunky Kit Kats that often now."

They both smiled, and a picture of Pete munching his way through the large chocolate bars and her nagging him, teasing him about his obsession came to her. She always told him that if eating Kit Kats were an Olympic event, he would have won a gold medal.

John fidgeted by her side. She could tell he wanted to say something.

"John?"

"This might not be the time or the place, but umm… Have you heard about the superintendent?"

She'd forgotten about him. *What the hell has he been up to now?* She shook her head. "No, surprise me, John."

"Whilst you and the chief were hunting down the Unicorn, he pulled in an old friend of his."

"I didn't know he had any. I mean, he did? And who was that?"

"Does the name Glen Waverley ring any bells?"

"It does. You mean the dodgy geezer who had to be moved, the one who turned up at Abromovski's party?"

"That's the one. He's been chirping like a dozen canaries for hours now. The superintendent *himself* has been questioning him."

"Has he, indeed? Anyone had a listen in on the interview?"

"I might have popped my head in once or twice. I figured you'd want to know if anything interesting reared its head." His eyebrow rose mischievously, and a sparkle appeared in his hazel eyes.

"The question is, John, did you happen to *pop* in at a convenient moment?"

"As it happens, I did. Waverley alleges the Unicorn blackmailed him. He insisted he was forced to attend the party. Going over the footage from the party, it definitely looked like he enjoyed himself to me. I didn't notice anyone twisting his arm up his back."

"Did he say *why* he was being blackmailed?"

"Something to do with that drugs bust that went wrong, you know, the case that forced his sideways promotion."

"Don't tell me. The Unicorn's shipment of drugs got busted, and he blamed Waverley then decided payback time had come?"

"That's the one."

"Okay, that's feasible. I guess that's one part of the case solved. Did he know anything about the other members of the *esteemed* group?"

"Pretty much the same story, the councillors and the planning bods attended one of these parties. The subsequent compromising photos meant, unwilling or not, they all had to attend and fall in with Abromovski's and Baldwin's plans. If they refused, the pictures would end up in the press. The same thing happened with the footballer. You know what they're like, got too much money, and they end up flashing it around never thinking of the consequences. They literally had him by the balls."

"And what about Judge Winwood? Was it his involvement with the Abdul Mansaud case which led to his corruption and subsequent blackmail?"

"Abdul Mansaud is apparently a good friend and business associate of—"

"Don't tell me, Baldwin, right? So it probably went: the judge received an invite to a party, got himself compromised, was blackmailed and coerced by the thought of a fistful of dollars, so to speak, from the profits of the auction. After that, he became the subject of a double blackmail—photos of his antics and the fixing of a trial."

"Yes. I suppose you've heard of the DVDs found in the judge's house?"

"Yes, I have. Not a good choice of 'must-see films' before you die, for either the judge or his wife."

"No, ma'am. Oh, here's the chief and superintendent, now."

"Does the chief know about Waverley?"

"Not that I know of, but it's likely, as he's been with the superintendent most of the morning."

"Yes, right. I'll go and join them. See you after," she said.

"I'm going back to the office after. Most of us are. There are a lot of loose ends to tie up."

"Loose ends can wait another day. Unfortunately, Pete only has one wake. I want all the team to be there. If anyone complains, point them in my direction. I'll put them straight with a few choice words, got it?"

"Ah, Inspector, how are you today?" Roberts asked as if he were visiting her on a mental health ward. His full dress uniform sat well on him, but she could've happily kicked mud all over him from the puddle at his feet.

"I'm well, thank you, sir, though I wished I was anywhere but here, of course."

"Hello, Inspector. I must say I agree with you. I hate funerals, but having to attend one of a colleague is worse than anything. I hope you're bearing up. I know how much Pete meant to you," the superintendent said.

"Thank you, sir. I'm doing all right." *Is the superintendent being nice to me? If so, why?* It was so unlike him. Lorne had always perceived him as being devoid of any human emotions other than malevolent ones. *What the hell is going on here?*

"Good, I knew you would. After the wake, will you join us back in the office? There are one or two points to go over concerning the Unicorn case."

The funeral passed in a daze. Her eyes felt sore with the effort of blinking back the stinging tears. She'd keep them for the privacy of her home.

It had been a good turnout. Pete would've been proud. Most of his colleagues were still going at it, having moved to the local. But she was now in the chief's office, sitting in a chair next to the man she'd always considered her arch enemy within the force. She sat in silence.

For the next ten minutes, the two men discussed *her* case and congratulated themselves on how *they* had successfully managed to solve it. She found the whole damn scenario bloody farcical. It just about summed up her career beautifully. Whilst she worked her butt off, her superior male officers took the credit for her endeavours. *Well, screw that.*

It was time to put an end to all this crap and the rest of the garbage that clogged up her life. She'd start by sorting out her marriage. Later tonight would solve that issue, she hoped, though confusion still pulled at her. Tom had been a changed man of late, more like the Tom she'd fallen in love with. She'd leave all that until later.

But for now, a far greater matter pressed: her career. She'd had her fill of infuriating petty mindedness. She'd had enough of stroking the male egos surrounding her. Now Pete had gone, there was *nothing* to keep her in this unappreciative, restrictive environment.

"Feel free to join in the conversation, Inspector," Roberts said, finally noticing her. He gave her a puzzled look, and she threw an identical one back at him.

She shrugged, mumbled a brief apology, and walked out of the room. Neither of her two superiors tried to prevent her from leaving. She headed back to her office, her head bowed, feeling downright miserable. The chief caught up with her in the corridor.

"Lorne?"

"Sir?"

"Would you like to share with me what the hell is going on?"

She mimicked him, folding her arms across her chest. She had two choices. Either she could blame her mood on what they'd just been through, or she could come right out and tell him her true thoughts.

He pre-empted her. "I know how hard it was for you today, Lorne, but you're not alone in that boat. Pete was well thought of and admired amongst his fellow officers. The whole station is mourning the loss of a superb officer. You need to show your British bulldog spirit in the face of adversity. Do you think you can manage that, for me?"

Lorne bit her lip several times. She swept back a few stray hairs behind her ear, dropped her arms down by her side, and straightened her back rather than answer him.

The chief smiled as she metamorphosed before his eyes. "That's my girl." His misreading of the situation amused her.

"For your information, sir, this has nothing to do with Pete. Well, maybe a little... actually, maybe a lot—" She stopped. *Don't say anything, Lorne, not until you've had time to think it through thoroughly.* Her inner voice warned, but she refused to listen to her logical side any longer.

"I'm on my way to clear my desk. I've finally come to my senses and realised how unappreciated and maligned I am in this male-dominated environment. I thought new laws about sexual discrimination had come in. Guess I was wrong about that. The force has its own way of dealing with women. They seem to think that promoting them and then knocking them down is the best way of keeping the male dominance in the force. You can argue till you're blue in the face, *sir*, but the facts are plain to see. I've just spent the last ten bloody minutes listening to two bull-shitting men stroking their over-endowed egos, and I have to say that in my book, it was the final *fucking* insult. I happen to think I did a remarkable job out there in the last forty-eight hours. I've had to work under extreme, adverse circumstances, and what praise did I have heaped on me? Nothing. Zilch. Absolutely shit all. Can you honestly say that *if* the same set of circumstances had disrupted your sad life that you would've coped as well as me? I doubt *that* very much."

There, it was said, all out in the open. Only, it hadn't come out exactly the way she had imagined it would or should.

The chief stumbled backwards. He looked shell-shocked, as if Mike Tyson himself had smacked him on the jaw.

"You're upset. It's been a fraught couple of days, in one way or another. After the wake, why don't you take a couple of weeks off to recharge your batteries? I'll clear it with the superintendent. I'm sure he'll understand. I'm sure he won't mind."

Lorne felt like shoving his sympathetic crappy words where the sun didn't shine.

"I couldn't give a stuff if he minded or not. I've told you my decision, Sean, and I assure you this, I ain't going to be changing my mind. Not in a couple of hours or a couple of months. I've had it up to here. I've done my time. I've chased my last criminal. I've lost my last partner in needless circumstances. I want out. I want my life back. *I want a life, full fucking stop.* And I know that I'll never have a life I can call my own whilst I'm working on a force that doesn't appreciate the hours and work I pour into it."

"Where the hell do you get that idea from?"

"I've just spent ten to fifteen minutes listening to you and the superintendent congratulating yourselves, haven't I? In all that time, my family and what I foolishly put them through went unmentioned. That about sums the force up in my book, Sean. You're all a bunch of self-congratulatory pricks that joined up for what they could get out of the force. Whereas, I look at things from a different perspective, I've always considered my role in the force to be a privileged one. I've always felt honoured to have been chosen and trusted by the British public to keep this country safe and protected. However, the criminals have taken it to another level, and I feel the force is lagging behind, some might even say the criminals have the police tucked up in their back pockets. If it hadn't been for Tony's help, this case would never have been solved. But listening to you two in there…" She stopped talking. She'd said enough. She was fed up to the back teeth of going over old ground, having to fight her corner. What was the point? If he didn't understand where she was coming from by now, he never would.

"Oh, Lorne, you're so wrong."

"Oh, Sean," she mimicked sarcastically then issued him with her final sucker punch. "I don't think so. Anyway, I have a gut instinct that you and the superintendent are congratulating yourselves too soon."

"How so? Not that we were doing anything of the sort, anyway."

"Like I said, I have a gut feeling. Sorry, I forgot, you're not Pete. He always knew how foolish it was to ignore my gut feelings, or a woman's dangerous sixth sense, as he used to call it. Somewhere out there, Baldwin is hatching a new plan. He *didn't* die in that blaze."

"Oh, not that old toffee. Well, we'll have to see what the forensics say about that, won't we? I'm imploring you to rethink your decision, Lorne. Today's not the day to make such hasty decisions."

"I'd say today is the *ideal* day, actually. My desk will be cleared in one hour, and my resignation letter sitting in your in tray."

She turned on her heels and left him standing there.

Chapter Sixty-Seven

It wasn't a cold night, but a chill ran through Lorne; she laughed it off. Though it had a sinister feel to it, she realised the situation she'd put herself in, meeting up with another man to discuss leaving her husband, and all the implications associated with that would stir up misgivings. She tried to empty her mind, allow the rustle of the trees in the park behind her to soothe her. Her eyes followed the path Jacques would take to emerge out of the gate. Several people meandered up and down it, but not him.

Seven forty-five. Where the hell is he? Not that she could say whether he did keep to time schedules or not. She'd never met him in this way before. Their meetings, if you could call them that, had taken place in the mortuary or the cafeteria nearby for a coffee. *Am I mad? Could you really fall in love with someone under those circumstances? Or am I blowing up my attraction for him out of all proportion?* Thinking about it, those times had only provided flirtation rights. Most of the deeper banter between them had taken place on the telephone. *He's my mobile phone lover. And I'm thinking of giving up everything for him. Yes, I am mad.*

Even though she'd had her phone on her mind, at that moment, its ring made her jump. She looked along the path again, thinking he'd be walking towards her, but he wasn't. She flipped open the lid. "Hello?"

"*Ma chérie…*"

"Jacques, you're not going to tell me you're standing me up, are you?" She gave a nervous laugh.

"I…" His voice trailed off into a moan.

"Jacques. What is it? Are you all right? Jacques?"

"He cannot speak at the moment, Inspector."

Oh God. She looked around, turning her body in a frantic movement, people dodged around her.

"Hey, watch where you're going."

"Look out."

She muttered apologies, walked towards the park gate, and held on to it for support.

"Ha, that put you in a spin, Inspector. You didn't expect to hear from me, did you?"

"Don't hurt him, please don't hurt him. He's just a colleague, nothing more. He doesn't deserve to be involved in this—"

"Oh, I think he's a little more than that. Planning to leave your husband for him, were you? In fact, Tom is lucky. It could have been him, if things had been right between you, but that would only solve a problem for you, not cause you one."

"You bastard!"

"One of the many names you gave me that went to my watery grave. Remember? I'm a dead man. No one but you knows I'm alive, oh, except this snivelling Frog, of course, but dead men don't have memories…"

A sickening crack sounded in her ear. "Nooooo… Jacques… Jacques…"

"They don't talk, either, or hear last endearments. Didn't you know that? Not as clever as we thought, are we? But then, haven't I always told you that?"

Her mind felt like a tornado twisting out of control. A vice squeezed her heart.

"Why?"

"Oh, you just got under my skin. No one gets away with that. Not even my father, may he long rot in hell. You've been like a puppy dog with your teeth sunk into my trouser leg. No matter which way I turned, you hung on, growling and snarling. I had to kick you in the teeth to dislodge you."

"Christ, destroy me, you mean. But you had your freedom. Like you said, you were a dead man…"

"Not to you, I wasn't, was I? Oh, no. You made noises, tried to convince everyone I still existed. And as my death couldn't be proven, they would have listened to you in the end. They'd have stopped thinking of you as paranoid and started to hunt me again. I don't want that. I want you to forget me. And until you do, until you promise me you will, one by one they'll die. Each and every one of your loved ones will die. Do you hear me?"

"I hear you." Her body trembled. She leaned heavily on the gate.

"That's good. Compliance at last, that makes me happy."

"Just tell me, why didn't you just kill me? Wouldn't that have sorted the problem?"

"Yes, but where would the fun of been in that? I enjoy the games. Most of the time, I'm surrounded by idiots, like those two I instructed to torch your father. I'd planned that as my ultimate gift to you. A final reminder of what I'm capable of, but they let me down. They hadn't the guts to go through with it. Well, one day, they'll be released from prison. I can wait."

The horror of this admission made her knees buckle. "But now, why not kill me now?"

"Because then it would end. I have very little to keep me amused. Yes, I'm rich beyond anything you could dream of, but the pleasure of living openly as a playboy doing all the things I wanted to do when the killing days would be behind me, you've destroyed. You identified me. Now all I have is to live in a country where extradition doesn't exist. My pleasures will be limited. I don't like surgery. I have undergone a lot. I didn't want to undergo more. All that is your doing. You have to suffer. That can't happen if you're dead."

A trickle of anger entered her. He'd killed two people she loved, and worse, had violated her darling daughter and left her scarred for life. He so nearly murdered her father in the most horrific way imaginable, and she cowered beneath him like a wreck, feeding his ultimate fantasy of having her suffer. Well, if he thought that, he had another think coming.

"Like you say you, fucking bastard, you can't live openly, not anymore. Well, you'd better dig yourself in deep, because I won't rest until I have you behind bars. So if I were you, I'd go, and go right now to one of those countries that will shield you, and live as a fugitive, because if you stay here, I will get you. I'll hunt you down until the day I die. And if that leads to a dead end because of extradition laws, I'll make it my lifelong aim to change that country's law."

"Ha, that's the Inspector Simpkins that I love, though I did enjoy the one on her knees, too. And that is where I'll get you. So down on your knees, you'll never get up again."

The phone went dead.

NOTE TO THE READER

Dear Reader,

I hope you enjoyed the ride?

But this is just the beginning…

Lorne is confused and eager to get on with her life after what The Unicorn put her and her family through.

However, Tony Warner is about to throw a spanner in the works when one day he shows up on Lorne's doorstep.

What he reveals astounds her…

He tempts her to join him on a dangerous mission. One that will satisfy her hunger for revenge.

An action-packed thriller that will keep you on the edge-of-your-seat.

Get your copy today.

http://melcomley.blogspot.co.za/p/final-justice-1st-chapter.html

Thank you for your support.

P.S. Reviews are like hugs to authors, we love hugs.

Printed in Great Britain
by Amazon

23999859R00139